CHASING GRACE

KEVIN MILLS

Published in Macon, Georgia by Mill Town Press
www.milltownpress.com

ISBN: 978-0-9887815-0-4
Printed in the U.S.A.
Cover Art design by David Wall

For Katie

For this reason a man will leave his father and mother
and be united to his wife, and they will become one flesh.

Genesis 2:24

Chapter 1

Saturday, January 24, 1998

I stood from my seat, a hard pew that once occupied a place in the church sanctuary. Nearly a decade earlier it was removed in a renovation phase, and now offered seating for those waiting just outside the massive, wooden doors leading into the side entrance. With an awkward, nervous gait, I walked down the hallway and found myself staring into a full-length mirror leaning against the thick, plaster wall. I adjusted my tie for the twentieth time that hour. I checked my coat, tugged at my lapels, and pulled my shirtsleeves out so each displayed exactly one inch of their starched material. It was the same routine I'd performed five minutes earlier.

"Enough already. You are as good as you're going to get. Quit worrying. Even an ugly guy like you looks halfway decent in a tuxedo."

"Thanks, Jimmy," I said, with as much sarcasm as I could muster. "You may want to try using this mirror when I'm finished. See if there is anything you can do to help your situation, although it will take much more than a tuxedo."

At that moment, Mrs. Juliet Sanders entered the room. Juliet served unofficially as the church wedding coordinator. She was never named to this position, but everyone knew that if you wanted to get married at First Baptist Church, you had better use Juliet to plan your wedding. She was the head of the wedding committee and had written the most recent edition of the "First Baptist Church Wedding Policy" handbook.

She was a large woman in her late forties who spoke with a very proper, very slow, and very strong Southern accent. She was known to be bulldog tough on irreverent groomsmen or tardy bridesmaids, and was highly desired by would be fathers-of-the-bride as protection against any potential mishaps on a daughter's special day.

Juliet's other official position in life was as the keeper and provider of all local news, especially that of the fascinating or scandalous variety. She had a tongue-in-cheek phrase she repeated often: "If you do not have anything nice to say about somebody, then come and stand next to me for a while." She was not necessarily malicious in her attitude and actions; she just seemed to thrive on the latest and greatest Mapleton gossip. She received great pleasure from her association with any wedding containing drama between family members or tension between future in-laws. She always charged for her services, but would gladly have worked for free in exchange for a promised scene or disturbance at the rehearsal dinner. Although I was unable to guarantee any drama, she very quickly offered her services for my wedding completely free of charge.

She cleared her throat and announced in a dignified manner, "Pastor Smith just arrived." When she said the word 'pastor,' it was pronounced 'paaastor.' She made one think he was the King of England the way she said his name.

"I was getting very worried," she continued. "We are just about to seat the grandmothers, and I had no idea if we were going to have a preacher. I was just about to ordain the church custodian and tell him he would perform the ceremony when I saw Pastor Smith walk in the foyer. I did not know if I should kiss him or slap him, but I'm certainly glad he finally made it. Not nearly as glad as Sammy the custodian, though. He just kept telling me, 'I ain't doin' no weddin', Ms. Juliet. Y'all can just fire me if you want, but I ain't gettin' up there and talkin' in front of all those folks.' I guess he thought I was serious about ordaining him to do the ceremony. Anyway, all is well now. Henry, you look very handsome. I think Pastor Smith went to the bathroom to put on his robe and will be here shortly."

Pastor David Smith was actually not a pastor, but a history professor. While pursuing his doctorate degree at William and Mary College, he and his wife began to attend a small church just outside of Williamsburg, Virginia. Shortly after their arrival, the pastor resigned and a member of the church asked David if he would be willing to fill in while they looked for another preacher.

"I'm studying to be a history professor, not a preacher," he replied.

But this member insisted that almost having a doctorate of anything qualified him to preach. He eventually capitulated to the insistent demands of this member and agreed to just 'fill in' until they found someone else. For the next two years, until he completed his degree, David Smith 'filled in' for the church. They ordained him into the ministry, and while it was never his full-time profession, he continued to do the occasional fill-in for a vacationing or ill pastor.

Dr. Smith had been my instructor for more than one class during my time as an undergraduate student. Moreover, he had agreed to serve as a mentor to me during a particularly confusing and troublesome time in my college career. He was, humanly speaking, chiefly responsible for my current situation, and was more than willing to make the drive to Mapleton and officiate at my wedding.

"And by the way," Juliet continued, "I took a peek inside the sanctuary and it is absolutely packed. There are even people standing against the back wall, and someone told me some cars are still pulling into the parking lot. The last time I saw this many people in our church was when we had the funeral for Charlie Davidson."

I had heard the story of Charlie Davidson from numerous people. Charlie was barely seventeen years old when he died. It was his junior year of high school. He was the star quarterback for the Mapleton Falcons, an AAA public school football team. Mapleton High was the only high school in Mapleton, a city of about fifteen thousand residents located in the western part of Georgia.

As is the case with most small Southern towns, Mapleton took great pride in their football team. Their stadium held four thousand spectators, not counting those who were willing to stand along the fence and watch the game from ground level. Season tickets and reserve seating were available for a donation of at least one hundred dollars to the school's athletic program. Every season ticket available was sold, although most of those who got the tickets did so by only giving the minimum donation. The funds generated were used to build a field house that rivaled many small college football facilities. Mapleton absolutely loved their football team, especially when they were winning. If a team ever made it to the playoffs, the stadium would be full of spectators. Residents of Mapleton often joked that a Friday night in the fall was the best time for a thief to rob a house. Not only was a full one-third of the population at the game, at least half of the on-duty police officers were there as well.

Charlie was the eldest son of the most prominent attorney in Mapleton. Charles Davidson was one of the two partners at Davidson & Spivey, the largest firm in the town. Charles and his partner, Jack Spivey, specialized in personal injury cases, although their firm handled everything from divorces to wills to real estate closings. The office had anywhere between four and six associates working in their office at any given time. They were known to pay their employees well, but they both worked long hours and expected the same from others in the office. Jack normally arrived at the office by six o'clock every morning. Charles never left before seven in the evening. When they compared notes, it was fairly certain they would know who arrived late and who left early.

In their twenty-year partnership, they had only once considered adding another partner. Brad Williams, a young lawyer from North Carolina and a graduate of Duke University and Wake Forest Law School, worked as an associate in their office for five years. Through most of law school, Brad intended to seek employment at a large law firm in Charlotte or Atlanta The only reason he landed at Davidson & Spivey was because he met and married a Wake Forest undergrad while he was in law school. Her father was the president of a local Mapleton bank and offered to buy them a home if they would move to Mapleton once they were married. Brad was not overly enthusiastic about moving to a small town in Georgia, but it made sense financially. He worked long, hard hours and after five years worked up the courage to approach Mr. Davidson and Mr. Spivey about becoming a partner. He had brought a lot of clients and even more money into the firm, he argued, and while he received a nice salary compared to other associates in Mapleton, he believed he deserved more. He had outlasted every other associate, he also noted, which was not too difficult since most left after a couple of years. He liked both partners, he said, and liked the firm, but if they could not give him the chance to become a partner, he would have to strongly consider looking into other options. Mr. Davidson and Mr. Spivey wished him well.

⟨────────────────⟩

Charles Senior was a native of Mapleton. He played varsity football for the Falcons from 1967–1969. His junior and senior years, he was the starting quarterback and took the first snap of every single game for both seasons. His son, Charles Edward Davidson, Junior was born in 1978. Charles Senior poured his limited amount of time into coaching every sports team his son played on. Whether Charlie was playing tee-ball, peewee football, or junior basketball, his father could be seen on the sidelines at every practice and game, wearing his suit pants, dress shoes, starched white shirt and his tie loosened around his neck. He was determined to live vicariously through his son.

Fortunately, Charles Junior inherited the athletic genes of his father. It became evident very early in his young sporting career that little Charlie was exceptional. He especially loved football, and when his father noticed Charlie's strong throwing arm, he procured the services of a former college quarterback coach from the University of Alabama. Charlie received personal lessons throughout the year as well as attending two football camps every summer.

By the time Charlie reached high school, there were few doubts that he would become the starting quarterback. He was quick, had some size on him, and most importantly had a rocket of a right arm with incredible aim. There were even whispers that perhaps Charlie would be able to lead the Falcons to a state championship.

During his junior year, Charlie exceeded everyone's high expectations and led the Falcons to an undefeated season. They breezed through the first game of the playoffs, fought hard for a victory in the next, and then won their third game 49–0. The whispers eventually became shouts. The next game would be the state championship match-up, and Mapleton was buzzing about the title they would hold after one more victory.

The Saturday night after the third playoff game, Charlie drove his car to Brian Taylor's house. Brian's parents had spent that day in Athens, Georgia, tailgating with friends before the Georgia–Auburn game. It would be well after midnight before his parents came home, so a few boys from the football team decided to spend the evening hanging out at Brian's. When Charlie arrived a few minutes after six o'clock, Brian showed him a small key and told him it would unlock his dad's liquor cabinet. Two other teammates arrived thirty minutes later. All four boys began to mix drinks and toast their imminent state championship title.

Just before ten o'clock, with a strong buzz and feeling a need to release some tension, Charlie stood up and announced that he was heading to his girlfriend's house. Ashley would be there, he bragged, because he told her earlier that he would stop by when he was done having fun with his friends. Brian offered to drive Charlie, but Charlie insisted that he was just a little buzzed.

"Plus," he added, "she lives just a mile or so from here. I'll be fine."

For nearly 30 years, Charles Davidson went to bed at the same time every night and woke up at the same time every morning. He never used an alarm clock, but virtually every morning his eyes opened at exactly five o'clock. On this particular day, he awoke at his usual time, went to the restroom, and then started down the stairs of his home, toward the kitchen for his ritualistic first cup of coffee. Just as he reached the bottom stair, the thought occurred to him that he could not recall Charlie coming home the night before. Charlie always woke his father to let him know he was home, regardless of the time. His parents were so pleased with his behavior, his grades, and his stellar athletic accomplishments that he was never given a strict curfew. The one thing his father asked was for Charlie to always let him know where he was and to wake him when he came home. Charles remembered his son telling him about going to Brian's house and then his plans to see Ashley before coming home. He just could not remember his son waking him when he came in.

He took another step toward the kitchen, thinking that maybe after his first cup of coffee, the memory would return. He stopped, and something in his gut made him turn around and head back up the stairs. If he could just look in on Charlie, see him sleeping in his bed, then he could ask him later about the time he actually came home. The door to his bedroom was cracked, and before he even opened the door, Charles noticed the bed was still made. He looked around the room and saw no sign of Charlie.

He immediately went to the phone and called Brian's house. A very sleepy Mr. Taylor informed Charles Davidson that Charlie was not there. Charles apologized for the early hour, but begged him to wake Brian. A few minutes later, Charles Davidson was informed that Charlie left around ten to go to Ashley's house. He then called Ashley's, again apologizing for the early hour, and went through the same questions, only to be told that Charlie never made it there.

"Are you sure?"

"Absolutely," Ashley's father said. "We were up late consoling our daughter who was extremely upset over being stood up by your son."

Charles Davidson then called the Mapleton chief of police, Bill Parks, at home on the one morning Bill had planned on sleeping in. Charles and Bill knew each other, although there were many times they found themselves on opposite sides of the courtroom. "Bill, I need you to get some guys out on Old Mill Road right now. Charlie did not come home last night."

"Did you consider calling the police station to make this request?"

"Bill, I need you to handle this for me now. I've got to find Charlie."

It was a few minutes before seven o'clock when Police Chief Parks received a radio call from one of his deputies. The officer had discovered a 1995 red Jeep Wrangler registered to Charles Davidson. The Jeep had apparently veered off the road, rolled down a steep embankment, and stopped abruptly when it collided with a large oak tree. The steering wheel had crushed Charlie's chest and, according to the officer, most likely killed him instantly. Chief Parks thanked the deputy and then made the difficult call to Charles Davidson.

———————

Three days later, on December 3, 1996, First Baptist Church of Mapleton was full beyond capacity. Although on a normal Sunday morning there were fewer than two hundred in attendance, the sanctuary could comfortably hold six hundred people. On that day, at two o'clock in the afternoon, there were more than nine hundred individuals seated and standing shoulder to shoulder in the sanctuary. As the crowd poured in, the funeral director eventually allowed people to sit in the choir loft and on the steps in the balcony. The fire marshal would normally have disapproved of this capacity-exceeding gathering, but his son played on the football team with Charlie and both he and his son were in attendance that afternoon. It seemed the whole town had gathered to mourn the loss of this young man who had been taken from them well before his time.

The Mapleton Falcons played for the state championship the following Saturday at their home stadium. They played their hardest; "For Charlie" was their chant and inspiration. Without Charlie's rocket arm, though, victory proved elusive. They lost 35–7.

———————

I'm sure there are as many people here." Juliet's voice brought my mind back to the present. "Maybe more," she continued, as if it was a source of great pride to have more people present than were at Charlie's funeral. "By the time the ceremony actually begins, I'm sure there will be close to a thousand people here."

About the time Juliet finished bragging about the

capacity crowd, Dr. Smith walked in, gave me a big embrace, then held me at arm's length with both hands on my shoulders. "Henry, it's great to see you again. Now, before we begin, I've got to ask, are you sure you still want to do this?"

"No," I said. "But I'm going through with it now."

"You know, you can still back out," Dr. Smith said.

"No, I can't,"

"Then I'm with you all the way." Dr. Smith looked over at Jimmy, then back at me. "You boys ready?"

"I guess" we replied in unison.

Dr. Smith opened the doors, and the three of us walked into the sanctuary of the First Baptist Church of Mapleton. We stood in our assigned places at the front. I could feel the sweat dripping down my back and seeping into my boxers. I looked around the room. Most were members of First Baptist, although for some it was the first time they had set foot into the sanctuary in years. Others were not members, but people I knew from the community. Many of the people in the room were complete strangers to me. Under normal circumstances, I would have assumed that they represented family or friends of the bride, but I knew that was not true in this case.

People were, as Juliet had indicated, standing against the back walls of the sanctuary. Some people were seated on the steps in the balcony. They all stared at me very intently. None smiled. They just sat or stood in breathless anticipation of what would transpire in the next several minutes. Although no one said a word, I knew what every single person was thinking. There was one question burning in their brains.

Why is our pastor marrying a whore?

There is a time for everything, and a season for every activity under heaven.

Ecclesiastes 3:1

Chapter 2
Wednesday, May 26, 1993

Jimmy and I sat in two white, plastic lawn chairs, looking out over the dark, eerie waters of Lake Norman. The chairs were perched on a lakeside dock located roughly a hundred yards or so from the house. It was our graduation night, and I was glad to have Jimmy as my best friend. We were different. Our families were different. But Jimmy had been an invaluable part of my childhood and teenage years.

I met Jimmy in Mrs. Sullivan's third grade class. It was September, and he was the new kid in school. His parents had gone through a bitter, expensive divorce the previous year. When the dust had settled and the lawyers were paid, his family was in so much debt they were forced to sell their home. Jimmy, his mom, and his younger sister moved from their four-bedroom, craftsman style home on a quiet street to a crowded two-bedroom apartment. His days of playing on his swing set, digging in his sandbox, and riding his bike down the street came to an abrupt halt. His bike was sold because there was no room in the apartment and the sandbox and swing set stayed with the house. The apartment complex had a small playground with a single slide and monkey bars, but it seemed to be the meeting place for a crowd of older boys from the complex. Jimmy and his sister soon discovered that early Saturday mornings were the only time they were safe from the bullying of middle school boys.

There were nine girls in our class that year. Thirteen boys sat on one side of the classroom, and nine girls sat on the other. Among eight-year-old boys, it is a well-known fact that all girls, with the exception of mothers, grandmothers, and aunts, are infected with the deadly, incurable disease known as 'cooties.' There are a number of vaccines for this disease–the most popular involving a circle and three dots–but no boy in his right mind would trust the effectiveness of that shot. The best way to prevent infection is absolute

Worst of all for Jimmy, the apartment complex was zoned for an elementary school different than the one he had attended since kindergarten. Thrown into a new school and a new class only magnified Jimmy's timid nature. Jimmy was not only the new kid, but all the other boys in the class had been together for the three previous years. Their group of twelve had been part of the same class since kindergarten. Jimmy made number thirteen.

avoidance of anyone known to be carrying the infectious malady. In the classroom and at lunch, there needed to be a minimum distance of eight feet between a boy and a carrier. At recess, it was best to stay at least one hundred feet away. It was a well-known fact that a sweaty girl was highly contagious.

Early in the school year, several boys in the class quickly learned of Mrs. Sullivan's tendency to place students in co-ed pairs, which meant a boy was in the painful position of being forced into dangerously close proximity to a cootie-carrier. In previous years, the even number of boys made this event less likely. Only in the event of forced interaction by a teacher would a boy be in a close position to a girl. Any instructions to "pair up" were met with an instant reaction of six boys partnering with six other boys. But with the addition of Jimmy, there were thirteen, an odd number, and one that would cause confusion throughout the school year.

Keith Batson was the tallest, the fastest, and probably the strongest boy in our class. The first week of school, Keith came to the conclusion that if the new kid, Jimmy, would just hang out with the girls, they would have an even ten, and the boys would have twelve. Keith announced his theory at recess. With Jimmy within earshot, Keith stood on top of a picnic table and loudly proclaimed to the class that from now on, Jimmy would be called, "Julie," and he could sit with the girls at lunch and play with the girls at recess. All the other boys immediately looked over at Jimmy, who was standing next to the swings by himself, about ten yards from the picnic table where the rest of the boys had gathered. Upon hearing his name, Jimmy looked over at Keith, only to then hear the announcement to everyone that his name would now be Julie. His mouth hung open and he stared in disbelief at the big kid and the incredibly cruel words coming out of his mouth. When the other boys all turned their heads in unison toward Jimmy, it was more than he could handle. His head dropped. From where I stood, I could see his shoulders begin to shake and a tear fall from his face onto the dirt below.

Several of the boys laughed. Others followed with a nervous kind of laughter, none wanting to be the next target of Keith and going along with the group so as to not be noticed. In the face of a bully, this is the code of the playground: blend in, go along, and play it safe.

For the first time in my life, I could not go along with the crowd. I did not laugh. When I saw Jimmy's reaction, I found no humor in the situation. We had always looked to Keith–the biggest and fastest kid in the class–as our leader. When Keith decided the boys would play kickball, we would play kickball. When Keith wanted to play football, we played football, and Keith was the quarterback. When Keith decided it was time for a class race, we raced and he won. No one had the guts to go up against Keith. He was the leader of the pack, and none had the courage to defy his leadership. . . .until that moment.

The unprovoked verbal attack on Jimmy had crossed the line. I simply could not understand the point of embarrassing this new kid in such a vicious way. During the first two days of school, Jimmy had barely spoken a word to any of us. At this point, all I had heard from Jimmy was "Here," spoken at the beginning of class each morning. He had kept to himself, obviously waiting for someone to let him into our circle of friendship. In a moment, that hope was destroyed. With just a few careless words, Keith had not only guaranteed Jimmy would be ostracized from our group for a long time, but that he would have the nickname, "Julie," for as long as he remained at our school. That moment had the potential to affect him for years to come, and I knew Jimmy needed someone to help him.

Keith was still standing on the top of the picnic table. His hands were on his hips, and he had thrown back his head, laughing at what he perceived to be his brilliant wit. The other eleven boys were gathered around the table, like subjects around the throne of their king. I quickly glanced over my shoulder and observed Mrs. Sullivan engrossed in a conversation with the second grade teacher, not watching our gathering of young boys. In my first moment of real courage, I took two steps forward so that my belt was touching the top of the picnic table. Keith stood atop the table, still laughing as he faced my direction. I drew back my arm and threw an upward punch as hard as I could. . .

My fist landed squarely in his crotch.

Keith immediately doubled over in pain. The fact that I'd punched him right in his prepubescent manhood would be a topic of conversation for years to come. While the punch itself was seriously damaging to Keith's diminutive manhood and ego, it was not what changed the power structure of our third grade Lord of the Flies. As he grabbed himself in pain, Keith screamed a high-pitched yelp, sounding like a cross between the scream of a three-year-old girl and the bark of a Chihuahua. All the other boys immediately laughed at the squeal emanating from Keith. When he heard the other boys laughing, Keith stood straight up with a pained look of shock and disbelief on his face. Billy Sanders was the first to notice the wet stain beginning to cover the front of Keith's tan corduroy pants. The stream slowly moved down one pants leg, stopping just above the knee. His eyes began to well with tears, and Keith quickly hopped off the table and ran bow legged all the way to where Mrs. Sullivan was standing. I could see him crying and pointing back in my direction.

When I told my side of the story to Mrs. Sullivan, I could see the edges of her lips curl slightly upward, forming a crooked smile across her face. She told me that I would spend the next three days sitting by her during recess, and that she would have to notify my parents about what I had done. I hung my head and simply said, "Yes ma'am." As I walked away, I thought I heard the sound of suppressed laughter.

That day, Keith Batson received a nickname. For the rest of his elementary school career, he was called, "Pee-ith."

That was also the day Jimmy and I became best friends.

It was our graduation night, and a select group from our class of over five hundred graduates gathered at a lake house owned by Derek Johnson's parents. I felt a great sense of peace as I listened to the steady rhythm of waves lapping against the dock. From our vantage point, we could see the whirlwind of activity happening inside the house perched on the hill above us. While it was extremely nice by my standards, it did not compare to his family's stately home in the Myers Park section of Charlotte, North Carolina. Located just a few miles from the uptown business district, Myers Park was developed in 1905 as a streetcar community for the wealthy families of Charlotte. Hundred-year-old willow oaks lined the main road, and grand estate homes from the 1920s and 30s sat on large, mature lots. Just off the main road were streets with houses not quite as grand, yet highly desirable.

Derek's family lived on one of those side streets in a large, newly constructed home sitting on a lot formerly occupied by a 1950s ranch home. They bought the home for the lot, tore down the old house, and built a 5,000 square foot house, which barely fit on the land where it sat. They easily could have paid half the price to purchase a home just a few miles farther away from uptown, but wanted the prestige and convenience of the Myers Park neighborhood.

I grew up in a house located in one of those side neighborhoods, only about a mile from Derek's family. The street and lot were similar, but our homes were vastly different. Our home was built in 1952 with none of the grand features of the stately mansions located just a stone's throw away on Queens Road West.

Our middle-class family living in an upper-class

neighborhood meant my friends came from far wealthier families. I spent countless hours at Jimmy's home located just a couple of miles from my own.

Jimmy's father worked for the First Union Corporation, which just a few years later merged with and changed its name to Wachovia. Jimmy's father was a senior vice president and for a period of time worked on the same floor as Derek's father. Both men climbed their way up the corporate ladder, although in much different ways. Mr. Johnson worked seventy-five hours a week, Monday through Friday, and played golf every Saturday and Sunday. Frequent business trips meant that Derek would often go for several weeks without seeing his father. Mr. Johnson was a great provider for his family, but to Derek was little more than a paycheck to support their lifestyle.

Jimmy's father, on the other hand, approached his job in a much different manner. Although he was well regarded in his position, he rarely put in more than fifty hours a week, which was an anomaly for someone working at his level. He was an exceptionally astute financial expert and somehow completed his work without being chained to his desk all week. Before his divorce, Jimmy's father played golf every weekend. When he came to Jimmy's mom, begging her to take him back, he did so with a broken 7–iron, a symbolic gesture of his willingness to cease playing this sport in order to win her back. With his parents reconciled, Jimmy's family was able to move out of the apartment and into a house. His mom insisted on buying a home zoned for the same school where Jimmy and his sister were attending. She did not want to add any more change to their already turbulent year. Her decision meant that I was able to continue going to school with my new best friend.

⌁━━━━━━━━━⌁

I adjusted myself in my seat, careful not to spill the Bud-Light in my hand. The adult libation was courtesy of Mr. Johnson. Earlier that day, he had purchased enough beer to stock the refrigerator in the lake house. The assortment of domestic and imported beers was a sort of graduation present for Derek and his friends. As people arrived at the house that afternoon, he diligently procured the car keys of everyone who entered. Even those who did not drive their vehicles were forced to hand over their keys. Mr. Johnson placed all the keys in two large Ziploc bags and announced that he would be back the next morning at seven o'clock. If any problems developed, he said, call the house and he could be back in thirty minutes. Under no circumstances was anyone to leave the house and go anywhere. "Otherwise," he said, "congratulations, be safe, and you kids have fun."

"I've always liked Derek's dad," I said. "I know they can be kind of snobbish about their money, but he seems like a nice guy. I mean, hey, he bought all that beer for us. He can't be all that bad."

"Mr. Johnson is fine," Jimmy said. "My dad always got along with him when they worked together. He is way too in love with his money and his toys, but he's okay."

"Jimmy, are you sure you don't want to drink a beer?" I asked. "I'll be happy to go get one for you. I mean, come on; it's graduation night, no one is driving, and best of all, it's free! No one will care if you drink one beer. I certainly won't."

"I know it would not be a big deal to you, but it would rock the worlds of the people inside that house. They would all scramble for their cameras, overcome with joy that the good Christian high school boy is partying like a rock star. I have no interest in getting the gossip mill running at full speed by drinking a can of that horse piss."

"How do you know it tastes like horse piss? Have you ever had a beer?"

"No and I've never tried horse piss either, but I've smelled both and they smell pretty much the same to me. So, I think I'll pass on that beer."

Although I cherished Jimmy's friendship, we had never seen eye to eye on religious matters. We were very different from Jimmy's family. They attended church every Sunday. Jimmy's father was on the church leadership board and was involved in discussions concerning any major issues. Jimmy and his sister attended youth group meetings, summer camp, and retreats. While our family had a loose association with church, the schedule of Jimmy's family seemed to revolve around their church activities.

Our divergent views on religious matters caused only a small degree of discord between us. There were occasions when our conversations took on a theological bent, but Jimmy always managed to refrain from a proselytizing tone in his speech. I was able to express my views without fear of judgment, and he was able to do the same. Jimmy was the only person I knew who was simultaneously very religious and very normal.

On that cool evening in May of 1993, I found myself extremely thankful for my friendship with Jimmy. A gentle breeze blew over the lake, creating small, uniform waves, giving the dock a steady, methodical, rhythmic bob. For several moments, neither of us spoke. We both seemed to be relishing that rare moment in life when responsibilities are few and freedoms are aplenty.

Jimmy broke the silence first. "It's going to be a great summer."

"Great summer," I replied.

Jimmy continued, "I promise I'll come visit you at Mercer, when I get a chance."

"You'd better."

"How's that beer?"

"Tastes like horse piss."

"Told you," Jimmy said with a smile.

My son, keep your father's command and do not forsake your mother's teaching.

Proverbs 6:20

Chapter 3

Saturday, September 4, 1993

It was early on Saturday morning, and my father had his golf bag in one hand and a thermos in the other. He was pointed toward the back door of our house, heading toward his car and the golf course for his regular Saturday game.

"Your mother tells me you're going shopping today."

"Yeah, there are some things I need to get for my dorm. You sure you don't want to come with us, dad?" I had a smirk on my face, knowing well his answer to my question.

"Funny! I'll see you guys at dinner tonight."

My father was a faithful provider for our family, a good husband to my mom, and was always there for me if I needed anything. But Dad was not the emotional type. Our conversations rarely dived below surface level discussions.

Once, when I was ten years old, my mom happened to overhear the braggadocio of a neighborhood kid as he held captive a small audience of fifth graders with the purported interactions between him and his girlfriend. Dustin Holbrooke was thirteen years old and lived just a few houses down the street from ours. Three friends, including Jimmy, had come to my house after school to play a rudimentary game of front yard football. Jimmy and I were leading the game 203–147 when Dustin came strolling down the sidewalk. He stopped and watched our competition, making his desire for us to include him quite obvious. After three more touchdowns and still no invitation extended, he called out, "Hey Henry, you guys need someone else for your game?"

"No Dustin," I said. "I think we are just about finished playing."

"Aww, that's fine. I'm really too tired to play anyway. I just spent the last couple of hours at Amy's house. Her parents were at work. We were alone."

Dustin was one of those guys who, although older than me, seemed to be much less cool. He had this insatiable desire to be liked by others, and would say or do anything to gain acceptance from his peers. While not an uncommon trait among the youthful, Dustin seemed to be especially concerned with the image he personified. He would aggrandize the events of any story to elevate his own particular part in the drama. Everyone understood this to be part of Dustin's personality, but at this particular moment not a one of us was concerned with this flaw in his character. He obviously had a story, and any ten-year-old boy gladly listened to a tale expounding upon the mysteries of the female anatomy. Our game was officially over, and we quickly gathered around this juvenile narrator, eager for any information he would share.

"Did you hold her hand?" . . . "Did you kiss her?" . . . "Did she kiss you back?"

A broad grin formed across Dustin's face as he enjoyed the attention he so desperately craved. So, for a full fifteen minutes, he described his afternoon rendezvous with Amy. The details of his experience happened to follow, nearly to the exact detail, the romantic scene between Patrick Swayze and Demi Moore in *Ghost*. Fortunately for him, no one questioned the veracity of Dustin's tale. We simply wanted details, whether they were created by him or by Hollywood.

Unbeknownst to any of us, the kitchen window was ajar, and my mom overheard the fabricated tale of Dustin's early entrance into manhood. While she seriously doubted this teenage girl actually exhibited the kind of romantic assertiveness as described by Dustin, she saw my hopeful expression that soon I would be so fortunate as to find such a girl.

My father came home that evening from work, and she told him that it was time for him to have 'the talk' with me.

As soon as I finished my supper, I asked if I could be excused to my room. I needed some time to process this new information imparted to me earlier in the day. Just as my mind began to replay the details of Dustin's story, I heard a tenuous knock at the door. The knob slowly turned, the door cracked open, and my father's head peeked into my room. He saw me on the bed and said, "Son, I need to talk to you for a minute."

"Yeah Dad?"

My father entered, closed the door behind him, and perched himself on the edge of my bed.

"Okay, so here's the deal."

My father liked to use that phrase a lot. Somehow it conveyed this sense that he had a handle on the situation, had thoroughly examined all the facts, and had ascertained the most effective and efficient way to address whatever problem lay before us. When he said the words "Here's the deal," he intended for me to listen to his great wisdom as he enlightened me with his summation of a complex situation.

"We are going to have this talk, but I'm pretty sure you've already learned a lot. So I'm going to cut straight to it. I will tell you something, and if you already know it, you just say, 'I understand.' Understand?"

"Umm, I think so." I suspected I knew the subject matter he would cover; my heart began to beat quickly and I felt my face become flushed. There is no emotional pain in the world worse than suffering through a parental sex talk.

"So, here's the deal. There are boy parts and there are girl parts," he continued. "You got that?"

My heart sank to my stomach. I had come to my

room immediately after dinner to recall certain details of Dustin's story. Any previously felt feelings were now officially annihilated by my father's opening statement.

"Yeah, Dad, I got it."

"Say, 'I understand.'"

"Okay. I understand."

"Good. Now, when boy parts and girl parts go together, that will produce a baby. You got it?"

"I understand."

"Now for the most important thing I am going to tell you tonight. I want you to listen carefully and tell me that you understand what I'm about to tell you. I have to go back in there and convince your mom that you get the whole birds and the bees thing. So I'm going to tell you something, and I want you to let me know that you understand me completely. Here's the deal: don't go putting your boy parts with any girl parts until you are ready to have a baby. You understand?"

My mouth fell open. I simply wanted this nightmare to end, and I was thankful for the expeditious manner in which he had handled this topic.

I replied, "I understand."

"Good! Now one more thing. Listen to me carefully. Here's the deal: if you and your friends want to talk about sex stuff, make sure you aren't standing next to the kitchen window. Good night, Henry. I would say sweet dreams, but I'm guessing that's a forgone conclusion."

My father was right. That night I dreamed I was in

the back of my mother's Ford Taurus station wagon with Demi Moore. She was kissing me, and I was completely frozen in awe of the experience. She pulled her head back and looked at me with the smirk of an older, much more experienced partner. I looked over her left shoulder, and I could see my mother staring at us through the kitchen window, her face displaying a scornful look of disapproval. I looked back at Demi, but she was no longer Demi Moore. Demi had turned into Dustin Holbrooke. He smiled and leaned toward me in an attempt at kissing. I recoiled in horror and woke up to the sound of my own scream. I lay still in my bed for a few moments, my heart beating rapidly, trying to process my nightmare. Before I could apply too much Freudian psychology to it all, I heard my mother calling me to breakfast. I quickly ran to the escape of food and conversation, hoping the dream would slip deeply into my subconscious and remain forever buried there.

My mother walked in the room just as my father's hand reached the doorknob. "Hank," she said. "I really wish you'd change your mind and go shopping with us. This is Henry's last couple of weeks with us. Don't you want to spend time with your son?"

"Of course I do, Mary."

My father turned and spoke directly to me. "I'll be back this afternoon and we can do whatever you want to do, Henry."

My mother knew that my father was not going to

suddenly cancel his golf game, but she enjoyed pouring on the guilt. As he walked out the door, she turned to me, smiled, and said, "Now he can't say anything to me about the money we are going to spend today."

I prayed for this child, and the Lord has granted me what I asked of him.

I Samuel 1:27

Chapter 4

Sunday, September 12, 1993

The pastor rose to give his final benediction. I was thankful the service was nearly completed. It was a beautiful fall day in Charlotte, and one of the remaining few I had to enjoy before leaving for college. My mother had insisted we all attend church services as a family, and with her oldest child's departure from home quickly approaching, she desperately wanted to capture opportunities for family bonding experiences. Our desire to keep mama happy necessitated our presence in the worship service.

We attended Eastover United Methodist, a sizable congregation in the prestigious Eastover section of Charlotte. My mother's family joined the church when she was three years old. My father grew up in a Presbyterian church in a small town located about sixty miles south of Atlanta. They met while both attending Mercer University in Macon, Georgia. They married the summer after their graduation, moved to Charlotte, and I was born two years later. In their first two years of marriage, they only attended the obligatory Easter or Christmas service with my mom's family. In those periods of time between the high holidays, my grandparents constantly pressured my parents to accompany them to their church. When my mom became pregnant, the entreaties frequently contained the phrase, "You know, a child needs to be raised in church."

Shortly after my entry into this world, the *cri de coeur* officially reached its climax. It was the Sunday after my first Easter, and my father had decided not to attend church that morning with my mom and grandparents. He'd made the compulsory appearance the week before, on Easter Sunday. He told my mother he needed to go to the office that morning and prepare for a Monday morning meeting. The truth was that he did not want to attend two Sundays in a row and risk acquiring the reputation of going overboard with the whole church thing. More importantly, he wanted to make sure he was home in time to watch the final round of the Masters Golf Tournament. He went to the office, as promised, then came home in time to settle in on the couch, watch golf, and occasionally nap during the commercials.

My mom took me, only three weeks old at this time, and met my grandparents at the morning worship service.

My grandmother prepared a big lunch and begged my mom to bring me to their house after the service. She had invited two couples from her Sunday School class so that she could proudly display her first grandchild to these unsuspecting visitors. They spent the afternoon eating, taking turns feeding me, and ogling me as I slept. It was just after four o'clock when my grandparents took my mom and me, back to our house.

My grandmother walked into the den about the time Jack Nicklaus was finishing the thirteenth hole at Augusta. My father was dressed in gym shorts and a T-shirt. Open on his chest was a half-eaten bag of potato chips. Although he was never a great golfer, he loved the Masters. When he was in high school, his father, my grandfather, was given two tickets to the 1966 Masters Tournament. He took my father, who was only fourteen years old at the time. It was the year Jack Nicklaus won in a playoff against Gay Brewer and Tommy Jacobs, winning his second consecutive and third Masters tournament. My father became a lifelong fan of "The Golden Bear" that Sunday afternoon.

For the rest of his life, he would vehemently argue his case that Jack Nicklaus was the greatest golfer who ever lived. Years later, when Tiger Woods began to stockpile one tournament win after another, I distinctly remember hearing my father say often, "That kid may just end up being the second best golfer who has ever lived." No matter what anyone else accomplished, in my father's mind, Jack would never be deposed as the king of the golf world.

He had fallen asleep a couple of times, but by four

o'clock found himself hypnotized by the television set. It was a tight match between Nicklaus, Johnny Miller, and Tom Weiskopf. My grandmother walked in and stood, with her hands on her hips, staring at my father slouching on the couch, sloppily dressed, with potato chip crumbs all around him. "Hank" she said. He did not budge. "Hank!"

"Please, Martha. I promise you that whatever needs fixin', I will look at it in just a little while."

With the precision of a United States Marine, my grandmother turned on her left heel, walked over to the television set, and very dramatically hit the power button. My father bolted from his prone position, spilling potato chips all over the carpet. "What the heck, Martha?" As crass as my father could be, he still managed to control his language around his mother-in-law.

"Hank, I'll turn the television back on after you answer one question for me."

"Please Martha, I beg you. Hurry up and ask your question. I want to watch the Masters. For Pete's sake, what do you want?"

"I want to know–when do you plan to have your son baptized?"

My father had no such plans at all. He had assumed that responsibility, along with the changing of diapers, feeding, bathing, and other general provisions for my welfare fell under the mom job description. His duties were not supposed to kick in until the child became old enough to play sports. He was, in his mind, there to provide a paycheck for the child and to fix things when they broke.

How to clothe me, what to feed me, when to change me, and who was to baptize me were decisions he thought should be left to my mother.

"I don't know, Martha. Have you checked with Nancy? She probably knows what the best thing is to do on that."

"Nancy is in the back, changing Henry's diaper and putting him down for a nap. She will be finished in fifteen minutes or so. I'll be more than happy to stand here and wait while the two of you discuss what Sunday would work best with your busy schedule so that you can be there for you son's baptism. We will probably have the whole thing worked out in the next thirty minutes or so, and then I will gladly turn the television back on so you can watch the rest of your sports show. Or, you could tell me right now that you'll be available next Sunday and that I can call Reverend Brown tomorrow and set the whole thing up. If you decide that will work, then as far as I'm concerned this conversation is over and I'll turn the television back on. The choice is yours."

My father would often tell me that I owed my Christian baptism to The Golden Bear.

We attended church services at least once a month, more regularly in the winter months. In the spring, summer, and fall, other events took priority over church attendance. There were weekend get-away's, visiting relatives, and as my sister and I grew older, countless baseball games and soccer matches. Much to the dismay of my grandparents, we never became overly active or invested in Eastover Methodist.

As we exited the front doors of the church sanctuary, I immediately felt the warm sunshine mixed with the crisp air. I rushed my parents and sister to the parking lot and our waiting car. I desperately wanted to enjoy one of my few remaining afternoons of freedom before beginning my freshman year of college.

He loved the young woman and spoke tenderly to her.

Genesis 34:3

Chapter 5

Monday, September 20, 1993

My father and I sat across from each other at The Charlotte Café, a restaurant located less than a mile from our house. Since I had entered high school, our family dined together at this establishment at least once a week. My mother's return to the work force had caused her to retire from her previous position as head cook of our household. With its selection of meats and vegetables, she believed the menu of The Charlotte Café offered the next best thing to a home-cooked meal.

"Are you nervous, excited, or both?" My father asked as he and I were waiting on my mother and sister to arrive at the restaurant. We had left the house in separate cars so that my mom could retrieve my sister from her soccer practice. My sister had just started her ninth grade year at

Myers Park High School, the same school I had attended. The practice was apparently running long, and so my father and I were waiting in a booth for the two of them to arrive.

"I think both, Dad. Probably more nervous than excited. Although I guess I should trust you and mom. Both of you loved the place."

It was the previous Thanksgiving, during my senior year in high school, when I came to the realization that my immediate future had already been predetermined. I had just recently received the results of my SAT's. While it was evident that I most likely would not have a future as a Rhodes Scholar, my score of 1280 was respectable enough for me to gain consideration by most universities. Because I'd lived in Charlotte my entire life, the wide spread presence of Carolina Blue intensified my enthusiasm for the University of North Carolina at Chapel Hill. Several friends in my class, including my best friend Jimmy, were planning on becoming Tar Heels that next fall, so there was a natural appeal for me to do the same. Roughly a two-hour drive from Charlotte, the school was located far enough away from home to have an adequate "buffer zone," and yet close enough to come home to deposit laundry and procure a home cooked meal. Armed with a decent grade point average and an SAT score in the very acceptable range, I discussed going to Chapel Hill as if it were a foregone conclusion.

The only barrier to my plans was the fact that my mother and father had both matriculated at a small Baptist school located in the central part of Georgia. They met during the fall of their freshman year while attending the weekly chapel service. The school required every student to attend a chapel service at 11:00AM on Wednesday mornings. The services were designed to indoctrinate the students in the ways of being academically Baptist, and were incredibly dull. My father often talked about how these chapel services succeeded in confirming his view that the Bible must be the most boring book ever to sell more than a hundred copies.

Students were required to attend, but there was no effective way to force them to pay attention. Newspapers were wide open, ostentatiously displayed in protest of the obligatory presence in chapel. Some students studied, some slept, and few suffered in silence. The next year the University decided to make chapel services optional.

It was a Wednesday morning in the fall of 1971 when my parents spoke to each other for the very first time. My father had noticed my mom on campus and admired her from a distance. That morning, as Mercer students begrudgingly filed into the chapel, my father saw my mom entering the pew directly across from where he stood. He quickly moved into the pew from the other side so that the two would eventually meet in the middle and sit next to each other during the service.

As chapel began, he wondered how to initiate a conversation with this girl he had esteemed from across the campus. He knew that his window of opportunity was available for one hour, and that quite possibly he may not have such a favorable moment again. The lecture that day was by a visiting New Testament professor from an Ivy

League school. As my father remembered the story, it was the most tedious, monotonous speech he'd ever heard. As the professor droned on for nearly forty-five minutes, my father racked his brain, trying to craft an opening line to get the attention of this girl seated next to him. The lecture eventually ended, and as the students were instructed to rise for the closing hymn, my father became keenly aware that his golden opportunity was slipping away. Under such pressure, he came up with what he thought was the height of cleverness.

As the student body stood to sing, "O God Our Help in Ages Past", my father leaned over to my mother and asked, "Come here often?"

My mother simply stared at my father and said, in her most proper southern accent, "Yes. Every week. Chapel attendance is required." She then turned her head and faced the front of the room.

The pipe organ paused at the end of the first verse and then quickly resumed its bellowing. My father, having had his advances thoroughly rebuffed, decided it was time to throw the proverbial Hail Mary. With nothing left to lose, he leaned down and whispered in my mother's ear, "There ain't a girl in this entire chapel as pretty as you. Even Diana Miller sitting over there would look homely if she was seated here next to you."

Diana Miller was a junior Phi-Mu with a voluptuous body, olive skin, long brown hair, and ocean blue eyes. She was most often seen with a gaggle of KA boys vying for her attention. Every male on campus admired her. Every female envied her. Any objective observer would have noted that Diana Miller would not have been the prettiest girl on campus only if Pattie Boyd or Cheryl Tiegs suddenly decided to enroll at Mercer.

My father held his breath. He knew that he would either be slapped across the face, or would have a date that night. While most stood and stared into space, a few good Baptist students obediently sang the words,

"A thousand ages in thy sight, are like an evening gone; short as the watch that end the night before the rising sun."

My father never averted his gaze from my mother. He waited patiently to see if the desparate play was a success or if his team would crawl back to the locker room in defeat. After what seemed to be an eternal five seconds, he noticed the corner of her mouth curl in an upward motion. The song ended and the organ thundered its final blast. The dean of students stepped to the pulpit to voice the closing prayer. The congregation would soon be dismissed and the object of his affection swept into conversation by the adjacent crowd of girls. As the dean finished his magniloquent appeal to the Almighty and bellowed a prolonged, concluding "Haaay-men," my mother turned and whispered, "Plunkett Dorm. Room two-fourteen. Pick me up at seven tonight." The split second after she relayed those glorious instructions to my father, she was whisked away to the cafeteria by a cohort of coeds.

My father repeated, "Plunkett, two-fourteen, seven o'clock" to himself over and over until he felt certain he had it memorized. As he exited the chapel, he was overwhelmed with joy from narrowly securing a date with this girl he had admired from a distance for the previous two months. Less than an hour later, shortly after finishing lunch, he suddenly realized he had never learned her name. She was a Chi-Omega pledge. He knew that fact from observing her wearing a jersey proudly displaying the two Greek letters. He thought about going to the sorority house and describing her to whoever answered the door, hoping that his words would be accurate enough to secure a name. But no girl would ever agree to keep that a secret, and he knew word would eventually get back to. . .'what's her name'. . . of his furtive mission. As he walked from the cafeteria back to his dorm room, he abandoned plan A and desperately tried to conceive of a plan B.

He reached his room and sat on the edge of his bed to contemplate his choices. He could, perhaps, simply show up for the date that night, go into the lobby of Plunkett Dormitory, call the room, and announce to whoever answered, "I'm here." But he knew that would be a crass way to begin a date, and that he may spend the entire evening with this girl not knowing her name.

He rubbed his eyes, then his temples, then his eyes again. When he looked up, his gaze landed on the tiny desk squeezed between his dresser and his closet. There, sticking up between two text books, was the campus phone directory. He slid into the metal chair, ergonomically designed to keep students from becoming too comfortable and sleeping instead of studying. He grabbed the directory, quickly turned to the first page, and spent the next hour reading every name until he found two identified as living in room two-fourteen of Plunkett Dormitory: Mary Thompson and Renee Barnes. He had it narrowed down to two names. Now he just needed to determine which name fit with his date for that evening. He could not simply walk to the front desk, ask for Mary, or ask for Renee, take the fifty-fifty chance he was right, and hope for the best. He had to find a way to know he had the right name.

He rubbed his temples for a while longer, struggling to determine his course of action. Suddenly, almost with no warning, the idea came to him. He picked up the phone and quickly, before he lost his nerve, dialed the number for room two-fourteen.

"Hello?" a female voice answered.

My father, with his best nasal, Boston accent, said, "Ya, uh, is Mary there?"

"This is she."

"Uh, Mary, this is John." He was trying his best to imitate the vocal inflections of President Kennedy, and so it made sense he would go by 'John.'

"Who?"

"John. I'm in your English class." He paused and held his breath that she, like most freshmen, was taking English.

"Dr. Brown's class?" *Thank God*, he thought. Dr. Brown taught English 101.

"Yes, that's it."

"I'm so sorry, but I do not think I recognize who you are," she stated.

"Uh, yeah, well, I sit in the back of the class. Listen, I missed class last week. I was sick all week long. Could I come by your dorm this evening and see your notes from class?"

"Umm...well, I guess you could. What time did you want to come by?"

"Maybe around seven?" There was a long pause on the other end. If she said yes, then his date that night would be with the lovely Renee. If she said she was busy, his escort would be Mary.

"John, look, I'm so sorry. I cannot for the life of me recall who you are and I'm just not comfortable meeting you."

So what did that mean? His mind raced, trying to come up with some question or comment that would force her to reveal her plans for that evening. Before his brain could craft a reply, she spoke again.

"I'm sure you can find someone else in the class with decent notes. I'm sorry. Plus, I have plans at seven tonight and would not be able to meet you anyway."

Mary. Mary Thompson. Mary Thompson, room two-fourteen, Plunkett. Got it.

"John, are you there?"

"Uh, yeah, thanks anyway Mary. Gotta go. Bye."

Some of my earliest memories are of my parents telling stories of their years together at Mercer. They both spoke with such affection and wistfulness that it should not have surprised me at all when, on that fall day, my father put up his hand, signaling the need for me to end my rambling on about going to Chapel Hill.

"So, here's the deal," my father said, utilizing his favorite phrase to communicate to me that he had already figured out what I should do. "Henry, you can go to any college that accepts you."

"Good, Dad. Because I think that with this SAT score, UNC will accept me."

"You did not let me finish. Here's the deal: you can go to any college that accepts you, but if you want me to pay for it, you are going to Mercer University, understood?"

My mother and sister rushed into the restaurant and sat down. I could see from the expression on my mother's face that she was disappointed over being late. Every family experience for the last month had been approached with an extreme amount of nostalgia. This was our "last" family meal together before I departed for college, and she wanted to relish every moment.

"Mary, what are you going to get to eat? We have been sitting here for twenty minutes waiting on the two of you. Be ready to order when the server comes."

"Hank, give me just a minute, will you? It's our last night together. I want to relax and enjoy it."

My father huffed but remained silent. He knew not to push my mother. This time meant a great deal to her. He fought his hunger pangs and took a drink from his glass. The next day I would be forced to listen to his musings on the chronic lateness of the female members of our family.

He will turn the hearts of the parents to their children, and
the hearts of the children to their parents.

Malachi 4:6

Chapter 6

Tuesday, September 21, 1993

We started our journey to Macon, Georgia early on that Tuesday morning. My father drove his Jeep Cherokee and I rode in the passenger seat, anxious about beginning my freshman year of college. We started our trip listening to WBT, the Charlotte news channel. Roughly twenty miles before reaching Columbia, South Carolina, as static began to intermittently cover the voice of Don Russell, my father reached over and pressed the power button on the radio, suddenly filling the car with silence.

"So, you excited about college?" He asked, attempting to initiate a conversation.

"I think so. I'm not sure. I have no idea what to expect. I guess you know better than me. Should I be excited?"

"You'd better believe it. You are about to begin the greatest four years of your life."

The journey from Charlotte, North Carolina to Macon, Georgia was, to that point in my life, my greatest bonding experience with my father. Unaccustomed to meaningful conversations between the two of us, I was shocked when he turned off the radio and began to tell me stories of his years at Mercer. I was enthralled with his tales of pledging a fraternity and the abuse he suffered from the hostility of upperclassmen. On that trip I learned that my father had deeply desired to major in art, but his father, my grandfather, insisted he get a degree in business. My father recounted taking my mother on a date to Coleman Hill, an elevated point in Macon overlooking the city. He packed a picnic supper of Vienna sausages, Saltine crackers, Velveeta cheese slices. They laid on a blanket, watching the sun settle on the horizon and the stars make their appearance in the night sky. He told me how he knew, after that evening, he would one day propose to my mother.

<hr/>

We arrived at Mercer University just before two o'clock. During the summer, I received a letter indicating my dorm assignment was Shorter Hall, room 102. The letter informed me of my roommate's name, Stanislaw Andrej Szukalski, and that he was from Buffalo, New York. The letter gave the address and phone number of Stanislaw. I contacted him in early July to introduce myself and discuss room arrangements. Much to my delight, I would not be saddled with the arduous task of having to pronounce his first or middle name. In that conversation, I learned that he went by the nickname, "Law." I also learned that his grandparents emigrated from Poland just after the second World War, and that he was thoroughly Yankee and thoroughly Roman Catholic. He had been recruited by Mercer's baseball program. He played catcher in high school, and had never heard of Mercer or Macon until receiving a phone call from the coach.

I would later discover that my future roommate was physically built like a cube. Standing just over five feet eight inches, he was nearly as wide as he was tall, and he possessed a culverin for a right arm. It was a rare occurrence for a base runner or ball to get past Law. Attempts to steal second base while he was positioned at home plate were most often unsuccessful.

My father parked his Jeep in the closest space he could find to Shorter Hall. During our father–son bonding experience on the road, he informed me that he had spent his sophomore year in Shorter Hall. "You're lucky to be on the first floor," he said. "I lived on the fourth. Here's the deal: come June, it gets dang hot on the fourth floor."

"You mean Shorter is *not* air-conditioned?"

"I'm sure it is now. That was in the 1970s. None of the dorms had air conditioning back then. I would be surprised if it has not been updated by now."

My father was surprised. I was distressed. The

heat and humidity of the September day hit me as soon as I opened the passenger side door. Even though I knew cooler weather was approaching, I found myself already agonizing over what the next May and June would bring. We walked into the dorm and located my room. We entered and immediately saw sprawled on the bottom bunk, in nothing but his boxers, my roommate Law. The shape of his body seemed to mirror the rectangular form of the mattress below him. His biceps were the size of my legs, and his legs had the same thickness as my torso. He wore a short, military–style haircut. Dark, thick hair covered his chest and stomach, giving him the appearance of having a swath of black shag carpet lying atop his body. His legs and arms were covered with hair as well. As he lay sprawled on the bed, he reminded me of a stuffed teddy bear wearing a pair of shorts.

He slept soundly and snored loudly. I knocked, a little tenuous at first, somewhat scared to wake the grizzly bear. I banged with more force, and this time the giant shifted. I gave one more quick, sharp pound on the door, and Law sat straight up in his bed, knocked his head on the bar located underneath the top bunk, and screamed a couple of expletives. He turned his head and saw us standing in the doorway.

"Mary, mudder of our Lord Jesus! Youse two done scared the living daylights outta me!"

"You must be Law," I said.

"Das right. And youse must be Henry. Pleased ta

meetchya. Dis youse fadder?"

"Yeah, this is my dad. Hank Miller. We just pulled in a little while ago."

"Pleased ta meetchya as well, Mista Miller. Hey, Henry, I gotcha key right heyr. Youse gotta buncha stuff? I'm happy to help ya unload. Lemme find some shoes."

"What about a shirt and shorts?"

"No way. It's so cursed hot down heyr in dis place I ain't wearing any clothes till deys tell me I gots to. Where's your car?"

My father quickly interjected. "Law, I think we just have a couple other bags. Stay right here and we'll go get them. I want to be able to say goodbye to Henry anyway."

"Whatever youse guys say. Nice to meetcha Mista Miller."

"You too Law."

My father and I walked back outside to his car, my father said, "Good Lord, I didn't want to have that naked Sasquatch out here walking around campus with us. Look, son, I wanted to do one thing with you before I left to go back to Charlotte. I want to take you by the old fraternity house, show you where it is, and see if any guys are there for you to meet. I'm not pressuring you at all, but I want them to know there is a legacy on campus."

We walked from Shorter Hall to fraternity row. Perched on top of a hill, looking out over the intramural field, sat the Kappa Sigma house, painted in red, white and green. On the right side of the front door was a large crest, and on the left side of the door were red letters, roughly four feet tall each. One letter clearly was a K. The second letter looked to me to be an upper case E, although not quite formed correctly.

"Dad, why is that E painted on the wall?"

"Isn't not an E. It's a Greek Sigma. Kappa Sigma. Walk up to the house with me. I want to see if anyone is home. You may want to let me do most of the talking."

My father walked to the front door and noticed it was slightly ajar. He gave a push and we walked into a foyer. On the walls hung large composite portraits of brothers from years past. Each framed amalgamation captured the four classes of students who matriculated that year as Kappa Sigma brothers. Their rigid poses and stern expressions solemnly bespoke their immortalization in time. The decades old black and white portraits with tarnished glass were on one side of the foyer. As the decades progressed, the composites became larger, eventually adding color, now, the most recent ones had the clarity of a contemporary photograph.

A boy stepped through a door, stopped, and was obviously surprised to see two people he did not recognize in the foyer. He was tall, skinny, and had a mop of dark brown hair on his head. For a brief moment, I expected a grunt or a "whatzz up, dude?" to come out of his mouth. Instead, with perfect diction, he reached out his hand to my father and said, "Welcome to the Kappa Sigma house, sir. I am Brother Chip Malone. Can I help you gentlemen with anything?"

I noticed my father did not return this fellow's

greeting with a normal handshake. There was something different about the way he grasped the outstretched hand, and this signal seemed to be instantly recognized by Chip.

"Nice to meet you, Brother Malone. My name is Brother Hank Miller, class of '75. This is my son, Henry, and he is just beginning his college career here at Mercer. I thought we might drop by and let me introduce him to a few Kappa Sigmas."

Chip reached over and shook my hand. "Nice to meet you Henry. You plan on going through rush?" His voice was so crisp and authoritative that for a moment I was unable to speak. I immediately felt gravely inexperienced as I stood before this self-assured college upperclassman. With a crack in my voice and the words stumbling out, I finally managed to say, "Uh, I think so, yeah, sure, when is it?"

"Oh, don't worry, they will explain it all to you in orientation. We are not allowed to do any pre-rush activities right now, but just be sure to find me when you come through the house."

My father shook hands again with Chip, although this time it seemed to be a normal two-handed grip, and said, "Thanks, Chip. I'm sure you will be seeing Henry again."

We walked back to my father's car. I reached in and retrieved two suitcases containing the remainder of the possessions needed for my first quarter in college. My father gave me a hug, a physical action not all that common between us. I suddenly had this surging desire to jump in his car and go back to Charlotte. I fought the urge, and we both said our goodbyes.

"Here's the deal," he said. "I've got to get back, but you call me if you need anything at all. And be sure to give those Kappa Sigmas a chance."

"I will."

"I love you, son."

I could count on one hand the number of times he had said that to me in my life. I could feel the swelling behind my eyes and my lower lip beginning to quiver. I quickly looked down, choked back my emotion, and said,

"Thanks Dad. I love you, too. Tell Mom and Sis the same."

As I watched my father's car pull away. I stood there on the sidewalk for a few minutes, wondering if community college and living at home would have been all that bad after all. After a few more contemplative moments, I headed back toward Shorter Hall. I entered the doors to the first floor in search of my hairy roommate, hoping he would know where we were to go for our first session of freshman orientation, and hoping even more that he would wear clothes.

Two are better than one, because they have a good return for their labor. If either of them falls down, one can help the other up.

Ecclesiastes 4:9-10

Chapter 7

Friday, November 12, 1993

Holding the newspaper, I said, "Law, here it is, on the front page of the newspaper. Man, if I were you, I would have insisted they not include my picture. The article makes you sound like a saint, but your ugly mug shot doesn't do you any favors."

"Youse jest jealous, Miller. Now give me dat paper so I'se can read it."

"Law, I'll be happy to read the article to you. You do not have to fake the whole literacy thing with me. I know you can't read and that your professors are only passing you because your baseball coach has some sort of blackmail on each one."

"Shut-up Miller and give me dat paper before I break youse arm."

I just laughed and tossed the newspaper to him. He quickly scanned the article, looking for the highlights and reviewing the accuracy of the story.

"Youse know, dat reporter got it jest right. Too bad dey didn't say anytin' 'bout you, Henry. Maybe some girl out dere would feel sorry for you and youse might actually get a date."

"Don't worry, Law. I'm just waiting on the right girl. I'm getting ready to meet her any day now."

The first day I met Law, I thought our roommate status would quickly dissolve and we would each find more suitable living arrangements. It was hard to imagine a bonding experience between myself and a hairy, muscle-bound, boisterous, dyed–in–the–wool Roman Catholic Yankee. My opinion quickly changed as we walked to our first orientation session together. Fortunately, Law had decided to put on a T-shirt and a pair of nylon warm-up pants. Every step he took, I could hear the rustle of his leg hair against the synthetic material. Just listening to him walk made my body itch all over.

We walked from our dorm, past Porter Gym, and into the Connell Student Center. The cafeteria occupied one side of the building and the Co-Op occupied the other. After the cafeteria closed, food could be purchased in the Co-Op. The upstairs portion of the Student Center contained a number of offices and meeting spaces. Our first orientation class was to be in one of the larger spaces on the second floor. Just before we made it to the stairs, Law grabbed my arm and pulled me against a wall, away from the pattern of heavy foot traffic moving through the building.

"Look Henry, befores we's go to dis meetin' I want you to know someting. I really did not want to come to dis school. Come on, a Yankee Pol like me–what bidness at all do I have comin' all de way down here to Macon, Georgia? But dis school offered me a full scholarship for baseball. Only college to do dat. Even gave me an extra stipend for spendin' money. No udder school offered anyting close to dat. My parents ain't rich, so it jest made sense for me to come here. But youse southern boys gonna make fun of me and I know dat. I don't talk like you and I don't dress like you and I sure as heck ain't going to get a southern girl down here to date me. But here is da deal. You seem like a nice guy and all. Youse didn't even ask me why I only agreed to bring a clock for da room and youse brought all dat other stuff. We jest didn't have any money for me to bring a lot."

Law paused. Seeing the confused look on my face, he shifted his weight and evidently decided to get to the point. "Dere are tree tings in life I'm really good at doin." He held up the finger of one hand and touched it with the pointer finger of his other hand. "One: Eatin'. Last year I won a hot-dog eatin' contest at a festival in Buf'lo." He then held up a second finger. "Two: baseball. For some reason I jest know hows to catch, trow, and hit a ball." Finally, he pointed to his third digit. "Tree: fightin'. I sent more guys from my neighborhood to the ER to git stitched up dan I can count. So, here's my promise to you. Youse help me figure out hows to navigate de culture here, and I won't let a soul mess wit'chu. I will be the ace in your back pocket all da time. Someone need a talkin' to, or jest a little ruffling, or a full out whippin', youse jest let me know."

I wasn't sure how to respond. I had no idea that I would need protection, and I was not sure if it was a wise move to enter into this verbal contract with my Neanderthal roommate. But I saw the look of trepidation in his eyes. Although burly and physically tough, he was in a foreign land and anxious about his future. If I had been completely honest with him, I would have confessed the same fears and that moments before I had wanted to leap onto the top of my father's car and ride back to Charlotte holding on to the roof rack. Instead, I smiled and reached out my right hand. As his enormous, hairy hand shook mine, I simply said, "Deal, Law."

Had I possessed psychic powers and been able to accurately see into the future, I would have been far less cavalier in my handshake with Law. Later that week I honored the wishes of my father and went through the ritual of rush week. All the male students desiring to be part of this college tradition gathered in the auditorium of the science center. The Dean of Students, Dr. Collier, walked solemnly to the podium, and silence fell over the room. Every eye was trained on this purveyor of information on how to become a fraternity man. He cleared his throat and, in a resonant voice, began to impart his wisdom to the anxious crowd.

"You will be divided in groups of twenty according to your last name. Your leader for the next two days will be what we refer to as a Rho Chi, or rush coordinator. He is a fraternity man, but has received stringent instructions that he is not to reveal the identity of his particular affiliation. Any support, outwardly expressed or tacitly implied, for any particular fraternity house will result in severe discipline. If you notice any violation of this policy, you are instructed to report it to me immediately."

Every student sat upright and motionless in the hard chairs of the auditorium. We were now well aware of the formal process we were about to enter into and the stern rules ensuring its integrity.

"You will spend one hour at each fraternity house. During the next forty-eight hours, you are not allowed to be present at any of the houses outside of this scheduled visit. No member of a fraternity is allowed to rush you outside of this time until the forty-eight hour period ends. Any violation of this policy will disqualify the fraternity from offering you a bid."

"At the end of the next two days, formal rush ends and the informal rush period will begin. You are allowed to visit any house of your choosing during the scheduled evening rush times. You are not allowed to be in the house during the day, nor are you allowed off campus with any member of a fraternity."

"I want to remind you of our University's policy against alcoholic beverages being served during the rush period. Any fraternity caught serving will be subject to losing its charter on campus."

"At the end of this rush week, you will have an opportunity to express your interest in receiving a bid from up to three of the fraternities. Of course, you are not required to seek bids from three. You may choose only one." Dr. Collier stopped speaking. A deafening silence fell over the room. His head dropped and for several seconds he stared at the podium, as if deep in thought. It seemed as if he were too overwhelmed with emotion to speak. After a long, very pregnant pause, he regained his composure and continued his oration.

"Boys, I want you to listen to me, and listen well. I implore you, *do not* request a bid from only one fraternity. You may be steadfastly confident in your desires and believe the brothers of a house possess the same affection toward you, and thus conclude there is no reason to waste the time with another fraternity. You may disregard my appeal as the foolish rambling of an old man who is ignorant of your unique situation."

He paused again, but this time his eyes stayed trained on the crowd seated in front of him. He looked around the room, his glance slowly moving across the classroom as if he were inspecting merchandise for purchase.

"One of you in here will come to my office in a week. You will either be so emotionally overcome with grief that you will attempt to share with me your experience through mucus and tears, or you will be so livid you will spend most of the time telling me how your small town lawyer daddy is going to sue the University. The source of your consternation will be rejection by a fraternity house, even though you were supremely confident that all the brothers believed you were God's gift to the fraternal world. Gentlemen, even if every brother signs a document in his own blood declaring his solemn promise to offer you a bid, request a bid from at least one other fraternity. It will save me and you both from having that awkward conversation in my office."

Heeding the advice of Dr. Collier, I requested bids of Kappa Sigma, Kappa Alpha Order, and Lambda Chi Alpha. I received bids from all three, but had no trouble making the decision to pledge Kappa Sigma. A phone call from my father in the middle of the week removed any potential ambiguity from the process. "Henry, I want you to enjoy your time in college. You are welcome to pledge the fraternity of your choice. But here's the deal: if you want me to pay for it, you pledge Kappa Sigma."

Law did not go through the rush process. I encouraged him to sign up for the events and told him about all the free food, but he was not interested. "Come on, Miller, youse know I ain't got 'nuff money for dat fraternity stuff. Plus all dese southern boys ain't gonna want me anyhow. I'm jest fine being on de baseball team."

Turned out it was a win–win for both of us. Law quickly became more than my roommate. We developed a strong friendship, and he was nothing if not extremely loyal to his friends. Even though Law was physically tough, his reputation as an irascible and violent soul reached mythic proportions just a few weeks into our first semester.

November of our freshman year, my pledge class decided to gather at Darrell's, a bar/restaurant located a short distance from campus. Most in our class had made the effort to obtain fake identifications declaring our years on this earth to have been at least twenty-one, thus affording us the opportunity to partake in alcoholic beverages. Our gathering that night was billed as one to discuss our pledge class project. This community service project was required of all pledge classes and if it did not meet the approval of the members in the fraternity, it would result in early morning called meetings to clean the house or perform calisthenics on the intramural field.

We gathered around several tables, ordered eight pitchers of beer, and met for two hours. At ten o'clock, Danny Newman decided he wanted to go back to his dorm and call his girlfriend, who was still in high school in his hometown of Sylvester, Georgia. I agreed to walk with him under the guise of watching out for a fellow pledge brother. If I had been completely honest, the reason for my early exit was my own homesickness and the desire to make a phone call or two myself.

As we left the bar, I noticed Law in a corner booth with a few of the baseball players. I gave a slight head nod and indicated I was heading back. He waved in acknowledgment.

While located only two blocks from campus, getting to and from Darrell's by foot was not an easy process. Between the bar and Mercer sat Tattnall Square Park, an old public recreation area with a few tennis courts, a playground, and an open field. The journey back to campus could be shortened by going through the park instead of using the sidewalk around it. This particular route was not well lit and was replete with rocks and uneven ground. Many a co-ed had suffered a sprained ankle after a night of drinking at Darrell's.

Desperate to call his girlfriend before she went to bed, Danny insisted we take the shorter route through the park. We walked past the tennis courts, past the playground and continued our stroll toward the lights of campus. A row of overgrown holly bushes sat in the middle of the park, providing a barrier between an athletic field and a natural area. We walked toward the field, to the right side of these bushes. A lonely street lamp hovered over the playground area, providing light to only a small portion of the park. Danny walked just in front of me, his trepidation over missing the opportunity to speak with his girlfriend increasing the speed of his gait.

We were a hundred yards from the end of the park and the protective bubble of campus when I suddenly noticed the movement of bushes directly in front of our path. I started to pivot to the right and change my course of direction when a figure suddenly emerged from behind the wall of greenery. Danny, walking quickly with his head down to focus on every step, did not notice the approaching figure. He let out a yell, just at the last moment before impact, as he saw the feet and legs of this person intending to block his path. The figure shoved Danny, sending him flying backward and falling to the ground with a thud. I instinctively reached down to help my pledge brother to his feet, but before I could get to him, the voice of his attacker spoke.

"Don't move. Stay right there on the ground. You get down as well college boy. Throw me both your wallets and I won't have to use this gun."

I looked up and saw the shadowy figure more visibly. He was a short, white man with a ball cap pulled down low on his forehead, wearing a dark sweatshirt and dark jeans. I could not see any distinguishing characteristics on his face, but I did notice the reflection of the moonlight across the barrel of what appeared to be a sizable handgun. Frozen with fear and unable to speak or move, I just stared at our attacker.

"You fellas deaf? I said give me your wallets now, or you gonna be two dead college boys."

At that moment, I heard what sounded like the low hum of an airplane taxiing on a runway. I turned my head to see the outline of a bulky figure running directly toward our assailant. Bellowing in a rage of fury, the individual leapt from his feet and became nearly horizontal to the ground. His head landed squarely in the middle of the attacker's rib cage and sent him flying into the bushes. This hero of the night quickly scrambled to his feet, then with just one hand, lifted the man up by his neck, and I heard that blessed voice of my Yankee roommate say, "Jest who youse tink youse messin' wit, huh?" I started to warn Law about the gun, but then I looked and saw the weapon in his left hand. During their struggle, Law had somehow managed to secure the gun.

The man's feet were dangling from the ground, and with his arms he started to fight back. Law took the gun, placed it under the man's chin, and in a voice that was eerily calm, said, "I'm jest crazy 'nuff to use this." The man froze, and Law threw him to the ground.

My roommate's picture appeared both in *The Cluster*, the Mercer campus newspaper, and in the *Macon Telegraph*. He not only saved two Mercerians from being victims of larceny and possible injury, but he helped the Macon Police catch a wanted criminal. He became a hero, but as the story was told and retold, his reputation as a violent, less than stable individual spread as well.

This aura of suspicion around Law worked to my advantage. As a pledge of a fraternity, I was subjected to the ritualistic rite of passage known as hazing. Brothers had what they viewed as an obligation to thoroughly vet all those who desired membership in their ranks. Hazing was a way to ascertain one's commitment to being a part of the group. Anyone who truly wanted membership, the logic went, would be willing to suffer any abuse necessary.

The University frowned upon this time-honored tradition, so all hazing had to be carried out away from the watchful eye of the administration. While most events of this nature were innocuous, they were also annoying. To be roused from sleep at midnight just to be told to deliver a bowl of ice cream to a drunk brother in another dorm caused a deficit in my sleep.

Law's actions that night in November not only became legendary, they also served as my protection against excessive hazing. No one wanted to call my room at midnight and risk waking the sleeping giant. The members were careful not to be too harsh with me and face the wrath of my tough, unstable roommate. Law's heroism that night in Tattnall Square Park not only saved me from a heinous criminal, it also made my days as a pledge virtually hassle free.

———————

Law picked up the paper again and decided to read the entire article. He finished, looked up at me and said, "Youse know what, Miller? Dey didn't mention a ting about how youse jest laid dere in the grass while I whipped dat boy."

"Yeah, that newspaper reporter said that she took one look at me and realized that I was most definitely a lover, not a fighter."

"Miller, now I know youse crazy."

Do not be deceived, God cannot be mocked. A man reaps
what he sows.

Galatians 6:7

Chapter 8
Thursday, April 14, 1994

We sat across from one another at The Bear's Den, a greasy spoon restaurant located just a block from campus. When a hiatus from the regular routine of cafeteria food became necessary, the Bear's Den became a welcoming oasis in the desert. For $4.95, a patron received a meat, two vegetables, a square of cornbread, and a drink. The libation of choice for most of the customers was the iced tea, heavily sweetened. Three-gallon urns located at a self-serve station allowed one to refill a Styrofoam cup as often as desired. The ten pounds I gained my freshman year of college was partly attributed to the seven hundred calories consumed through a straw while at this establishment. The other culprit was the self-serve ice cream machine in the

Mercer cafeteria.

As I took a long drag of tea through my straw Law said, "I jest don't see how youse can stand that stuff. Why don't youse people down here jest drink pop like the rest of the world?"

"First of all, Law, it's not 'pop.' Like I've told you before, it's Coke. Regardless of what soft drink you choose, it's Coke. There is regular Coke, Diet Coke, Dr. Pepper Coke, and Orange Coke. The only exception to this is Sprite, but even then you would say, if someone asks, 'What are you drinking?' your reply is, 'a Coke.' Then when they say, 'What kind?' you say, 'Sprite.' Does this make sense?"

"So whatchu people say for Pepsi?"

"We don't. Nobody drinks Pepsi."

"What 'bout Snapple?"

"Never even heard of it."

"Youse people need some culturing."

"Yeah, Law, we are the ones who are uncultured."

Eating a meal with Law was less of a dining experience and more like watching a Saturday night World Wide Wresting Federation cage match. He did not extend his arm from his side, acquire the food with his utensil, then transport the fare from his plate to his mouth.

In his opinion, this form of dining wasted far too much time in getting the sustenance from his plate into his stomach. Law sat at the table with the upper half of his body hunched over his meal. His arms wrapped around the circumference of the plate so that his hands met at the northern rim of the circle. From that position he was able to virtually inhale his meal, using his paws simply as a guide for the process. Any attempted purloining of food by a naïve prankster was met with a swift and effective backhand. Law would not even raise his head until the process was completed. More often than not, I was just finishing my first bite while he was leaning back in his chair, emitting the first of many belches, and declaring his satisfaction with the meal.

This day was different. Law barely touched his food. He sat across from me, bent over his plate, with one arm by his side and the other moving green beans around with his fork.

"So whatcha think theyse people gonna do to me? Come on, Henry. Youse know these people down here. Youse daddy went to dis school. Youse knows how all dis stuff operates. If youse my real friend, youse will shoot straight wid me."

"Law, it goes without saying that you have been a great friend to me. I'm going to do everything I can to help you, but I have no idea what can be done. I'll speak on your behalf, but it sounds like this thing may be really bad for you. I'm just trying to shoot straight with you. If it works out the way I think, you will most likely lose your scholarship."

The week before, Law had introduced me to a traditional Polish celebration known as "Dyngus Day." Always on the Monday after Easter Sunday, this strange Polish–Catholic Festival celebrates the end of the restrictive observance of Lent. One might compare the intentions to Mardi–Gras, but with less revelry and occurring after rather than before the Lenten season.

"I tell ya, Miller, it's kinda like dat Cherry Blossom ting youse people have here, jest wit a whole lot more drinkin' goin' on."

In the early 1980s, Macon began a week–long celebration of the spring-time appearance of the cherry tree's pink and white blooms. By that time, Macon claimed to have over 300,000 Yoshino cherry trees planted throughout the city. Normally around the third week in March, these trees would explode with tiny blossoms. Throughout the city, there are entire streets lined with these trees, virtually forming a pink and white canopy for the passing motorists.

The Monday morning after Easter, I awoke to the sound of polka music. I looked down from my top bunk and saw Law, in nothing but his boxers, lying on the floor with a cassette player next to his head. In his left hand was a bottle, and in his right hand was some sort of stick with furry, grayish-white catkins placed sporadically along its length.

"Law, man, it's seven-thirty in the morning. What in the world are you doing?"

"Celebratin'."

"Celebrating what? The invention of really bad music."

"Shut-up, Miller. Don't make fun of polka on dis day. T'day is Dyngus Day."

"Doris Day? You mean that old actress? Why in the world are you laying on the floor talking about Doris Day?"

"Not Doris Day. Dyngus Day. It's someting we

celebrate back home in Buff'lo. Big deal dere amongst us Polacks."

"What is that you are holding?"

He lifted the bottle in the air. "Dis here is a Tyskie beer. It's a Polish beer, and I've been saving it for dis day."

"What about that branch with those little silver deals all over it?"

"Dis here is a pussy willow. I had my mudder mail it last week. Dis is what we use to celebrate. Guys throw water on girls dey like, girls hit guys dey like wit dis here, a pussy willow."

"Law, how many of those beers have you had already?"

"Only dis one, Miller. Too early for more dan dat, but dere will be more to drink tonight, and I even have a couple for you."

Law carried that pussy willow with him to class, to lunch, and even to baseball practice that afternoon. He would share tales of past Dyngus Day celebrations to anyone who would listen. His Polish and Northern heritage was a source of great pride, and he did not care who was annoyed by his bizarre antics.

The week after his solitary celebration, he received a letter in his university mailbox from Dr. Freeman, his professor of English 102. Dr. Freeman was a sixty-something year old portly gentleman who had served in his pedagogical post for over three decades. He had himself matriculated at Mercer, left to secure two advanced degrees at the University of Georgia, and immediately returned when offered an associate professorship. A decade later he was named the chair of the English department, and had ruled over his department as a fascist dictator for nearly twenty years. He took great pride in the number of freshmen who were forced to repeat his English 101 class. A smile would form and his chest would swell when he overheard the line, "Flunk with Freeman," a phrase oft repeated by some frustrated freshman.

Dr. Freeman came from extremely humble beginnings. As the son of a sharecropper from Waycross, Georgia, it was only possible for him to attend Mercer University because of the generosity of a favorite uncle. He arrived on campus in 1951 and realized his own inadequacy in the sophisticated world of higher education. He was, as the term was used, nothing but "poor, white trash." Although he had no money and almost zero understanding of the conventional standards of social behavior, he did possess an incredibly keen mind and a work ethic stronger than any in his class. He vowed to study hard, to observe carefully the world around him, and to forever elevate his stature in the social circles of southern culture.

He succeeded in this task, and upon meeting Dr. Freeman, one would assume he hailed from a wealthy Atlanta family whose ancestors had possessed large plantations and fought the fires of Sherman to save their valuable properties. He possessed such hubris and propriety that one doubted he ever performed such base human functions as going to the bathroom or belching.

His face was round and his skin pale and smooth.

At no time of the day did it ever appear he needed to shave. His fleshy jowls folded over his starched white shirt, giving the impression that the circulation of blood to his head was reduced dramatically. More than just overweight, he appeared to be extremely soft to the touch. One could imagine his torso serving well as a down pillow. It was difficult to picture Dr. Freeman ever performing any physical labor, playing sports, or participating in any activity that would cause him to sweat.

What was not immediately noticeable, but became quickly apparent by casual study, was the thick toupee he donned atop his round, corpulent head. Any cursory inspection showed the synthetic texture, slightly coarser than his natural hair on the sides and back of his head. Evident as well was how awkwardly the toupee lay at a slightly different angle from the God–given hair underneath. While the manufacturer of the cranial adornment had created the appropriate blend of grey and brown hairs, the attempted deception was futile. The full, thick head of hair adorned by Mr. Freeman was quite obviously only naturally achieved during a much earlier time in his life.

His voice was slightly higher than a normal male voice, and his accent thoroughly southern. He spoke with proper diction, thoroughly enunciating each letter in a word, sometimes allowing his voice to hang on a letter for a second or two longer than necessary. When addressing a group of students, he would emphasize and prolong the "a" in class, just long enough to give him extra time to form his next thoughts. "Now, claaass. We are looking today at the proper use of the comma in the English language." His careful, steady pronunciation of each word gave one the impression that Dr. Freeman had received his English inculcation by Dr. Henry Higgins himself.

One might have listened to Dr. Freeman and initially believed him to be harmless. Normally after the first lecture, any unsuspecting student would be disabused of this notion. His tongue was quick and deadly. He was known to castigate a student for an incorrect answer or an incomplete assignment without ever raising his voice, and yet utterly destroying a young soul. His manner of accentuating his speech and emphasizing pointed questions came from his ability to open his eyes wide and bore a glaring hole through the object of his wrath. Rare was a student who could look Dr. Freeman directly in the eye for more than a few seconds.

Law was one of those rare students. He appeared, in nearly every way, to be the antithesis of Dr. Freeman: a well-educated, slightly effeminate, Presbyterian, proper southern gentleman versus a poor, Catholic, crass, macho Yankee. Underneath his facade, Dr. Freeman understood just how much Law reminded him of another freshman student from forty years before. The painful reminder of his own past embarrassment fueled the desire to rid his class, and quite possibly the University, of Law's presence.

On the first day of class, when Dr. Freeman listened to my roommate butcher the King's English, he mistakenly assumed Law would be yet another casualty of his introductory course. What he did not know was that Law possessed that same tenacity for success he'd had many years earlier. While his verbal skills were lacking, Law wrote with the grammatical precision of Emily Post. He had been trained in English by Sister Mary Jaworski, whose longsuffering and persistent nature eventually resulted in the proper education of my roommate. While he still spoke with the tongue of a drunk Navy ensign, his written communications were nearly flawless.

During the first week of the fall quarter, Dr. Freeman began his lecture by stating, "Now claaass, today we will discuss the proper use of the infinitive in the English language. I do pray your high school grammar instructors instilled within you an appreciation for the proper use of the infinitive." His eyes turned toward the class roster sitting on top of his desk. "Let's see...Miss Jackson." He allowed a dramatic pause to hang in the air just long enough for the named student to absorb the impact of both public identification and the anticipation of an ensuing interrogation. Dr. Freeman cherished these moments and the power he possessed over the psyches of these neophytes. "Can you illustrate for us the proper use of the perfect continuous infinitive in a sentence?"

Sherry Jackson sat there, her face quickly becoming a dark shade of crimson. After a few seconds of embarrassing silence, she replied in a weak voice, "No sir, I cannot."

"Miss Jackson, where did you attend high school?"

"In Blakely, Georgia. Early County High School."

"And Miss Jackson, just who was your twelfth grade English teacher?"

"Mr. Hall. He was also the head football coach."

"I see. Just how did your high school football team fare during your senior year?"

Sherry was painfully aware of the trap being set for her by these targeted questions. She also realized she had no choice but to answer and hope the interrogation would end quickly.

"Very well, Dr. Freeman. We won the region."

"And for that I'm sure Mr. Hall received accolades from the entire town for his superior coaching abilities. Unfortunately, his expertise in the athletic arena has been of no benefit to you today, in this classroom. May I recommend to you a trip to our fine library and the encouragement to spend some time reviewing the fundamental rules of this language we call English? I would also encourage you to attend an Early County football game on your next weekend excursion home. At the conclusion of the game, I would ask you to find this Mr. Hall and offer him a firm slap across the face for this incredible disservice he has bestowed upon you and the other students from your part of the world."

Sherry stared for just a moment at Dr. Freeman, unable to fully determine whether or not his instructions were meant to be literal. Finally, understanding his sarcasm and the fashion in which he had impugned the educational value of her high school career, she hung her head and became enamored with the top of her desk.

No student in the class smiled or spoke. There was an incredulous gasp emitted by a girl seated in the back of the class. None could believe the way this professor had demeaned poor Sherry in such a public manner. Dr. Freeman stood there, with a slight smirk on his face, studying the faces of the crowd before him and determining who would be his next victim.

Law sat adjacent to Sherry and became indignant at this intentional humiliation of a classmate. Unable to conceal his outrage, he mumbled, "jerk," so that only the students in his immediate radius were able to hear his comment. A few were unable to restrain a slight chuckle over the expression of their shared sentiment.

Dr. Freeman, upon hearing the laughter and understanding Law to be the source of this amusement, turned his stare toward my roommate, smiled, and said, "You, young man. Perhaps you would care to enlighten us on the proper use of the perfect continuous infinitive?"

Law did not speak. Dr. Freeman, along with his classmates, assumed this was because he did not know how to use the perfect continuous infinitive. But they were wrong. Sister Mary had drilled into the brain of Stanislaw Andrej Szukalski every known rule of English grammar. Incorrect answers to her questions often resulted in a wooden ruler quickly slapped across the back of his hand. He soon discovered just how the threat of this sharp pain enabled his mind to recall the instructions given in Sister Mary's previous lecture.

Law paused because he wanted a minute to weigh his words. He understood well that the next sentence he contemplated speaking would ensure his need for a perfect performance in order to pass the class. Any assignments requiring a subjective evaluation by Dr. Freeman would result in the lowest possible mark.

"Young man, did you attend Early County High School as well?" Dr. Freeman's smirk stretched more broadly across his fleshy face.

"I went to school in Buff'lo, New Yok."

"Ahhh yes, I hear now the abrasive inflection in your tone and the mysterious deletion of r's from your words. I'm sure your teachers were completely unaware themselves of the proper use of the perfect continuous infinitive."

That did it. It was bad enough for this obese elitist to humiliate his fellow student, but to malign the reputation of Sister Mary Jaworski was absolutely intolerable.

"Perfect continuous infinitive," said Law, imitating with near perfection the voice of Dr. Freeman, "is the use of the phrase, 'to have been' along with a perfect participle. An example sentence is, 'The professor seemed to have been wearing a toupee.'"

The smirk quickly escaped the face of Dr. Freeman. A crimson shade began to rise from the fleshy folds of his neckline, in an upward fashion, toward the aforementioned apparatus atop his head. His eyes grew wide, and his cold stare aimed straight at my roommate. Dr. Freeman cleared his throat and continued his questioning.

"The continuous infinitive."

"I imagine he would really like to be slimmer," Law replied with perfect diction.

Dr. Freeman's face grew even more flush. He locked eyes with Law, who refused to avert his gaze. *Bring it on*, he was intimating. *Bring it on.*

"The passive infinitive," growled Dr. Freeman.

"The student does not expect to be given an A in his English course."

Until this point, the class had remained silent during the verbal volley between Law and Dr. Freeman. Law's last sentence, illustrating the proper use of the passive infinitive, somewhat lowered the level of hostility and turned the attack on Dr. Freeman back to himself. With the tension slightly subsiding, Jeremy Berger let out a soft chuckle. The short laugh became an impetus for other giggles, and pretty soon the entire room was filled with laughter. The only two expressions that did not change were Law and Dr. Freeman. They simply stared at one another, daring the other to blink first.

When the laughter quieted, Dr. Freeman broke his stare, looked back at the class roster on his desk, and identified the name of this gadfly who sat so bravely before him.

"Mr. Szukalski, I know not whether you are a prophet or the son of a prophet, but it appears you have accurately predicted the future. Furthermore, the entire class can express their gratitude to you for ending this lecture early. A lecture which, by the way, will be the subject matter on your first English quiz tomorrow. Good luck."

He grabbed his roll, turned on his right heel, and exited the classroom. The entire class did thank Law. They each confirmed a willingness to earn an 'F' on their next quiz rather than suffer another moment of embarrassment at the hand of this sadist professor.

Law managed to attain a 'B' as his final grade in the course. He easily would have flunked, except Dr. Freeman had clearly indicated on the first day of class that eighty percent of one's grade would be derived from grammar quizzes. Law never scored less than ninety-five.

Law vowed to never again register for a class taught by Dr. Freeman. The schedule of course offerings listed Dr. Freeman as the instructor of English 102 during the winter quarter, but Dr. Matthews as the instructor during the spring quarter. Law kept his promise and waited until the spring to tackle the intricacies of the second required English course.

When he and the other Mercer students returned from that scheduled respite from academic pursuits known as spring break, news spread quickly that the beloved Dr. Matthews had suffered a heart attack and would be on indefinite leave from the university. On the first day of his English 102 class, Dr. Freeman strode into the classroom and introduced himself as the replacement in the unfortunate absence of Dr. Matthews. Law felt his heart sink into his nether regions. English 101 largely focused on grammar and had an objective nature to the grading system. English 102 had a greater emphasis on writing. This meant grades attained were subject to the capricious opinions of the instructor.

He had the option to drop the class immediately, but decided to wait a few weeks to determine the degree of acrimonious sentiment still directed toward him by Dr. Freeman. *"Perhaps"*, he thought, *"the previous three months served as enough time to mollify any previously felt animosity."*

The first major assignment given to the class was to complete an essay on a choice of works from a twentieth-century African-American literature list. Law chose, *A Gathering of Old Men,* by Ernest Gaines. Set on a Louisiana cane plantation in the 1970's, the novel explores the societal structure and racial tensions of the old south. Law was fascinated by the novel. A neophyte to southern culture and history, he became prodigiously inquisitive of his southern born friends on racial attitudes and expectations.

"A lot has changed in thirty years" I continually reminded Law, but he continued to press the subject and seek affirmation of his personal revulsion over the historical narrative of southern culture.

He found a willing subject in Daniel Sterns, a sophomore baseball player from Atlanta, Georgia. Daniel completed his required English courses the previous year and had also been fascinated with African-American literature. Expressing the same feelings of disgust towards racial bigotry and the civil rights abuses of previous decades, Law and Danny spent several hours together in discussions of this topic. Law became vigilant in his study and passionate in his opinions concerning the past injustices committed by both private citizens and government institutions.

Law wrote a reflective essay on the Gaines novel. On Tuesday of the next week, he received a letter in his university mailbox. Mercer's official seal was glaringly stamped on both the envelope and the letterhead. The contents of the letter were brief, requesting Law to attend a meeting in Dr. Freeman's office at two o'clock on the following day.

The next day, at the appointed time, Law anxiously made his way to the second floor of Willingham Hall and into Dr. Freeman's office. There he found seated both Dr. Freeman and Dean Collier. Dr. Freeman was behind his desk, and Dean Collier was in a metal chair pulled to the edge of the massive wooden structure. Their eyes were focused on documents spread in front of them. Dr. Freeman was speaking and pointing to a document while Dean Collier nodded his head. Upon hearing Law enter through the doorway, they looked up, immediately ceased their conversation, and simultaneously sat back in their chairs.

"Mister Szukaaalski. Right on time. I ah–assume you know Dean Collier."

"Uh, yes sir." Dean Collier nodded his head and extended his hand to Law to offer a perfunctory handshake.

"Listen, Mr. Szukalski," Dr. Freeman continued, "I am not one to speak in parables, so I'll get right to the point. I believe you have committed plagiarism. Tell me, do you know a fellow student named Daniel Sterns?"

Law sat there in shock. He stuttered for a moment, eventually found his voice, and replied, "Uh, uh, yes sir. He plays on de baseball team wit me."

"Have you discussed with Mr. Sterns the book, *A Gathering of Old Men?*"

"Uh, yes sir. He's de one who helped me decide to write my essay on dat book."

"Did Mr. Sterns also loan you his copy of the essay

he wrote on the novel?"

"What? Oh, no sir! I never looked at any essay he wrote. We jest talked, I promise."

"Mr. Szukalski, I have before me your essay and the essay written last year by Mr. Sterns. The contents of both are remarkably similar. Mr. Szukalski, I will certainly give you the credit you deserve on your grasp of English grammar rules. In my years of teaching, I do not believe I have seen a student with quite as prodigious a memory as you obviously possess. And yet, what you have in a formidable ability to recall, you lack in the creative department. The ideas in this essay are not original with you. I believe you stole these arguments from Mr. Sterns."

Law sat, unable to speak. Dean Collier was obsessed with cleaning something from the underside of his right thumbnail. He never looked up at either Dr. Freeman or Law.

"You say you did not read Mr. Sterns' essay. I believe you are lying, but my opinion as to your truthfulness may be irrelevant. A verbal transfer of ideas and the use of those as one's own can constitute plagiarism as well. Dr. Collier has agreed to convene the judicial disciplinary council tomorrow afternoon. They will receive copies of your essay and the essay by Mr. Sterns. You will be allowed to present your case, but I suspect it will be an exercise in futility. You are to appear before the council at four o'clock. If you have any questions, please direct them to Dr. Collier. Good day."

Dr. Collier rose to his feet, nodded at both Law and Dr. Freeman, and quickly exited the room. Law, still stunned from the revelation of his alleged crimes and impending trial, sat immobilized in his chair. Dr. Freeman, utilizing his power of the unblinking gaze and sensing the vulnerability of the prey before him, looked at Law with great amusement. My roommate began to rise out of his seat to make his exit when Dr. Freeman broke the silence.

"Mr. Szukalski, if I may. Last week I saw you carrying around some ridiculous branch with white balls of fur stuck to it. May I ask you why?"

"It was a pussy willow, sir. It's from back home. We use it in a traditional festiv'l called Dyngus Day. It celebrates de end of Lent."

"Ah, Dyngus Day. Sounds entertaining and I'm sure someone would be interested in hearing you expound more on this obviously very holy festival. If you are curious, Mr. Szukalski, your so-called Dyngus Day is the reason you find yourself in this current predicament."

"Sir? I don't understand."

"See, I initially read your essay and decided to confer upon you a D minus. It was not that your paper lacked a comprehensive review of the material or a substantial basis for your opinion. You did, however, reveal your complete ignorance of southern culture and the proper progression of socially accepted norms. In short, the grade I would have assigned was a result of my extreme irritation over a Yankee pontificating profusely about our way of life."

Dr. Freeman paused, leaned back in his chair and placed his arms behind his head.

"Monday a week ago, as I sat here in this office, finishing the grading of these essays, I happened to look out my window and noticed you with that ridiculous branch, obviously giving an education on the purpose of said object to Mr. Sterns. At that moment, it hit me. I remembered reading a similar critique of my heritage, but not from some Yankee carpetbagger. This critique came from a southern boy–a champion of the 'New South.' I had suffered through Mr. Sterns' diatribe last year when I gave this assignment in my second quarter class. I retrieved the copy I had made of his paper and, although not quite as bitter in tone, your content is remarkably similar. I then realized a D minus was much too generous a compensation for your efforts. Thus, you may blame Friday's dispensation of justice in part upon the commemoration of your native tradition."

The lunchtime crowd was beginning to gather in the Bear's Den. Lawyers, construction workers, factory workers, and police officers entered the doorway and queued up for their food. Class distinctions and social barriers seemed to be nonexistent in the acquisition of a lunch laden with cholesterol.

Law recounted this story to me and then continued, "I tell ya', Henry, I never looked at any paper of Daniel's. He and me jest talked, ya know? We talked a lot 'bout our ideas and stuff, but he never told me he wrote 'bout dose ideas. I guess more sank into dis head of mine dan I reckoned would."

He paused, looked at me with eyes pleading for my assistance, and continued, "So whatcha tink dese people gonna do to me? Come on, Henry, I need some help!"

"Don't worry, Law. I've got a plan. I've got a plan."

Nothing outside a man can make him 'unclean' by going into him. Rather, it is what comes out of a man that makes him 'unclean.'"

Mark 7:15

Chapter 9

Friday, April 15, 1994

The previous day, my brain had been consumed with finding a way to rescue my roommate from what would be certain expulsion from the university. I knew Law was being completely honest with me. While physically tough, he was virtually incapable of telling a lie. He possessed a certain guilelessness when it came to personal interactions and was completely void of duplicity. If Law was unhappy, he was quick to express his displeasure. If Law became angry, it was readily apparent to all. He did not possess the ability to bury his emotions and save his wrath for another day. He was wholly unfamiliar with the shrewd ways of a crossed southerner and the ability to conceal one's enmity with a cheerful countenance and a counterfeit smile. He had yet to fully comprehend the calculated scheme of a blessed revenge and how a smile and an embrace could accompany a proverbial knife in the back. Law was a "what you see is what you get" kind of guy, and in the seven months of our acquaintance I had never witnessed any degree of subterfuge in his actions.

I, on the other hand, understood well the methods of attaining retribution for transgressions against one's personhood. I had observed, especially in the female members of my own family, how a disapproving action could produce a deathly silence. My mother was the paradigm of a woman who could hold her tongue while quietly calculating a deadly revenge.

During my formative years I witnessed, on more than one occasion, my father making a public transgression against my mother. The offending comment would most often be related to my mother's cooking, penchant for shopping, or habitual tardiness. While my father was laughing at his perceived wit, my mother's eyes would glare in his direction, then slowly a slight upward curl would form on just one corner of her mouth. My father, suddenly recognizing my mother's stare, would then make a perfunctory statement expressing his lack of seriousness. He would turn to my mother and say, "Honey, you know I'm just joking, right?" She would respond with a seemingly kind but curt, "Of course, Hank, everyone knows you are joking." There was something in the way she said his name–almost in a formal, detached manner–that privately indicated her retribution would be coming at some unsuspecting point in the future.

One evening my parents hosted a gathering from his office at our home. It had been a busy week, and so my mother wisely decided to have the meal catered. As the guests approached our dining room table and began to select various items for their plates, one lady called across the table to my mother and said, "Lord, this is wonderful food. Mary, did you cook all of this?"

Before my mother could answer, my father grunted and said, "Are you kidding me? Mary has retired from cooking. I have her Christmas present hidden in the oven." My father continued his chuckling, quite oblivious to the nervous glances and groans of his guests.

My mother cut her eyes at him, gave a devious smile, and sarcastically said, "Well, Hank, I'll be sure to check the oven before I pre-heat it. I would hate to burn any of those wonderful gifts you always get for me." She held her gaze and her smile, and my father just grumbled and continued the process of piling food on his plate.

The next morning my father had scheduled his regular Saturday golf game. Years before, he had developed a ritual of putting a long, tubular stainless steel thermos in the freezer the night before his morning golf game. The last thing he did before leaving the house and heading to the golf course was to take four cans of Coors Light beer, open the cans, and pour the contents into the thermos. This thermos fit perfectly into the side pocket of his golf bag. The frosted thermos would keep the drinks cold for several hours. Once he arrived at the course, he would order one beer, in a cup, and then throughout the round continually refill that cup from his bootlegged container. This would both save him the expense of purchasing over-priced beer and ensure he would have his favorite libation.

As he rushed into the kitchen on this particular morning, running behind schedule and needing to quickly prepare his drink container, my mother reached into the freezer and handed him a full thermos. "Here," she said. "I saw you were running late so I went ahead and poured the beers for you."

"Thanks, honey," he replied. "You're the best. See you this afternoon."

It was on the fourth hole, as he and his buddies waited on the incredibly slow foursome ahead of them to finish putting, that he extracted from his bag the still cold thermos. He poured the liquid into his nearly empty cup and noticed a slightly odd smell wafting in his direction. Assuming it was something from the lake directly in front where their carts had stopped, he replaced the container and thought nothing more about it. He returned to the cart, grumbled about the plodding pace of the geriatric group still on the green, and reached down for his drink. He turned his cup upward and took a long, badly needed gulp. The delay in smell and taste caused him to consume several ounces before the putrid stench overwhelmed his senses. He gagged and dramatically spewed a mouthful onto the golf cart windshield directly in front of him. His playing partner leapt out of his seat and screamed at my father, "Hank, what in the world are you doing?"

"Dang it, dang it, dang it, dang it!" my father repeated

over and over. "She put vinegar in my thermos. Lord it stinks! And now it's everywhere. Dang it, dang it, dang it."

My father's playing partner refused to ride in the cart due to the horrendous smell, choosing instead to walk the remaining five holes until they were able to secure a replacement cart at the turn. My father's round was ruined, due in part to being so jolted by the experience and by having to purchase, at ridiculously inflated prices, four beers from the golf course club house.

Later that afternoon he walked into the house, tossed his thermos into the sink, looked at my mother and simply said, "Funny."

"Oh, honey. You know how I am around the kitchen. If I messed up, I do apologize." She then walked toward their bedroom with a broad grin on her face, satisfied that her message had been effectively communicated.

My entire life, I'd observed my mother and her passive-aggressive manner of handling conflict. Her influence upon my own way of addressing uncomfortable or contentious situations affected me more than I understood. Instead of expressing my emotions in the heat of battle, I tended to make every effort to pacify the immediate situation, withdraw, and then plan my attack for the most opportune moment.

In the case of Law's dilemma, my ability to passively and subtly inflict pain upon another would serve him well. Law only understood the full-frontal method of attack. I would serve as his tutor, faithfully instructing him in the more effective and deadly techniques of the unsuspecting and ambiguous attack. I would allow him to observe a delicate, precise, and underhanded approach to dealing with one's enemies. As an additional benefit, he would only be able to gain the full knowledge of my ingenious plan several weeks after the events of that Friday afternoon. With Law's ineptitude in the realm of truth stretching, duplicity, and bold-faced lying, I needed him to have complete deniability if questioned on the succeeding events.

The judicial council was scheduled to meet at four o'clock that afternoon in a room located on the second floor of the student center. I awoke earlier than usual that morning to begin making the proper arrangements. In order to make adequate preparations, I was forced to enlist the aid of Autumn Cheetwood, a junior pre-med major from Fitzgerald, Georgia. Autumn had long dark hair, an olive complexion, greenish-brown eyes, a small nose, and full, pouty lips. Her well-proportioned, athletic figure resembled a small hourglass. Most importantly, she possessed an infectious smile and an amiable nature, quite naturally being an object of great admiration and desire from the male population on campus. She kindly rebuffed these advances, though, due to her romantic relationship with an older fellow who was in his second year at the Medical College of Georgia.

I'd met Autumn during the second quarter of my freshman year. She had waited longer than usual to take a required course on the New Testament. Most of the class consisted of freshmen looking to dispense with the obligatory prerequisite before moving on to classes of greater interest. Unlike my fellow Mercerians, I found the course to be quite fascinating, and thus applied my energies to studying and mastering the material given. While Autumn was a veritable master of biology and chemistry, she struggled in understanding the theological threads of the New Testament and the progressive exegesis of Paul Tillich, Rudolf Bultmann, and other academicians who approached their study of the Bible with a great degree of skepticism.

Shortly after the distribution of the first examinations and the revelation by the professor that I had attained solitary status as an achiever of an 'A,' Autumn quickly sought my assistance. She required a high mark in this class, she said, and was determined to not allow a less than perfect grade to become a possible barrier to her admittance into the Medical College of Georgia. Her destiny was to join her boyfriend there and for both of them to become medical professionals. She was not about to let Matthew, Mark, Luke, or John stand in the way of her long-time dream.

Following class, I heard a soft, friendly voice call my name. I turned to see Autumn peering at me with flirty, pleading eyes. Finding myself completely overwhelmed at hearing this upper-class goddess speak my name, I suddenly discovered my tongue's inability to form even a simple syllable.

Fortunately, she filled the awkward gap of silence and said, "Hey, you seem to get this stuff pretty well. Any chance I could study with you sometime?"

By this point my jaw had regained some sense of feeling and I was able to form an eloquent "uh-huh" in response.

"Great," she replied. "How about after lunch on Wednesdays, in the library?"

Again, I somehow managed to reply with another affirmative grunt.

"Okay, I'll see you then. Just meet me in the lobby."

I stood in that same location for several minutes, simply staring into space and mumbling the occasional "uh-huh" to no one in particular. I eventually managed to regain my composure and continue my trek to the cafeteria.

I met Autumn the next week at the appointed time, and we began a shared investigation of New Testament theology. Despite my awkwardness in our initial conversation, Autumn and I quickly developed an amiable relationship. The romantic tension that normally exists in a male-female friendship was greatly suppressed by her unquestionable devotion to her boyfriend and the undeniable fact that she was out of my league as a potential dating partner. With the amorous aspects of the relationship dispelled, we were able to pursue well our academic studies and enjoy one another on a purely platonic level.

I called Autumn on that Thursday evening, gave her a quick summary of my roommate's predicament, and enlisted her assistance for the following day. Being an upperclassman, Autumn had the option of living off campus. She and her roommate lived in a newer apartment complex located a mile from Mercer. Not only were her medical and culinary skills essential to the success of my plan, but I needed access to a full kitchen as well. Autumn agreed to lend me both her talents and her apartment. I arrived early that morning, made the proper preparations, swore her to complete secrecy, and then headed back to campus just before lunch.

During that academic quarter, I had observed a particular morning ritual of Dr. Freeman. When he was asked to assume the teaching responsibility of Dr. Matthew's English 102 class, he did not realize this class began at the noon hour. This meant he had exactly a twenty-minute break between his ten-thirty class and the starting time for the unplanned class. The instruction period was to be one hour and ten minutes, which meant Dr. Freeman would not be able to eat lunch until well after the one o'clock hour. For a man of his stature and girth, it was virtually impossible for him to wait until that belated period of the day. Moreover, Dr. Freeman had a certain discriminating taste, and refused to dine on some portable snack he could keep in his office.

On several occasions, I had noticed Dr. Freeman leaving his classroom immediately following the conclusion of his ten-thirty class. He would walk at a hurried pace from Willingham Hall to the Connell Student Center and into The Lair, a small cafe located just outside of the main cafeteria. His expeditious travel to and from the Student Center was, undoubtedly, the greatest physical exertion of his week. He would request a large chocolate chip muffin, sliced, with a pat of butter in the middle and placed in the microwave for exactly thirty seconds. While the server behind the counter prepared the muffin to his specifications, he would select an extra-large cup and fill it with ice and Coca-Cola from the self-serve fountain machine. He would then pay for both items and quickly return to his office in time to enjoy his mid-morning snack before beginning the next instruction period.

Nick Secada was a pledge brother from West Palm Beach, Florida. Nick and I were not particularly close, but Nick possessed a certain boldness when it came to engaging in less than honorable actions. I contacted Nick on Thursday and asked if he would be willing to help me with a difficult situation, and he immediately agreed to assist. On Friday morning, he procured an eight-foot folding table from underneath a stairwell in the student activities center. He placed this table by the entrance to the Connell Student Center, just inside the building and outside the doors to the student cafeteria.

Nick went to the student activities office and secured enough white butcher paper to adequately cover the four by eight table. He then pasted a poster board sign to the front of the table with the words, "Help Kappa Sigma support the Macon Children's Center." The Children's Center resided in an old, large home in downtown Macon and provided a safe environment and after school activities for underprivileged children. Many Mercer students and faculty members supported this charity. It was not uncommon to see fraternities, sororities, or other student groups raising funds for the center.

After diligently working that morning in Autumn's kitchen, I arrived back on campus at exactly eleven o'clock. I met Nick in the Student Center at the predetermined location with my culinary preparations in hand. On the table I put out a display of sugar cookies, chocolate chip cookies and blueberry muffins, all placed in individual sandwich bags or wrapped in cellophane. In front of each there was a sign indicating the cost of purchasing a bag of cookies or a muffin: one dollar for a bag of three cookies and one dollar per muffin. All proceeds were, of course, designated for a good cause.

Behind the table, covered with napkins, I kept hidden the *piece de resistance* – a plate of beautifully arranged chocolate chip muffins. At exactly the right moment, they would be placed upon the table in splendid glory. These muffins were carefully and scientifically prepared with a very slight but specific variation to the traditional recipe. Instead of actual chocolate chips, a certain chocolate laxative was substituted. Instead of vegetable oil, castor oil was used. The sugar content was increased to ensure the camouflaging of any differing tastes or odors, regardless of how mild they might be. According to my assistant, the breakfast items were virtual colon-busting, stool-stimulating, diarrhea-producing, chocolate-filled hand grenades. One muffin, she estimated, would require long-term occupancy of a lavatory within four to six hours after consumption.

We arranged the table to our exact specifications by eleven-fifteen. Few students or faculty moved through the student center at this hour; most were either in class, preparing for class, or still sleeping. The heavy traffic would begin around eleven fifty-five, when students who did not have a noon class would join the rush to the cafeteria. Nick stood by the glass double doors at the front entrance to the building. At exactly eleven forty-five, he saw the rotund figure of Dr. Freeman appear on the sidewalk, waddling as quickly as he could toward the student center. Nick rushed back to the table, reached underneath, and pulled out a large portable stand "borrowed" from the custodial closet. Using heavy-duty poster board, we created an official-looking sign with the words:

THE LAIR IS TEMPORARILY CLOSED DUE TO A GAS LINE ISSUE
WE APOLOGIZE FOR THE INCONVENIENCE

Nick placed the sign in a conspicuous location just outside the entrance to The Lair. Just as he had the sign properly arranged, Dr. Freeman came barreling through the double doors on his routine mission to satisfy his morning hunger pangs. He turned the corner, with his head lowered, and quickly continued his journey toward the entrance to The Lair. About five paces from the sign he looked up and came to an immediate halt. As he comprehended the words before him, I noticed his breathing increase and the back of his neck turn from its normal pale to a reddish hue. It was obvious this news and the resulting disruption to his dietary routine caused him a great deal of consternation. He placed his hands on his hips, let out a huff, and looked around, I assumed, in search of some employee to publicly castigate for this egregious offense.

I quickly knelt down and retrieved the plate of chocolate chip muffins, each individually wrapped in cellophane and strategically placed in pyramid fashion on the serving dish. I then called out to no one in particular, "Help support the children's center. Cookies and muffins available here."

Like a prairie dog lifting his head to investigate an unusual noise, Dr. Freeman turned, looked in our direction, and quickly moved toward our table and the wares for purchase. "What kind of muffins do you have?"

"We have these blueberry muffins, which I like a lot," I said. "We also have these chocolate chip muffins. I'm not really a fan of chocolate chips, but someone said it was the best chocolate chip muffin he'd ever had. Would you like blueberry or chocolate chip?"

"I'll take a chocolate," he huffed.

"Okay, one chocolate muffin. That will be one dollar."

"You lads say this is for the children's center? Well, if it is for a good cause, then I will take two muffins. I want to do what I can to support the children's center."

I paused momentarily. My medical assistant

had calculated the probable outcome based upon the consumption of only one muffin. The physical results of ingesting two muffins were completely unknown. Autumn was not around for me to quickly ask the pertinent question weighing heavily on my mind. So, with very little thought, I replied, "Umm, sir, we have limited purchases to one per person."

"Do not be ridiculous. Here are two dollars." He then snatched two of the gastrointestinal explosives and hastily headed out the doors and back to Willingham Hall.

I stood in stunned silence for several moments. I finally looked over at Nick, who had a broad smile across his face. He shook his head and said, "Sure hope he uses some restraint and stops at just one. Otherwise, he is gonna have one tore up backside."

At three-thirty that afternoon, Nick and I returned to the student center. The judicial council was scheduled to meet in a room on the second floor. Nick had in his backpack several prepared signs made from black magic marker and printer paper. At three forty-five Nick went to his post by the glass double doors and watched for the approaching Dr. Freeman. After waiting a few minutes, he noticed the good professor ambling at a slow and struggling pace on the path from Willingham Hall to the student center. In one hand he held a manila folder, and the other hand was resting on the lower curve of his corpulent stomach. He would walk a few steps, stop, breath, pause a moment longer, then resume his amble. He continued at this labored pace, giving Nick enough time to hurriedly complete his pre-assigned task.

I made my way up the staircase to the second floor of the student center and entered the first men's restroom. I found the water shut-off valve for the toilets, turned them to the "off" position, and then flushed the toilets so that no water was left in the basin. I then went to the entrance door and placed a sign reading, "Temporarily Out of Service." I rushed to the other men's restroom and repeated the same process. Nick quickly did the same in the two restrooms on the first floor. As I exited the second men's room, I noticed Dr. Freeman struggling up the staircase. He looked ghastly pale and, even from a distance, I could see large beads of sweat on his brow. He reached the top step and immediately turned to the left and toward the restroom. He arrived at the door, noticed the sign, but went in to investigate for himself the state of usability. I then saw him exit the restroom and walk toward me and the other men's room on the second floor. His pace was much quicker, determined, and his gait was short and choppy, as if he were trying to carry a baseball between his thighs. I walked in his direction while saying to no one in particular, "Man, I cannot believe that one is out of order too. And someone sure has left a mess in there."

Dr. Freeman stopped dead in his tracks. Realizing the precariousness of his situation and the expedient need to find a working restroom, he turned and headed back down the stairs. I followed him, but kept a distance between us. He stumbled toward the first downstairs restroom, only to find the same sign posted in front of him. He stopped, apparently trying to recall the location of another restroom. He turned toward the exit doors in search of a place to relieve the acute pressure deep within his bowels.

Suddenly he stopped. He had reached the point of being completely unable to restrain the building tension within any longer. The laxative laden muffins had overwhelmed his ability to control the erratic and forceful movement of his intestines. In the middle of his stride, the very natural human function happened at the most inopportune time. He hung his head for a moment, trying to get his bearings and to determine his course of action. Any movement could possibly cause another reaction from his bowels, but to remain standing in the same place could bring unwanted attention upon his strange behavior. He stood, statuesque in his posture, weighing the few options he had in this precarious situation.

Realizing the futility of somehow salvaging the situation, he turned and began his exit toward the glass double doors and the path that would take him to the parking lot. His waiting car would carry him home and to a fully functional toilet. As he made each step in a careful, judicious manner, the indomitable force of gravity began its pull on the embarrassing culprit. A portion managed to wiggle through the length of the right pant leg, exit just above the shoe, and settled on the tile floor of the student center. Another step through the glass doors produced a similar occurrence and once again resulted in a small amount of the mobile matter finding a resting place on the sidewalk. This process continued to repeat itself for several more yards as Dr. Freeman hung his head and hurriedly made his way toward his vehicle, leaving a trail along the concrete path.

Ms. Doris Williams had been employed at Mercer University for as long as anyone could remember. She began her employment as a teenager, working in the dining hall first as a dishwasher and later as a head cook. Her affable manner and strong work ethic did not go unnoticed by other department heads, and anytime a supervisor had a vacancy to hire a new employee, he or she would inevitably try and steal Ms. Doris from her position to come work for them. By the time I arrived on campus, Ms. Doris was well into her senior adult years, had outlived two good-for-nothing alcoholic husbands, and Mercer had become her family as well as her employer. She had ascended to the position of supervising guest services, which meant she handled the arrangements for visiting dignitaries, assisted moms and dads on parents' weekends, and greeted alumni during homecoming weekend. Her daily task involved managing the welcome desk located near the entrance to the student center. Anyone needing directions or information about the campus would find Ms. Doris more than willing to assist in any way possible. She had been known to leave her post and walk a confused parent to the other side of the campus just to ensure the bewildered individual arrived at the correct destination.

On this particular afternoon, she had stepped

outside for her routine smoke break, taken ten minutes before the top of every hour. During the Dr. Freeman fiasco, she was seated on a bench in a secluded alcove working diligently on a menthol cigarette. She completely missed seeing the events unfold just a few feet from the desk where she presided most hours of the day. As she made her way back from her designated smoking area and walked up the steps, through the glass doors, and into the student center, she began speaking quite loudly.

"Oh, Lawd! Them gooses done made a mess out there on that sidewalk! Heavens to Betsy! Oh Lawd, now would you look at this! Some goose done been here in the student center. Lawd, he done made a mess. Who done gone and let a goose inside my building? Oh, Lawd, would you look at the mess he done made! Gonna stink up the whole place. Lawd, we need to call somebody now to clean this up and get this goose outta here. He probably done made a mess all over this building. Lawd have mercy!"

At almost the exact same moment Ms. Doris was vociferating profusely about the goose's invasion of the student center, Dr. Collier declared a necessary delay in the trial of Stanislaw Szukalski. Without the evidence that was to be brought by Dr. Freeman, there was nothing to discuss.

It was only later that I would realize the full impact of the day's events. Not only would my scheme save my roommate from possible expulsion, it would also be the impetus to forever change my life.

Then I acknowledged my sin to you and did not cover up my iniquity. I said, "I will confess my transgressions to the Lord." And you forgave the guilt of my sin.

Psalm 32:5

Chapter 10

Wednesday, June 15, 1994

When I began my freshman year of studies, Mercer operated its academic calendar on the quarter system. Under this method of study, a student generally enrolled in three classes for each of the three quarters of an academic year, while the more common semester system required five or six classes per term.

While this proved to be a great advantage during final exams, there did exist one major disadvantage of matriculating at one of the few remaining universities in the nation operating under the quarter system. The third quarter of the academic year normally began sometime in the month of April and did not end until the first week of June. Friends from other universities began their summer break sometime between the beginning and middle of May, a full month ahead of the time I was able to complete the final exams of my third quarter studies. This late date of exiting school meant my odds of procuring employment for the summer were normally very slim. Those few employers willing to hire short-term help had secured any needed personnel long before I was available.

This fact was of very little concern to me until phone conversations with my father began to always contain the phrase: "So here's the deal, you need to get a job this summer." I well understood the very remote chance of me being able to find employment during my first college summer break.

I completed my final exams and my first year of college study on a muggy Monday evening. My father arrived at Mercer just before lunch on Tuesday and helped me load my few belongings into his Jeep. An hour later, we began the journey home to Charlotte. The conversation was not as enlightening or as endearing as the trip in September. The discussion seemed to center completely around possible job opportunities for the summer.

"Here's the deal," my father repeated more than once. "You are not sitting around the house all summer long and just playing video games. A guy who works with me has a brother who owns an electrical supply company. They are always looking for people to stock the warehouse. It's hotter 'n Hades in there, but it'll be good for you. If you don't find something by the end of the week, I'm calling him and getting you a job."

The thought of hauling wire inside a metal hothouse all summer was more than enough motivation for me to commence with an immediate, rigorous search for alternate employment. Fortunately for me, this quest became completely unnecessary. The summer job gods must have smiled upon me and taken pity on my late search for temporary work. The night I arrived back in Charlotte, Jimmy Rawlins called to tell me of a position open at a Blockbuster movie rental store. Since he was enrolled at the University of North Carolina at Chapel Hill, a semester school, he had been home for a month and had managed to secure summer employment at the store. While it paid only minimum wage–$4.25 per hour–there was the fringe benefit of free movie and video game rentals, which would be quite advantageous for a college student, bored at home and accustomed to staying up late. More importantly, though, the duties of this position were performed inside an air-conditioned environment and did not require a nearly constant execution of strenuous physical labor.

"Why in the world is this job available? Seems like it would have been taken a long time ago."

Jimmy went on to explain how a fellow employee, Joey Stinson, had been arrested for driving under the influence earlier that week. His parents forced him to take a job in his father's construction company. It was hard labor, chiefly involving the carrying of lumber and other supplies from the trucks to the tradesmen. He would be so exhausted at the end of each day-his father reasoned-he would have no energy or desire to be out at clubs or bars.

"So I told our manager that I could get someone in here tomorrow to take Joey's place, and that you are a really good guy and he would not regret hiring you. He agreed to give you an interview at ten in the morning. You gonna be there?"

It took me less than a second to consider the proposal. "You bet, Jimmy. Thanks for looking out for me. I'm glad we get to work together this summer."

I was hired that morning and asked to begin my first work shift later that afternoon. Fortunately, I was assigned to work alongside Jimmy. The manager had great trust in Jimmy and had given him a set of keys to the store, allowing Jimmy to close a few nights each week. I began working at four o'clock that afternoon and was scheduled to work until the store closed that evening. It was Jimmy's assignment to train me during the times of slower store traffic. He showed me how to use the computer system, scan movies for check-in and check-out, and replace movies and games returned to the store. It was, for the most part, an uncomplicated and undemanding job. I was thankful to not be employed at the electrical supply company or carrying bags of cement in the Charlotte summer heat.

At the end of my first day's work, I walked outside with Jimmy as he closed and locked the front door of the store. It was late, but I was still very much awake. I had in my hand the John Madden Football '93 video game for Sega Genesis, courtesy of my new employer. Jimmy asked me to spend the night. His house had a large bonus room, and we knew we could stay up late playing a video game without disturbing his parents.

We arrived at his house and settled into a barn-burner match up between Oakland and New Jersey. After a few minutes of playing, Jimmy paused the game, turned to me, and said, "I hate to interrupt our match, but I've got to know something. What the heck is wrong with you? Are you not happy I got you this job?"

I was thrilled Jimmy had helped me secure employment for the summer, and was surprised I had not been able to adequately mask my recent melancholy. I guess I should have known that of all people, Jimmy would be able to see through the façade, but I thought I had been able to hide the deep, internal struggles of my soul.

"Jimmy, it has nothing to do with the job, and I was sincere in my thanks for putting in a good word for me."

"Then why are you in such a funk?"

"Jimmy," I continued, "it has been a rough couple of months."

"Girl problems?"

"No. Well, no more than the usual problem of can't get a girlfriend. But that isn't anything new."

"Then what is the issue?"

"Are you asking me this because you are behind by three touchdowns and know you are gonna get whipped, or do you really want to hear my junk?"

"Probably some of both, but I know I don't want to

work all summer with a killjoy. I would have asked someone else if I'd known you were going to be in a mood like this. So won't you go ahead and lay it on me so I can tell you what to get over."

I took a deep breath and laid back on the oversized beanbag I'd settled in earlier for the video game brawl. I put my arms behind my head and launched into my story. "You remember me telling you about my roommate Law?"

"The Polish Catholic Yankee boy who saved your sorry rear from getting mugged?"

"Yeah, that's him. He flat broadsided that guy. In addition to the life saving assistance he provided me, he has been a good roommate. He got into some trouble a couple of months ago. It wasn't his fault, mostly. He found himself in the cross-hairs of a narcissistic bigoted professor who did not like Law because of his views, his background and because he embarrassed the fool out of him in class one day."

I recounted to Jimmy the events of the previous April and my sabotaging Law's trial before the disciplinary committee. Jimmy was drinking a Coca-Cola, and when I related the details of Dr. Freeman's episode in the student center, he began laughing hysterically and sprayed me with a mouthful of Coke. Once he regained his composure, he smiled and said, "I've got to tell you, Henry, I didn't know you had it in you, but the old man sounded like he had it coming."

I paused, breathed deeply, and continued my story.

"He may have, Jimmy, but the next day I thought I'd just about killed a man."

Jimmy just stared for a moment before finally speaking. "What in the world are you talking about?"

"The next morning I went to breakfast in the cafeteria. Law slept in, completely exhausted by the events of the previous week. Another freshman, Daniel Watkins, prepared his plate and sat at my table. We are only casual friends, but on Saturday mornings there is hardly anyone in the cafeteria. All the people who live close to Macon seem to go home for the weekend, and those remaining on campus normally do not wake up before lunch."

"So Daniel tells me about this girl he has just started dating–this cute little Phi Mu from Savannah–and how much he is in love and how one day her name will be Mrs. Watkins. I'm sitting there, listening to this drivel, trying to eat my eggs without throwing up. Then he said something that really caught my attention. He said that this new girlfriend works part time at the Medical Center in the emergency room. She mainly does filing and answers the phones at the reception desk, but if she is working an evening shift she will help with the intake of patients. So he tells me that the night before, he went to meet her during her break and she tells him that Dr. Freeman had come in that evening just after supper, complaining of some serious stomach issues. She said that she gave him some forms to fill out and that as he reached for the clipboard, he fell over right in front of the reception desk. She said that doctors and nurses were scrambling all over the place and later that an ER doctor said something about stomach bleeding and they were running all kinds of tests. He said that she was real upset by it all and that from everything she saw, it looked like Dr. Freeman wasn't going to make it. She had never taken a class with Dr. Freeman, but he seemed like such a nice old man, she said, and she was heartbroken that the school was losing such a good professor."

"I tell you, Jimmy, my heart dropped right into my stomach. I could not believe what he was telling me. Daniel just laughed and kept on talking. He was more upset about his girlfriend not wanting to come see him when she finished her shift than he was over the news about Dr. Freeman. He moved onto some other subject, but I did not hear a word he said. I quit eating and just sat there, I'm sure white as a ghost, thinking that perhaps I had just committed murder. This man was going to die, and it sounded like it was directly related to the stupid prank I'd pulled to rescue my roommate from expulsion. Sure, I wanted to sideline Dr. Freeman. I wanted to keep him from being able to speak that afternoon before the disciplinary committee, but I certainly did not want to kill the man. And then Daniel lays this bombshell on me and I'm suddenly facing the reality that I may have committed murder! Jimmy, I was dying inside. Absolutely dying. I had my last bite of eggs stuck somewhere in the middle of my chest, so I made some excuse and told Daniel I had to leave. I dumped my tray and went back to my room."

"Law was still asleep, which was good. I climbed into my bed and tried to go to sleep myself, but it was impossible. I kept thinking to myself over and over, 'I may be a murderer.' Part of me was extremely worried about what would happen if there was an investigation and somehow they traced the laxatives back to my chocolate muffins. I kept picturing the police coming to my room, the arrest, a trial and my parents being overwhelmed with grief over their son becoming a jailbird. I mean, a picture of a very dim future kept flashing before my eyes and really had me upset."

"But what got to me even more, and this is hard to explain, was that I, Henry Miller, was no longer a good kid. Jimmy, you know me as well as anybody. It's not that I'm completely innocent, but I'm really a good guy. Maybe not compared to you–since you are a saint and all–but when you compare me to most of the guys who went to high school with us, I look pretty good. I mean, it's not by my own choosing, but I've never gotten past first base with a girl, and that certainly makes me look like Billy Graham compared to most guys I know. I've had a few beers, but never enough to get drunk. I've never failed a class or been suspended from school. Sure, I don't go to church as often as you, but at least I go on occasion. The way I figure it, I've been good enough that God has to be fine with me."

"But then this happened." I paused and looked at Jimmy, trying to read his reaction. He did not speak, but his expression invited me to continue my story. "Even though it was unintentional–and I'm sure that meant something to God–I knew there was no way God could look at murder and be okay with it. My good-guy status was shot. If I'd really killed Dr. Freeman, then I was officially a bad person. I'd never thought of myself in that light before. It was wrecking my soul."

"That Saturday I stayed in my room most of the day. Law still had no idea about anything. He just assumed Dr. Freeman did not show up that afternoon for the disciplinary committee meeting because he was detained. All he knew was that the absence of his accuser had bought him some time, and with enough time elapse he just might escape punishment after all. He was so relieved to have this respite from his troubles, he decided to spend the afternoon having fun. He asked me to go play Ultimate Frisbee with him and some other baseball players, but I told him I had to study. I called my parents and talked to them for a while, but I was too scared to tell them anything. I thought about going to see a Catholic priest. I'd heard Law talking about his priest back home and how those guys are sworn to secrecy, but I wasn't sure how to get to a Catholic church and if I did, if the guy would even see me since I'm not Catholic."

"I went to the library to see if any other students were around and had heard anything about Dr. Freeman. I thought that maybe I could get an update without seeming too inquisitive and possibly implicating myself. I sat at a table and overheard some girls talking at the table next to mine. One of them evidently lived in the dorm room next to

Daniel's girlfriend and had met her in the hallway when she came home from work. She was obviously quite upset. They stayed up and talked, and this girl told the others how they prayed together for Dr. Freeman and the doctors."

"She continued talking and appealed to her study partners to join her in praying. Daniel's girlfriend had called the hospital that morning to get an update, and he'd taken a dramatic turn for the worse. She said he was in ICU and they were calling the Hospice people in to help him in his transition."

Again, I paused, hoping Jimmy might interject and tell me that I had not intended any of this to happen and that, in fact, I was still a good guy. Instead, he just sat and listened, willing me to continue my story.

"I overheard this conversation, threw my books into my backpack, and quickly made my exit. As I walked back to my dorm, tears streamed down my face. I'd never felt that way before. My soul was being crushed under the weight of overwhelming guilt, shame, and self-condemnation. I wanted to run to the hospital, find Dr. Freeman, and confess everything to him. Maybe, I thought, the old curmudgeon would somehow find it in his heart to forgive me of my sin before he passed away and relieve my crushing guilt. But then I knew that would lead to being caught and charged with his murder, which would make for a very bleak future. I was torn. I could not live with the knowledge of my own culpability, but could not face the consequences of confessing. I was completely consumed by this dilemma. I felt as if my soul was being ripped in half."

"The next morning I decided to go to church. I'd not been to any church in Macon since arriving at Mercer, but I thought perhaps attending a service would help alleviate my aching soul. There is this small Methodist church within walking distance of campus. Since I didn't have a vehicle and really did not want to ask anyone to give me a ride, I decided to just walk over to this church by myself. I felt so out of my element, walking in alone to this new place. Honestly, I was nervous someone would ask me to stand, introduce myself, and tell everyone my biggest sin of the past week. Fortunately, at no point in the service was there a time of visitor recognition. The people were nice and I recognized a few Mercer students, although I could not call any by name. I did not really understand most of the sermon, but somehow in that service I felt like God spoke to me and told me exactly what I needed to do. In some inexplicable way, His will for my life and for my situation became crystal clear."

Jimmy spoke for the first time. "What did He tell you?"

"He told me to confess. To own up to the murder of Dr. Freeman. To go and tell the authorities what I'd done. It was better to spend years in prison and have my soul free than to avoid jail but live with my soul in bondage."

"So I walked back to campus, a little lighter in my step after making that decision. I went to the cafeteria. I'd not eaten anything since Saturday morning–since I'd received the news about Dr. Freeman. My stomach had been tied in such knots, I knew eating was a virtual impossibility. But after church and the peace that came from my decision, I suddenly became keenly aware of my hunger pangs. I walked into the cafeteria and noticed Daniel talking to a freshman girl. I assumed this was his girlfriend and the source of information on the demise of Dr. Freeman. I walked over to their table. Daniel introduced me to his girlfriend, and I said, 'Nice to meet you. Daniel told me about your experience on Friday night and Dr. Freeman's hospitalization. I heard someone say that hospice had been called in. Have you heard anything today?'"

"She just sort of chuckled, which I thought extremely odd, and said, 'Yeah, I heard some news. I called over there this morning and found out that he is not dying at all. He has a bleeding ulcer, something he's had for a long time, and that he had been sick and that is what made him pass out on Friday night. The nurse on duty told me that he was much better by Saturday evening. She said he has been sitting up in his bed all morning barking orders at every nurse, orderly, and doctor who dares enter his room. He is constantly pushing the nurse call button and demanding food that is actually edible, or for the hospital to subscribe to a cable service that carries the BBC network, or for a hot cup of tea, or some other ridiculous demand. The nurse told me that the staff is considering putting a constant Valium drip into his IV just to shut him up. They also said that he has faked a number of near death experiences before, and just like other times told the doctors on duty that he had stage-four colon cancer and that is why he was bleeding. They ran tests and he does not have cancer, just a severe case of cantankerousness.'"

"Jimmy, when she spoke those words, it was like the roof of the cafeteria opened, the clouds parted, and the rays of the sun focused their energies right into my soul. I tried to mask my jubilance, not wanting them to suspect anything, but I guess a wide smile formed on my face. Daniel and his girlfriend assumed it was over the part about the hospital staff and their dealings with the intolerable Dr. Freeman. 'He is just a crazy old fool, isn't he?' Daniel said. 'Crazy, just crazy,' I said and then excused myself from their table."

"I left the cafeteria so overcome with joy I wanted to kiss the first person I saw. Unfortunately, the only person walking down the sidewalk was Mr. Ralph, the seventy-five-year-old custodian, and I decided to hold onto my outward expression of joy for another time."

"I went back to the room and Law was not there. I needed to spend some time in the books, so I decided to take advantage of the quiet Sunday afternoon and study in my room. Excited over the news of my newfound freedom from guilt, I thought I would be completely back to normal. But I wasn't. Something inside me was still just..."

I was not sure how to finish the sentence. Even though it had been two months since my nerve-wracking weekend, I still had not been able to fully process and identify the source of my distress and anxiety. I should

126

have been completely relieved, but there was still a tension within me I could not explain.

Jimmy spoke up and attempted to finish my sentence for me.

"You mean peace? Something inside of you still lacked peace?"

"Yeah, kinda like that. I mean, I was off the hook for the murder of Dr. Freeman, but the more I thought about it, the more I realized I could have killed him. I didn't, but what if I had? Fortunately events turned out differently, but in my foolishness I allowed him to take two muffins and double the laxatives. Not knowing his medical history, I very well could have been guilty of murder. The more I thought about it, the more I realized that perhaps I'm not really a good person after all. And that fact has been bugging me to death for the last several months. What is wrong with me?"

Jimmy cocked his head and a smile formed on his face. I could tell he was measuring his next words very carefully. He reclined on his beanbag, looked up at the ceiling, and began to speak.

"Nothing at all," he said. "There is not a thing in the world wrong with you. You are more normal than you know. You and I haven't talked religion a lot over the course of our friendship. You seem to get real glassy-eyed any time I bring up anything to do with Jesus or God. That is why I've always backed off from pushing you too hard on the spiritual stuff."

"Alright, I promise I won't go glassy-eyed. What are you talking about?"

"Your opinion of religion, Christianity, church, well, it's all been very superficial. You think it's something that everyone needs just a small dose of to make them a little better, a little more moral, a little more accepted by God. It seems to me that your opinion has been that people need to be religious, but don't get too serious about it. Don't go overboard or anything, just get enough God to make you a better person."

"But it sounds like now you have discovered something. Everyone–you, me, Billy Graham, Mother Theresa–everyone is born, well, bad. We all have natures that rebel against God. That is what you have felt deep within your soul. Maybe you have not committed any really big sins up to this point in your life, but you now realize just how capable you are of evil." Jimmy paused and let that truth seep into my mind. After my experience with Dr. Freeman, I now understood exactly what he meant.

"That is what a relationship with Christ is about. Jesus died on the cross to pay the penalty for all the sins you've ever committed–from the very small to your nearly homicidal act. When you become a follower of Christ, you get forgiveness for those acts, and you spend the rest of your life learning what it means to follow him. Does that make sense?"

"Yeah, makes perfect sense. I'm just having trouble getting my brain around the fact that I'm a bad person."

"A lot of people do. We all want to believe that deep down we are good people. But deep down we are all rebels."

I sat there for a while, just staring at the wall. Maybe Jimmy was right. Maybe I did need some serious help from God.

"Jimmy, I need some help. Please tell me what my next step needs to be."

"I can't, Henry. You know what you need to do. This is a decision you have to make on your own. I cannot make it for you. But I'll pray for you, right here, right now, and I'll stay right here with you, all night if I have to, while you make this decision. And I'll be your friend either way, but I am certainly praying and hoping you make the right choice."

We continued talking for a long time. It was nearly two o'clock that morning before we turned out the lights and went to bed. It was the first night I'd slept soundly in months.

To Timothy my true son in the faith.

I Timothy 1:2

Chapter 11

Tuesday, October 4, 1994

That September, I strode onto the campus of Mercer University with a newfound confidence. My summer in Charlotte had been the greatest of my life. I spent the summer drilling Jimmy with questions about the Bible and his own faith in God. I went to a college Bible study sponsored by his church. I learned so much, but more importantly, I discovered a formerly elusive inner peace.

More than acquiring some new head knowledge, I actually felt the love of God encompassing my very being. I realized I was more than just a product of the evolutionary cycle; more than just a chance happening on a tiny planet in a vast solar system; more than just a collection of protons and neutrons existing in a happenstance world. I believed in purpose, intentionality, and meaning for my life. It changed my attitude and my perspective toward people and events. No longer did I possess the very myopic view of my world, where each situation ranged from being either gloriously wonderful or strikingly horrible depending solely on my narrow judgment of the facts. I had suddenly gained a panoramic view of life, and this shift in my orientation toward the world served me well.

Law and I decided to be roommates again. Sometime in the middle of the previous May, the plagiarism case against him had been dropped. Dr. Freeman possessed a suspicious nature and determined that Law was the source of his incredibly unfortunate and terribly embarrassing physical malady on that Friday in April. A senior student and confidante of Dr. Freeman privately told me, "Dr. Freeman thinks your roommate put some kind of Polish Catholic voodoo spell on him, and that is why he messed all over himself that day. Said that he could never prove it, though, and he's not taking any more chances anyway. He said he is going to give Law a passing grade and pray to Mary, Joseph, Jesus, the Holy Spirit, and God the Father that the boy never crosses paths with him again."

Every Tuesday and Thursday afternoon of that fall quarter, my mind was filled with stories, dates, and various factoids surrounding the founding of the United States of America. I had registered for and was enrolled in an early American history course taught by a large African-American

132

professor.

Dr. David Smith hailed from Charlottesville, Virginia. As a young man, he became intrigued by and fascinated with the historical points of interest located in his vicinity. Upon graduation from high school, he enrolled in UVA, studied American History, and graduated with honors. He then went on to receive his Masters and Ph.D. Dr. Smith was considered one of the foremost scholars in the nation in the area of early American history. Mercer University took great pride in having a man with his credentials serving on the faculty.

Dr. Smith not only possessed a breadth of knowledge, he was greatly adored by his students. He was a tough professor, but extremely fair, and displayed a kind, affable, and respectful attitude toward all of his students. Dr. Smith was a lamb with those who wanted to learn and a lion with those who were insouciant. A student willing to put forth the study and effort would not fail his class–he could be sure of that. Students attempting to breeze through their studies would find a nice big "F" stamped across their final exam.

The early American history course he taught during the fall quarter of 1994 covered the period of time from the European settlement of the New World through the years just before the American Civil War. In early October, Dr. Smith taught a long segment on the Puritans-those men and women from England who settled into what would be known as the Massachusetts Bay Colony in the early 1600's. The influence of this group on the entire New England area was so impactful, according to Dr. Smith, any student who wanted to understand the mindset of the colonists needed to understand the beliefs and motivations of these early settlers.

At the conclusion of this segment, Dr. Smith gave the class an assignment to write a paper on the material covered, focusing specifically on connecting the belief system of the Puritans to their governance of the New World. I reviewed the reading materials and composed what I thought was an excellent paper.

Two weeks later our assignments were returned, and at the top of my paper, in red ink, a nice fat "D" stared back at me. I quickly flipped through the document, seeing no other marks until I reached the last page. At the bottom, in nearly illegible writing, Dr. Smith had scribbled the words, "See me in my office."

Unnerved by the summons, I walked toward Dr. Smith's office with no small amount of trepidation. Sure, he was a favorite among students, but the memory of Law's near expulsion after being called to his professor's office was still fresh in my mind.

I slowly made my way up to the second floor of the Langdale building in search of Dr. Smith's office. As I turned the corner and headed toward his doorway, I heard the sound of suppressed laughter. I continued toward his door, expecting to find Dr. Smith engaged in conversation, either with someone or on his phone. I reached my destination, looked into his office, and noticed Dr. Smith crouched under his window, his large body shaking as he attempted to subdue his own laughter. I stood there motionless, unsure of what I was witnessing or what my response should be. After a few moments, Dr. Smith turned his head and noticed my presence. He took his massive forefinger and held it perpendicular to his lips, signaling for me to remain quiet. He then waved me over and gestured for me to crouch beneath the window with him. I did as instructed.

"This is my cheap afternoon entertainment," he whispered, barely audible even though we were nearly face-to-face. At that moment, I observed a large plastic object at the feet of Dr. Smith. With only a cursory glance, I was able to quickly identify it as an oversized water pistol, appropriately dubbed the "Super Soaker." Armed with this water-filled weapon, one would be well prepared for any liquid-laden battle.

"See that sidewalk?" Dr. Smith continued in a hushed tone. "As soon as you see some people coming around the corner, let me know. I will pop up, spray a few rounds up in the air, and then we get to watch their reaction."

Just as he was finishing his sentence, a cluster of girls strolled around the corner, laughing and talking. I whispered back, "Five girls, dead ahead."

Dr. Smith stood, took careful aim, then pulled the trigger of the water pistol several times very quickly. He then returned to his crouched position, but able to see just above the bottom portion of the window. The sprayed water rose upward several yards until the inevitable force of gravity pulled the fluid back toward the earth. Dr. Smith was obviously not a novice in the art of long-distance spraying. The ammunition hit the mark, causing the girls' conversation to abruptly halt and become a cacophony of shrieks and squeals. Their yelps and confusion over the source of the spray brought great joy to Dr. Smith. His massive frame ducked down further underneath the window, shaking as he once again attempted to cover the sound of his laughter.

Once it was apparent that the girls had moved on, Dr. Smith motioned for me to sit in one of the two small chairs adjacent to his desk. He fell into his massive leather chair and launched immediately into the reason for my presence.

"Mister Miller," he began with a resonant voice. "I appreciate you assisting me in my afternoon entertainment. I trust your silence in this matter. Last year some students discovered my possession of a Super Soaker and ambushed me in class with their own water pistols."

"Now, for the reason you are here. I see that you read my note at the end of your last paper. You are probably wondering why I gave you a D. Don't worry, that is a temporary grade, if you so desire. Your writing style is excellent, probably the best in the class. You covered the subject well. The paper, under normal circumstances, would have been an A paper."

"Uh, thank you sir, I think." I paused, unsure if anything further needed to be stated.

"So, you are wondering why you received a D instead of an A. Here is why – you danced around the belief system of the Puritans, but you completely missed the foundation for what made these guys tick. You even quoted some from the Bible, but you never connected the dots."

He leaned forward in his chair and rested his enormous arms on the front of his desk. "So, Mister Miller, here is my proposal to you. I would like to have a private tutoring session with you. I think you almost got, but not fully comprehended, the religious foundation of these early settlers. You have been such a good student thus far, and I think you have a tremendous amount of talent. But I cannot, will not, allow you to get an A if you miss this critical point."

"At the end of this tutoring session, I will allow you to rewrite the paper. You can use most of what you have already, so I do not believe it will take you much time. But after we meet, I believe you will want to change several portions of what you have written. This is no guarantee, but my guess is you will receive an 'A' on your second attempt. This will, of course, replace your previous grade. So what do you think, Mister Miller?"

"Yes sir, I mean, of course, sir," I stammered. "When do you want to do the tutoring session?"

"Do you have time right now?"He asked.

"Yes sir."

That afternoon began a mentoring relationship that changed my life. Dr. Smith explained the Biblical foundation for the practices of those who left their homeland to come to the New World. He connected the dots for me in a way I'd not seen before. I absorbed this instruction, took copious notes, and later re-wrote a paper worthy of an A grade.

At the end of the tutoring session, I shared with Dr. Smith my experience of the previous summer. "These passages from the Bible you just read," I said, "this is the first time I've seen those. I'm extremely interested in learning more. I had a God-experience this past summer, but there is so much I do not know. It seems you have an incredible grasp of the Bible."

I glanced downward, pausing and working up the courage for my next words. "Dr. Smith, is there any way you could find the time to give me a few more of these tutoring sessions? Either on the Bible or history or anything else you want to discuss?"

He leaned back in his chair–so far that I thought it would tip over under the weight of his massive body. He placed his arms behind his head, looked up at the ceiling, and drew a deep breath. "Tell you what, Mister Miller. You show up here next week at the same time with a Bible and a notebook. We will see how it goes. If you do not waste my time, I will not waste yours. If you are serious about learning, I will tutor you. See you next week."

I sought the LORD, and he answered me; he delivered me
from all my fears.

Psalm 34:4

Chapter 12

Sunday, February 12, 1995

I met with Dr. Smith virtually every Tuesday afternoon for the remainder of the fall quarter. Every week he would spend thirty minutes talking and flipping through pages of the Bible. I filled several pages in my notebook as he gave me truths and scripture references in rapid-fire succession. At the end of his half-hour instruction, he would say, "So Mister Miller, what questions do you have?" I would then go back and read the questions I'd scribbled in the margins of my notebook. From the end of October to the first of December, I grew from being a neophyte in my understanding of the Christian faith to possessing a moderately deep theology.

When I returned to Mercer's campus after the

Christmas recess, I went to Dr. Smith's office to inquire about continuing our Tuesday afternoon sessions. I found him seated behind his desk, leaning his head over a large textbook.

"Dr. Smith," I said softly, feeling somewhat embarrassed about interrupting his study. "Happy new year. I hate to bother you, sir, but was curious about whether or not you would be able to meet next Tuesday."

"Mister Miller," he bellowed. "Of course we can meet. I've already thought about what we are going to cover this next quarter in our sessions. We are going to walk through every book of the Old Testament. I want you to have a basic comprehension of the content and background of all thirty-nine books. I suspect this study will take us into the spring quarter, if that is fine by you."

"Oh, yes sir! Again, I really do appreciate you doing this."

"Mister Miller, I have a question for you. I have been asked to be a guest preacher at a church not too far from Macon. My cousin lives in Mapleton, Georgia, just over an hour drive from here. She is an associate attorney in a small law firm there. One of the partners in the firm is a member of First Baptist Church. She evidently ran her big mouth one day and told this partner that I have preached on a few occasions, and now they have called me and asked me to come for a 'Race Relations' Sunday. Guess I was the only black preacher they could find. Anyway, my cousin really likes this partner and put a whole lot of pressure on me to accept the invitation. So, I did, and it looks like I will be preaching at this church next month."

"My question for you, Mister Miller, is if you would like to come with me. My wife told me that it is too much to try and get the children dressed and ready, then drive to Mapleton, then expect them to behave in church. She has told me that I will be traveling alone that day, but I would rather have some company. Plus, it will give us a chance to cover some new material. What do you say?"

"Uh, sure Dr. Smith. I really appreciate the invitation. I look forward to it."

***

Dr. Smith drove a white 1991 Buick Park Avenue, a vehicle seemingly incompatible with a man in his middle thirties. I sat in the passenger seat of the car, listening intently to my history professor talk. "Mister Miller, I'm fully aware that I'm driving a senior adult mobile. There are a couple of reasons for my current vehicular situation. The first is quite obvious. I am a big man, and the Park Avenue is a big car with a comfortable ride. Secondly, my father-in-law gave it to our family. He bought the car, drove it for a year, and decided that since his golfing buddies all drove Suburbans, he needed one as well. So, the price was right, and that is why I'm driving this land yacht. And I tell you, Mister Miller, once you get married and have a few children, you really do not care what others around you think. You just want to survive each day."

Shortly into the trip, Dr. Smith began to describe in great detail the sermon he was planning to preach that morning at First Baptist Church. He needed, he said, to rehearse it out loud, and since I was a captive audience, I would get the benefit of hearing it twice that morning.

"Mister Miller, I'm talking this morning about the power of forgiveness. They want me to come preach because I'm a black man and this is their Sunday to focus on improving relations between blacks and whites in their community. Well, the only way this can happen is when people learn to forgive–to forgive past atrocities, forgive acts of cruelty, even forgive attitudes and inherited perspectives. The first step toward reconciliation must be individual forgiveness."

"And here is why forgiveness is so important: it really is not for the other person. You get that Mister Miller? This is a life lesson I hope you never forget. God wants us to forgive one another not for the sake of the person who has offended us, but for our sake. Bitterness can tear up your soul. The quicker you are able to forgive, the better your life will be."

Shortly after he completed the dress rehearsal of his morning message, we arrived in Mapleton, a typical county seat, small town in Georgia. We were able to locate First Baptist Church without difficulty. At a four-way intersection off the main square sat three churches and a funeral home. On one corner was First Baptist; across the street sat the First Presbyterian Church; First Methodist was across the other street; and diagonally across from First Baptist was the Garvin Funeral Home.

This business was housed in an antebellum home

rumored to have been built by a cousin of Joseph Wheeler, a confederate general during the civil war. The story had been told that the home had once served as the gathering place for a group of generals just after the Atlanta campaign and the burning of that city by William Tecumseh Sherman. Of course, no one in Mapleton would actually refer to General Sherman by name. Anytime they discussed the history of that battle, which was fairly often, the phrase "that little fire ant" was used in place of his proper name.

Dr. Smith pulled into the parking lot at exactly ten o'clock, an hour before the morning service would begin. We exited the car, walking around the side of the building and toward what we assumed was the front entrance of the sanctuary. Two older gentlemen stood outside wearing overcoats, wool caps and heavy gloves. The men walked in our direction with hands extended.

"You must be Dr. Smith," one man said. "My name is Dwight Norman, and this is Melvin Bragg. We are so glad you made it today. Let us get you inside where it is warm. We need to find the pastor. I know he is anxiously waiting for you."

At that moment, coming from the direction of the parking lot, a voice called out, "Dr. Smith, Dr. Smith." From the portico where we stood we could see an older gentleman, who I would later learn was the pastor of the church, hurriedly making his way toward us. From his office window he had observed Dr. Smith exiting his vehicle, and had come out a side entrance in order to greet us. Dr. Smith turned, saw the man calling his name, and then began to walk toward the pastor.

In his haste, and unfamiliar with his surroundings, Dr. Smith did not notice the two brick steps descending to the parking lot. Looking ahead and waving his hand, he suddenly found himself stumbling from his elevated position toward the gutter running in between the front portico and parking lot of the church. He attempted to regain his balance by shifting one foot back toward the step. In his attempt to mitigate the embarrassing and potentially injurious situation, he landed his left foot directly into the gutter. The action prevented him from falling face forward, but caused his foot to settle onto uneven ground between the gutter and the parking lot. He bellowed in pain as his ankle twisted. In his attempt to relieve the searing pressure and discomfort, Dr. Smith fell onto the brick steps. He immediately made the effort to stand and regain some measure of dignity, but the moment he placed weight on his left foot, he collapsed to the parking lot.

At that moment the pastor arrived at his side. "Dr. Smith! Dr. Smith! Are you okay?"

"Yeah, I'm okay. Well, not really. Pastor, I broke my ankle in college playing a pickup game of basketball." He paused and then looked down at his foot. "It was this ankle, and it felt exactly like it feels now. I'm not a medical doctor, but I believe I need to see one as soon as possible."

"Of course, of course. We will have someone to drive you over to Columbus. They will have a doctor in the emergency room there. Oh, Dr. Smith, I'm so sorry this has happened."

"Do you want me to drive you in your car, Dr. Smith?" I asked. "I can follow someone if they will lead the way."

Dr. Smith nodded his head, then suddenly stopped. He had a pensive look about him. I assumed he was wondering whether or not he wanted a college student driving his vehicle. He turned to the pastor and two ushers and asked if they would excuse us for a moment. "Sure, we need to go and find someone to help us get you loaded into a vehicle," the pastor said. The three men scurried away, diligently focused on their mission.

"Henry," Dr. Smith said once the three men were gone. It was the first time he had ever called me by my first name. There had always been an air of formality in our relationship. I was not sure, until that moment, if he actually knew my first name.

"Henry," he repeated. "I want to ask you to do something that I know will scare you to death. I woke up this morning praying about this message I was to preach today. But something did not feel right. I could not place my finger on what it was. For a while, I thought God wanted me to change my message, but somehow I knew that was not the case. Still, there was this uneasiness within me about preaching today. God was telling me that He had a different plan, although He would not reveal that plan to me. Until now. Now I know what His plan is."

Completely unaware of the direction of the conversation, I quite naively asked, "What is His plan, Dr. Smith?"

"Henry, God wants you to preach this morning."

I blankly stared at my professor for several moments. Finally, a grin formed on my face as I replied, "Good one, Dr. Smith. Good one. Seriously, what is His plan?"

"Henry, I am serious. I knew somehow this whole thing involved you in some way. Why do you think I went over my sermon in painstaking detail this morning? I would not have done that, except something within me kept nudging me to share my message with you. You have a sharp mind and a strong memory. I bet you can preach what I shared with you word for word."

During our sessions together, Dr. Smith had noted something about me: I possessed what was virtually a perfect photographic and auditory memory. Not only could I read a book and recall virtually every word, I could remember, in exact detail, conversations I'd had years before. This characteristic was both a blessing and a curse. As much as I tried, I could not forget hurtful words, spoken either by me or others. Those memories often haunted me and reminded me of all the mistakes I had made. The inability to forget caused, at times, a great deal of pain.

Conversely, the nearly perfect memory was advantageous, especially in my academic pursuits. I had perfect scores on any exams requiring the recollection of facts and dates. In history courses, such as the one taught by Dr. Smith, I normally attained the highest grade in the class. The dates of settlements, battles, proclamations and protests were all seared into my memory like brands on cattle.

"Dr. Smith, you cannot be serious. I've never spoken

in front of any group larger than a class. You want me to stand before these people I do not know and . . . *preach*? I would be so nervous and–let's face it–there is no way they would take me seriously. I'm a twenty-year-old kid. What in the world would they say when they see me up there speaking in front of the group? Dr. Smith, please don't ask me to do this."

"Henry, I'm not asking you to do this."

"Okay, Dr. Smith, now I'm really confused. I thought you just asked me to stand in for you."

"I did, Henry, but it's not me. Henry, I really sense God is the one asking you to do this. I cannot begin to explain it all to you, but from the first day you came to my office, God laid it on my heart to pour myself into you. He has some big plans for you. And Henry, this is just the start. If this were just me asking you to do this, then it would be fine for you to refuse. But Henry, do not refuse God. That is a dangerous thing to do."

I was completely stumped. What in the world could I say? My mentor insisted God was calling me to this task. For several moments, I simply stood there with a lugubrious expression, hoping to elicit his sympathies and convince him to release me from this assignment. It was useless.

"Henry, when the pastor gets back here, I will explain to him what we are doing this morning. He will assent to having you speak, I'm sure. Now, once I've spoken with him, I want you to take your Bible, go into the pastor's office, and spend the next thirty minutes praying. And Henry, remember this: you are not the one responsible for what happens in there. God has asked you to do this, and He will take responsibility for the results."

———————

At ten minutes before eleven o'clock, Pastor John Lindsey knocked on the door of his own office and entered. I would later have the opportunity to learn a great deal about this man standing before me. Pastor John, as the church affectionately referred to him, was seventy years old and had served at the church for fifteen years. He had endeared himself to the congregation through a willingness to be available at any time for any need of a member. He was known to sit for hours with anxious family members waiting to hear about the surgical results of a loved one. He would visit often with shut-ins and those in the hospital or nursing homes. He spent very little time preparing for his Sunday morning preaching, but people were quick to forgive his often disorganized and superficial sermons because they knew Pastor John would be there for them when they needed him.

When he walked into the office I was seated behind his desk, my Bible in front of me, praying like I had never prayed before. I looked up as he walked over to me. "Kid, you'll do just fine," he said. "Dr. Smith assured me of that."

We left his office and walked into the sanctuary of the church. The design was typical of the many Baptist church sanctuaries constructed throughout the southern United States in the years immediately following World War Two. The baby-boomer generation and their parents were ardent church-goers, resulting in most churches seeing a sizable increase in their attendance throughout the 1950's. These congregations needed more building space to accommodate the burgeoning crowds, and many new sanctuaries were constructed during this period. They all seemed to have the same basic design: a rectangular room with high ceilings, four gold chandeliers hanging over pews placed parallel to the front and back of the room, a high platform in the front of the church, and a small balcony in the rear. The room communicated a certain formality. The pastor was exalted above the crowd and spoke from a place of authority. Others sat in rows of dutiful silence, maintaining a level of strict decorum.

The sanctuary of First Baptist followed this exact model. I estimated that approximately six hundred individuals would fit into the room, including the space for thirty or so choir members in the loft behind the platform area. As we made our way to the wooden chairs situated just behind the pulpit, I quickly guessed that there were less than a hundred and fifty present. People seemed to be perfectly spaced throughout the pews, most likely sitting in the same places every Sunday.

As the imminent conclusion of the choral piece approached, I dropped my head and silently prayed. "God, you and Dr. Smith seem to have some sort of plan. I do not have a clue what it is, but You have got to help me here."

The choir completed their portion of the worship service, and the music director signaled for the fifteen members to be seated. She then turned in my direction and motioned toward the pulpit, as if I'd somehow forgotten the task to which I'd agreed. I stood and slowly walked to my place, positioned my Bible on the top of the pulpit, and took a deep breath. Every eye was locked on me, and a deafening silence filled the room. I swallowed hard, cleared my throat, and began to speak.

"I'm the scab."

The congregation chuckled, remembering the recent National Football League players' strike. The replacement players were dubbed "scabs" by the fans and media. While they were willing to play for little pay, the moment the players' union and management were able to agree on suitable terms, these replacement players were without employment.

"You heard your pastor recount the story of Dr. Smith's stumble off of your front portico. He tapped me to take his place this morning. All I can say is that I sure better get an 'A' in his class for doing this."

The congregation again laughed, and I felt the tension within me begin to ease. It was a friendly crowd and, more importantly, I was actually able to get words to form on my tongue and speak with minimal hesitation or faltering.

"Look, I am just a white boy from Charlotte, North Carolina," I continued. "I have no expertise in the area of racial reconciliation. But I have learned recently what the Bible says about forgiveness. There is a great reason God is so adamant about burying grudges and resentment toward one another."

I recounted the sermon, nearly word for word, that Dr. Smith had shared with me only a couple hours earlier.

I then concluded with words not from Dr. Smith, but from my heart. "Last summer I had a life-changing experience. For the first time, I understood what it means to be forgiven by God for all the wrong I have done in my life. For a brief period of time, I thought I had committed an action as grievous as they come. I was overcome with guilt and fear. God used that process to draw me to Him and to help me realize my need for forgiveness. Through the death of Jesus Christ, I was forgiven for every sin I've ever committed or will commit in the future."

"It is only out of that enormous grace shown to me that I am also able to forgive others. No one has offended me in a fashion worse than God has been offended by my sin. It took the crucifixion of Jesus to make restitution for my wrongs. As much as people have hurt me, no one has ever nailed me to a cross. And yet, that is exactly what my sin did to Jesus Christ. Still, he was willing to forgive me."

"How can I then hold a grudge against someone who has wronged me? I have been forgiven of so much; I must be willing to do the same."

I paused, took a breath, and leaned onto the pulpit. "You may be thinking, 'There is no way I can forgive. I've been hurt too badly.' You are correct. You cannot forgive in your own power. But through the grace of Jesus Christ, you can find the ability to forgive. It's something you must do–not for the other person–but for yourself. Perhaps this morning you need to take that first step toward forgiveness by planting yourself at the foot of the cross. Sit and absorb what took place at the cross, then out of that allow forgiveness to flow."

I then closed my Bible, turned, and walked back to my assigned chair on the platform. No one moved for several seconds. Evidently I was supposed to pray, introduce a song, and give some sort of formal invitation to make a spiritual decision. I was unaware this was expected of me. After a few moments of silence, the pastor rose from his seat on the first pew, walked up the steps to the platform, and invited anyone who wanted to accept Christ to come forward. He then informed the congregation of the closing hymn and invited everyone to stand. As the congregation began to sing the first words of "Just As I Am," I exhaled for the first time since the fall of Dr. Smith.

I was thankful the service was over and more thankful my part was not a complete disaster. A church member drove me to Columbus to meet Dr. Smith. Fortunately it was just a bad sprain, and we were able to leave for Macon shortly after my arrival. I hoped I would never see the town of Mapleton again.

"For I know the plans I have for you," declares the LORD, "plans to prosper you and not to harm you, plans to give you hope and a future."

Jeremiah 29:11

Chapter 13

Thursday, April 17, 1997

During March of my senior year the entire student body seemed to get lost in a haze of melancholy resulting from a protracted and especially dreary winter in middle Georgia. The same black clouds darkening the sky hung metaphorically over the dormitories, the cafeteria, and the classrooms. Most of the students settled into a routine of serious study, interrupted only by the occasional basketball game or fraternity party. There were few things during that winter quarter that brought a sense of excitement to campus. The whole place seemed to be devoid of color, conversation, and jubilation.

Suddenly, one glorious day in the middle of April, the cloud cover broke and the sun shone her beautiful, gleaming rays onto the campus. The temperature rose fifteen degrees from the previous day, and the countenance of the entire student body lifted. Discarded for the season were the wool sweaters and heavy coats of the female population. In their place were sleeveless blouses, mini-skirts, and an assortment of other much more interesting attire.

Heather Anderson was a junior engineering student from Savannah, Georgia. While we were not close friends, we did congregate in the same social network. Heather was well liked by the girls on campus and nearly always invited to parties and other gatherings, but had not found herself on the receiving end of many romantic inquiries during her time at Mercer. She was slightly overweight and a touch out of style. She wore thick glasses, had ashy brown hair, and her clothes always seemed to be mismatched and old fashioned. The boys on campus referred to Heather as "friendly, but frumpy."

Unbeknownst to everyone but her roommate, she joined a local fitness center when she returned to Mercer after the Christmas break. Every afternoon she left the campus for a period of time, then returned just before the cafeteria opened to serve dinner. Her baggy attire hid her frame from the watchful eyes of her fellow students, keeping them completely unaware of the fact that Heather had lost fifteen pounds during the winter quarter.

She spent spring break at her home in Savannah. Her cousin came from Atlanta to visit for the week. Her cousin was a year younger than Heather and attended the University of Georgia. The two spent the week going to the beach at Tybee Island and attempting to bask in the sun in spite of the cooler-than-usual weather. On one particularly chilly and overcast morning, Heather's cousin suggested a "shopping and style" agenda for the day's activities. They would go to the local mall, look for some clothes, and make an appointment at a hair salon. Additionally, she convinced Heather to make an appointment at a local eye exam center to see if she could possibly be a candidate for contact lenses.

As the entire campus sprang to life after the winter hiatus, students gathered in the quad or outside the cafeteria in social clusters, seemingly discovering anew the existence of their fellow classmates.

On this particular Thursday morning, the first week of the spring quarter, I was standing just outside the student center. I had a twenty-minute break between classes, and was attempting to use every moment to enjoy the newly discovered sunshine. Law, my roommate for all four years of my college experience, was standing beside me. We both leaned against the iron handrail leading up the steps into the student center, and Law was giving a running commentary on the sights of the morning.

"I tell ya, Miller, youse guys here in Georgia better tank da good Lord for dis weather youse got now. In Buffalo, we'se still drowning in snow dis time of year. Snow piled up higher dan dis building here."

As Law was reporting on the miserable conditions in his hometown, the doors leading into the cafeteria opened. Through the exit walked Heather Anderson, wearing a white, sleeveless, button down blouse and a short, khaki skirt. Her formerly dark, dull hair had been transformed into a brilliant, shiny blond, hanging like a gold frame around her face. Contacts replaced her eyeglasses, revealing her cool, ocean blue eyes. Her now slightly bronzed skin tone showed the results of absorbing the pigment darkening rays of the sun, and her choice of outfit revealed a newly found sense of style.

Most important, though, was the indisputable evidence of her physical exercise during the previous months. Her tan, shapely legs and muscular arms conveyed both athleticism and femininity. She was now, by virtually any measure, anything but frumpy.

Law was in the middle of his commentary on the weather when he caught sight of Heather sauntering past our post. Thinking he was whispering, but in fact well within her range of hearing, Law gasped and then exclaimed, "Mary, Joseph, Peter, Paul and all dat is holy, would youse look at her? Thank you Lord for dis weather. Dese girls are finally wearing decent clothes. Hey Miller, youse recognize dat girl? Mother Mary, is dat Heather Anderson? What in God's name happened to dat girl? Man, she sure did change. Miller, youse should have asked dat girl out when youse might have had a chance wit her. Ain't no way she'd consider youse now."

"Thanks Law. Appreciate the encouragement."

"I'se just sayin' Miller. Man, dere goes your chance wit her. Miller, I don't know if we'se ever gonna find you a girl."

Over the Christmas break, Law had become engaged to his high school girlfriend, Cecilia Krakowski. She was, according to Law, "de finest Polish Cat'olic girl in all of Buff'lo." She attended Canisius College, a Catholic School in Buffalo, and was scheduled to graduate one month before Law. They planned to get married in June, and Law had already asked me to be a groomsman in his wedding. "Youse ever been part of a Cat'olic wedding, Miller? We know how to do it right, I tell ya. I can't wait to show you all de fun tings my mudder and fadder have planned for us dat weekend."

Law, upon receiving the greatly desired "yes" from Cecilia, believed his mission before graduation was to get me into a serious dating relationship. He constantly pushed and prodded me toward any female who met the qualifications of possessing both brain waves and a pulse. After several unsuccessful attempts, he finally announced that the brain wave qualification had become optional. He was determined to get me hitched before we walked across that stage at graduation.

"Tell ya what, Miller. Meet me right here after class. We will get food and den sit out here and watch de girls go by. Surely dere is some girl at dis school who will go on a date wit you. We just gots to find her, I guess."

"Sorry, Law. Dr. Smith asked me to grab lunch and eat with him in his office. I'll see you back at the room later on."

Dr. Smith and I continued our weekly meetings throughout my time at Mercer. During my junior and senior years, we met on a near weekly basis to discuss the Bible, history, religion, or philosophy. The education I received from Dr. Smith was just as valuable to me as anything I received in the classroom.

At the end of my sophomore year, because of the influence of Dr. Smith, I made the decision to major in History. I chose this field because of my interest in the subject, but well understood the limitations this particular major would place upon the prospects of my future employment. I had no desire to teach history at the high school level, and I was not sure I possessed the willingness to continue my education in order to be able to teach at the collegiate level. While I received superior grades in my major, my future career path remained undetermined for quite some time.

During my junior year, I watched several senior fraternity brothers struggle through the process of taking the Law School Admission Test and applying to various law schools throughout the country. When Rick Louden, whose grades were far inferior to mine, managed to get accepted to the University of Georgia Law School, I was determined to take this same path for myself. My grades were among the highest in my class, and in November of my senior year, I made a better than decent score on the LSAT. The combination of my grades and this test score would assure my acceptance to law school. My desire was to return to North Carolina, so I applied to and was accepted at the University of North Carolina at Chapel Hill. By the spring quarter of my senior year, my plans were set, giving me a certain sense of inner security concerning my future.

I pushed on the slightly ajar door of Dr. Smith's office with my brown-bag lunch in one hand and a twelve-ounce can of Coca-Cola in the other. Dr. Smith sat behind his desk, his chair leaning back as far as it would bend, feet propped on the edge of his desk, and a textbook held securely in his lap. He dropped his feet to the floor, sat upright in his chair, and waved me into his office.

"Mister Miller."

Whenever Dr. Smith saw me for the first time in a day, he somehow managed to drag out the syllables of the "mister" portion of his address to me while dropping the "r" at the end of the word. It was pronounced "Mista" and the 'a' was held for several nanoseconds longer than normal.

"Dr. Smith, always good to see you. I'm looking forward to having lunch with you today. I am curious, though. Why did you change the format of our meeting?"

"Because today's topic will require a more conversational method of discussion."

"Oh, I see. So, what is the topic for today?"

"Henry Miller."

I stared at him for several seconds, expecting him to say more. Dr. Smith remained seated with a deadpan expression on his face.

Finally I said, "Sir? I'm sorry, I do not understand."

"Henry, today, I want to talk to you about your future. Please, have a seat."

I pulled a chair beside his desk and opened my bag, revealing a turkey sandwich and a bag of potato chips. I began to unwrap my sandwich, although I realized my hunger pangs had quickly been replaced by an overwhelming uneasiness.

"Dr. Smith, I think I have told you everything I know about Chapel Hill's law school program. I'm not sure what else I can tell you."

"Henry, why are you going to law school?"

"First of all, Dr. Smith, because they accepted me. Secondly, what else would I do with a history major? If I had majored in something like engineering or accounting, sure, there would be a number of companies where I could submit my resume. But with a history major, I just about have to pursue another degree."

"I understand what you are saying, Henry. But I'm actually trying to ask you a much deeper question. Let me cut straight to it: do you believe God has called you to law school?"

Dr. Smith's question hung in the air. It caused me to immediately stop chewing my food, place my sandwich on the desk, and sit upright in my chair. I certainly believed in God's guidance for my life, and I even believed God had a plan, but I had never really stopped and considered whether or not He had called me to law school. It was just something I was doing because, quite frankly, I needed to have a career. I had never really stopped to consider God's involvement in the whole thing.

Attempting to engage Dr. Smith with a thoughtful answer, I replied, "Well, God has certainly called me to work, and so this choice seems to be a good path to a job."

Dr. Smith was not deterred by my flippant response. "You could get a job tomorrow as a waiter or selling goods at a department store. That is not my question. Do you have a sense that God has called you to become an attorney?"

I realized there was no easy way to avoid this direct question. "Well, honestly, I guess I have not felt some sort of mystical calling by God. I want to help people and earn a good living while doing it, so this seems to fit. But I have not heard an audible voice of God saying, 'Henry, go to law school.' It just seems like the best decision."

"Henry." Dr. Smith leaned back in his seat and took in a slow, deep breath. "Henry," he repeated. "I want to talk honestly with you, and I want you to keep an open mind. I think God has something different for you. I knew this shortly after we began our sessions together. I believe God revealed it to me early on, and laid it upon my heart to spend all these hours meeting with you. Then, last week, as I was reading my Bible and praying, God spoke to me. It was so strong and so directly from Him, there was no denying it. Lord knows, I tried. I tried my best to put it out of my mind. I went about my business that day and tried to forget that nudging from God. But it hung there in the back of my mind, like a nagging thought that would not go away. All day long it was there. As much as I attempted to dismiss the thought, I could not get away from it."

"Then, that evening, I received a phone call, and I knew that I'd better deliver the message. I actually became a little scared of what might happen to me if I did not. I started thinking about Jonah and that big fish. God had a message for Jonah to deliver to some people, but Jonah refused to deliver it. So God had Jonah thrown overboard and then a big fish swallowed that fella whole. This whole past week I've been nervous about riding past the Captain D's; not knowing what would happen until I delivered this message that I'm giving you today."

I let out an awkward, nervous laugh while continuing to stare at the top of Dr. Smith's desk.

"Henry," he continued, "I believe God has called you to be a pastor. He wants you to preach. Now listen, I see the look of shock on your face and the smirk beginning to form, like this has got to be some practical joke. But before you say anything, hear me out."

"Normally, Henry, in a case like this, I would encourage you to continue your education. That is the most logical step for someone sensing that call of God. But let's face it: from a purely human perspective, you should go to law school. You've already been accepted to a great school and you would have a lot of success, I'm sure. So I'm not talking about what makes sense. I've already said that I believe God is up to something big. So what makes sense, from our vantage point, may not be the best choice here."

"So, Dr. Smith, what is the best choice?"

"Henry, my cousin called me last week. You may remember that my cousin is an associate in a small law firm in Mapleton, Georgia. One of the partners is a member of First Baptist Church, and that was how they got my name two years ago when they asked me to come preach. That partner's name is Richard Davis. He served on the deacon board at the time, but now it seems Mr. Davis has a new position in the church."

Dr. Smith paused and stared at me. He appeared to be measuring his words very carefully, perhaps even a little unsure if he should continue. My curiosity was getting the best of me, so I decided to give him the verbal push he needed.

"What position is that?"

Dr. Smith took a deep breath and continued. "You remember meeting the pastor of First Baptist when we went to Mapleton two years ago? Of course you do. He retired just a couple of months after you preached. The church has been without a pastor now for nearly two years. The truth is, they are a struggling church. The church has been around since before the Civil War and has a long history in that town. But the church, at some point, became very complacent. They quit trusting in God and became very satisfied with their little religious club. As a result, they have found themselves in their current situation."

"Which is what?" I asked.

"My cousin says that the church is on life support, almost completely dead, and everyone knows it but the membership. Ten years from now they are going to be forced to either sell or abandon their property. Fifty years ago that sanctuary was filled with five or six hundred people each Sunday. You saw the crowd two years ago. They've probably dropped another fifty since then. Mr. Davis told my cousin that every Sunday morning feels like the funeral of a person who has outlived all of his friends and only a handful of people show up for the ceremony. They are down and discouraged, and yet very few people in the church realize the severity of the situation. It's like they just keep doing what they are doing, but expect that somehow things will turn around."

I looked down and noticed my foot was nervously tapping the floor. "Okay, so it looks bleak. What does this have to do with me?" I thought I may have a clue, but I was silently praying I was wrong.

"Henry, I actually spoke with Mr. Davis by phone last night." He again paused, took a breath, and leaned forward on his desk. I looked up at his expression. His eyes were filled with such earnestness it made it difficult to hold his stare. I suddenly became interested in taking another bite of my barely eaten turkey sandwich, giving me the excuse I needed to divert my eyes from his sober gaze.

"Henry, they want you to come and interview with them. They think...no...wait, let me be very honest here. Henry, they *believe* you are to become their next pastor."

Even though Dr. Smith spoke with a solemn voice, his words hit me like the punch line of a bad joke. An awkward laugh reflexively exploded from within me.

"Dr. Smith, you cannot be serious. I have not graduated yet! I've certainly never worked in a church. They would be crazy to hire me as their pastor!"

"Henry, I would have said the exact same thing, except for the fact that deep within my soul, I knew God was up to something here. Let me tell you something else Mr. Davis said: the Sunday you preached, according to him, was the only time he felt any life in the church at all. Your sermon, your authenticity, and your humility were a breath of spiritual life in a dying church. He said everyone on the committee agreed with his assessment. That morning worship service burned into their collective memory, and they have discussed it more than once."

"Henry, I know this is an extremely strange option for you to pursue. Here is what I'd like for you to do. Number one, just spend some time praying. There is no way you could ever take on a job like this unless you knew God was calling you. You need to spend some time talking to and, more importantly, hearing from God."

"Number two. I want you to speak with Mr. Davis. Just hear him out and see if anything he says resonates within you. If so, then go and interview with the committee. If not, then you'll be living in Chapel Hill this fall."

"So, once you are able to get your heart beating again and some color back in your complexion, I'll be more than happy to pray with you. Then you can do whatever you feel is best."

The Lord does not look at the things people look at. People look at the outward appearance, but the Lord looks at the heart.

I Samuel 16:7

Chapter 14

Friday, April 18, 1997

I placed the call to Mr. Richard Davis from the phone in my dorm room. We spoke for over an hour. At least four times I told him, "You guys are absolutely crazy for even considering me." At least four times he responded, "You are absolutely right. Why in the world would we consider a not-quite-graduated kid with no ministry experience to come and be the pastor of our church?"

Through the course of the conversation, I was able to gain some insight into how this committee had arrived at this decision. There were five individuals serving on the pastor search team. They began their search process by advertising in the denominational newspapers and by contacting the Baptist seminaries. Through these contacts they received over one hundred resumes from individuals who were interested in becoming the next pastor of the

First Baptist Church of Mapleton, Georgia. They went through the normal process of reviewing the resumes and winnowing the stack down to a dozen.

They began making contacts, but doors closed on every possibility. Each individual contacted had either secured other employment, or as the members of the committee investigated a candidate, they would discover deal-breaking skeletons in the closet. One particular applicant, Mr. Davis told me, had left two former churches due to having extramarital affairs in both. In an interview with another potential pastor, the applicant confessed to the committee his uncertainty as to the existence of God. He believed the Bible had much to say on how humans should interact with one another, but dismissed passages relating to God or an afterlife. The committee interviewed one candidate who showed a great deal of promise until they checked his references and discovered that he possessed an incredibly poor work ethic. He apparently had a habit of parking his car in the church parking lot, and then having his golfing buddy pick him up several blocks away. They would spend several days during the week playing golf, and if anyone asked, he would point to his car being at the church all day long and say, "I was studying" or "I was in the sanctuary praying." A church secretary finally discovered his scheme and relayed the information to the chairman of the deacon board. The next week, when they could not locate him in the church, the chairman and two other deacons went to the local golf course and waited for the pastor to finish his round. They fired him in the clubhouse.

The search committee became extremely discouraged and began to wonder if their church was destined to be without a pastor. As the months turned into years, the church continued to experience a decline in attendance and offerings. The search committee would meet with the finance team once a quarter, each time being informed of their need to again lower the salary package offered to any potential candidate. After nearly two years, the morale of the committee reached a low point. Mr. Davis told me that most of their meetings became group therapy sessions. Instead of pursing the task assigned to them, they spent their time together commiserating with one another about the state of the church.

Shortly after Christmas of 1996, as the committee was beginning to close in on the second anniversary of being without a pastor, their conversations took a dramatic turn.

Mrs. Mabel Johnson was the senior member of the search committee and had been a part of the church her entire life. At eighty-five years old, she remembered when the sanctuary was full every Sunday, and she had witnessed the decline over the last several decades. Mabel's husband had been a stalwart leader in the church until a sudden heart attack in 1976 had taken him from her. For the last twenty years, Mabel had seen it as her duty to be a person of prayer on behalf of the church. She awoke every morning at exactly nine o'clock, grabbed a cup of coffee, and began her prayer time. Her morning prayers focused on praising God and thanking Him for His blessings. In the evenings, she would devote herself to praying for the needs of others. Most nights she stayed up well past midnight, diligently going through her journal and the handwritten notes she made to remind her how to pray. Anytime God answered a prayer, she would turn to the page in her journal where the need was first recorded, put a check mark beside the request, and then make a notation to the side indicating the date and manner the prayer was answered. Her notebook was a virtual cornucopia of testimonies concerning the faithfulness of God.

In January of 1997, the committee met on a particularly cold evening in the home of Mr. Davis. The conversation quickly began to meander down its customary path of despondency and discouragement. Mrs. Johnson, as was her usual manner, just listened. After fifteen minutes or so of gloom and melancholy, Mrs. Johnson cleared her throat and began to speak. The rarity of hearing her voice caused the other four members to listen with rapt attention as she spoke.

"I want to share with you what the Lord has been telling me," she began, almost in a whisper, causing the other committee members to lean forward in their chairs, straining to hear her soft voice. "For nearly two years now, I have been praying every day, without fail, for this group, for our search process, and for the individual God would eventually bring to be the next pastor of our church. For over a year, God was silent on this matter. I prayed faithfully, but I did not receive any indication from the Lord that He was even listening to my prayers. But I knew He was. I've been around a long time and I knew God was listening, but the time was not right for me or us to know His will. We have been through several candidates, and God has clearly shut the door on each one. So I began to pray to God in a new way, asking Him if we were missing something in the process. And about three months ago, I finally heard from God."

The remainder of the committee members leaned forward even more, anxiously waiting to hear about this divine revelation.

"One evening I decided to devote my entire prayer time to this matter. I had been praying for about an hour when, all of a sudden, an inescapable image began to consume my thoughts. I would attempt to dismiss it, but it would not go away. Over and over and over this picture returned to the forefront of my mind. I finally realized that maybe the Lord was starting to reveal something to me. So I began to pray and ask the Lord if He was telling me something."

"After another twenty minutes of praying, God began to bring clarity to my mind. The picture I had seen was of that college kid who preached two years ago. The Lord revealed to me that it was not an accident at all, and that it had been His plan from the very beginning. He also told me that the college kid was now in the process of graduating, and that he would become our next pastor."

According to Mr. Davis, the other four members of the search team began to shuffle and squirm in their chairs. Only out of respect for Mrs. Johnson did they not all break forth in laughter and insist on immediately moving on to another topic.

"Now I know what you are thinking," she continued. "Because I thought the exact same thing. 'This does not make sense. Why in the world, Lord, would you want us to hire this young man?' He is young enough to be my great-grandson. How could he be old enough to serve as my pastor?"

"Then, and this does not happen to me often, God directed my heart to a passage in the Bible. It was not an audible voice, and yet it was an impression on my mind and heart that was clearer than anything I've ever heard with my ears. I turned to the passage and read it." She paused, swallowed hard, and then quickly choked back her tears. "I closed my Bible and started weeping before the Lord. It was one of the most powerful God moments I've ever had in my...well, let's be honest here...very long life."

Mrs. Johnson then reached for her tattered Bible and opened it to a previously marked page. "The story comes from First Samuel and concerns the choosing of a king to follow Saul. The prophet Samuel was given the assignment of anointing the next king of Israel. God told him this king was to be from the house of a man named Jesse. ...Samuel went to Jesse's house and saw his oldest son: a large, strapping young man. Samuel thought to himself, 'Surely this is the one the Lord has chosen.' But God spoke to Samuel and said the following words."

Her reading glasses hung on a chain around her neck. She pulled them up to her face and began to read from her Bible.

"*But the Lord said to Samuel, 'Do not consider his appearance or his height, for I have rejected him. The Lord does not look at the things people look at. People look at the outward appearance, but the Lord looks at the heart.'*"

"The Lord had not chosen this son, or any of the other sons who were present. When Samuel was at the point of desperation, believing he was at the wrong house, God directed him to ask Jesse if there were any other sons. 'Just the youngest,' he replied. 'He's just a runt, out in the field tending sheep.' They called for this son, a boy named David, and when the young lad walked in, God once again spoke to Samuel."

Mrs. Johnson looked down at the open Bible in her lap. "*Rise and anoint him; this is the one,*" she read aloud.

She closed her Bible and once again allowed her glasses to dangle around her neck.

"I know you may be thinking, 'Well, the old bat has finally lost her mind,' but I want you to know how much I believe this is from God. I do think we need to call him and go through the process of an interview, but if I'm right on this, he will no more be able to resist the Lord than we can. If this is a God thing, then it will happen."

"So, if you four would simply indulge an old woman and join me in praying about this. Go back and read that passage and then just spend a lot of time praying. If God does not direct all of our hearts in the same manner, then I will hush my mouth and will not bring it up again. But I'm convinced He will. I'm convinced He absolutely will."

"Henry," Mr. Davis continued after relaying that portion of the story to me. "Mrs. Johnson was correct. God did convince us. All of us. So, there you go. What do you think?"

I was speechless. I told Mr. Davis I needed some time to pray, but deep within my spirit I already knew the answer to my prayers, and it scared me to death.

The Lord says: "These people come near to me with their
mouth and honor me with their lips, but their hearts
are far from me. Their worship of me is based on merely
human rules they have been taught.

Isaiah 29:13

Chapter 15

Sunday, June 15, 1997

After graduation, I moved my few belongings in the bed of a borrowed pick-up truck from my Mercer dorm into a one-bedroom apartment located in the only apartment complex in Mapleton. For many years, First Baptist owned a parsonage located a mile from the church. The pastor of the church and his family were allowed to live in this house free of charge. In the early 1980's, just before hiring my predecessor, the church decided to sell the home and use the funds toward some necessary maintenance needs of the church property. It was argued by several members that not only did the church need the funds from this sale, but also that allowing a pastor to have this free rent was just too extravagant of a salary package. With a majority in agreement, the church decided to divest itself of owning any residential property.

In the months between my acceptance and the official beginning of my role as pastor, I received a crash course in sermon preparation and delivery from Dr. Smith. This private tutoring session occurred three times a week and involved a focused study on the New Testament book of John. "What the people in that church need," Dr. Smith relayed to me, "is a good dose of Jesus. We, I mean you, are going to give them just that. Before you graduate, I'm going to have you prepare eight sermons from John's gospel. You will preach these sermons to me, here in this office. With that memory of yours, you'll be just fine preaching to those folks in Mapleton."

Armed with a quiver of prepared messages, I began my first Sunday in the pulpit of First Baptist with a sermon from the first chapter of John. At the appointed time in the service, after a particularly excruciating solo by the part-time music director, I stood behind the pulpit and read the poetic and compelling words written nearly two thousand years earlier:

"In the beginning was the Word, and the Word was with God, and the Word was God. He was with God in the beginning. Through him all things were made; without him nothing was made that has been made. In him was life, and that life was the light of all mankind. The light shines in the darkness, and the darkness has not overcome it."

I then proceeded to deliver a well-crafted message on the divinity of Jesus Christ, the nature of the Trinity, and the plan of salvation created by the triune God at the beginning of time. It was a homily I had rehearsed many times in my head. I preached without notes and with great passion. I ended the sermon with an appeal for the listeners to understand the great love Jesus Christ displayed in coming from Heaven into this dark world so that we might experience salvation. I closed with prayer and returned to my seat on the platform behind the pulpit.

I then looked down at my watch and realized I had preached for exactly four and a half minutes.

Miss Mary Westwood, the part-time music director, sat in a front pew. After I had voiced an "amen" and returned to my seat, she quickly looked down at her watch, shrugged her shoulders, and walked up the steps of the platform to lead the congregation in the closing hymn. Unfortunately, the pianist had left her post to find a restroom, believing she had more than enough time to relieve herself before her services were again required.

While returning to the sanctuary after completing her mission, she heard the sound of the congregation singing a cappella. She rushed back to the piano and was able to begin playing as the congregation started singing the second verse.

Somehow, in my nervousness, I completely forgot long portions of my already prepared text. I knew that during the last verse of the closing hymn, I would be required to make my way to the foyer of the sanctuary and stand there as the congregants made their exit. I considered leaving through the side door, running to my car, and leaving the town of Mapleton, never to return.

But then the voice of Dr. Smith boomed in my head. In a calm, yet resonant tone, I heard him say, "God will see you through this, Henry. You just keep following Him."

Convinced by the voice in my head to abandon my escape plan, I quickly made my way to the foyer and stood by the set of double doors leading out of the church. I heard Miss Westwood give the final benediction, and the pianist began to play the postlude. The inner doors opened and the congregants began to casually file out of the sanctuary and make their way toward my position by the exit. Mr. Donald Stinson, a retired high school math teacher and lifelong bachelor, was the first to reach me. He stuck out his right hand, slapped his left hand on my shoulder, and nearly shouted, "Son, I tell you, you keep preaching that short, you are going to be the most popular preacher in town! We are actually going to be able to beat the Methodists to the restaurants today. Kid, you are all-right in my book!"

Not knowing what else to say, I simply smiled and thanked Mr. Stinson for his kind words. Another couple came by and voiced the same sentiment. An elderly woman told me, "You gave some good points, there, boy, but you were done preaching before I was done listening." Several others came by and either introduced themselves for the first time or reminded me that we'd met at the church reception held for me the previous day. I noticed in my peripheral vision Richard Davis standing a few yards away from me, apparently waiting for the conclusion of my cursory congregational evaluations. When the foyer emptied, he walked over to me and said, "You have plans for lunch?"

"Honestly, I've not even thought about eating. All I could think about was surviving this morning."

"Good. Follow me to my house. My wife has something for us."

Over a meal of fried chicken and vegetables, they shared their stories with me. Richard and his wife, Elise, were both from a small town in the mountains of eastern Tennessee. Richard's family was so poor that when the Great Depression hit this country, they barely noticed. They struggled to meet their basic needs before the Depression, and they continued to struggle after the Depression. Richard's father was an alcoholic who did a decent job providing for his family when he was sober, and a miserable job providing when he was drunk. As the years progressed, he found himself drunk more often than not and the family's meager fortunes diminished even further.

Elise's father was a bi-vocational pastor. When she was twelve years old, he became the pastor of Ebenezer Baptist Church in Van Hill, Tennessee–the church Richard's mother, siblings, and when sober, father attended. Richard was fourteen years old when he first laid eyes on Elise. She was, like him, wearing clothes that were even more tattered and old fashioned than the tattered and old-fashioned attire worn by everyone else in the church. But, she possessed a natural beauty and, when she showed it, a strikingly sweet smile. She captured his heart on that day, and Richard became quite enamored with the preacher's daughter.

Elise's father had not finished his seventh grade year in school and had never quite mastered the skills of reading and writing. He could sign his name and he recognized a few words, but not enough to read a complete sentence. Every Saturday night he would instruct Elise's mother to select a passage from the Bible and read it to him. She would read the verses three or four times out loud. Elise's father would close his eyes and picture the phrases in his mind. He would play her words over and over in his head until he had the passage memorized. The next morning he would open his Bible and pretend to read the passage to his congregation before preaching on the selected text. Elise and her family were the only ones who knew her father's secret.

Unlike Richard's father, Elise's father was an ardent teetotaler. He preached often against the devil's drink and the evils it accompanied. While this was the vice he most often addressed, he had a long list of other sins he targeted–young people going to the movies, women wearing make-up, anyone voting Republican–and he would often talk about the vices while sitting on the front porch of the church, smoking his hand-rolled cigarettes. Rarely had Elise ever heard a sermon on mercy and grace, and she never witnessed a father showing anything but discipline in his home. He was strict, distant, and seemed to care little about her needs or feelings. Every conversation she had with her father was critical, centering on her manner of dress, hairstyle, or the fact she was seen talking with some boy in church. She grew up believing God to be a harsh, judgmental, condemning God who anxiously waited to cast her soul into hell.

Richard and Elise began to date, in secret, when he turned sixteen years old. For one year they hid their romance from the ever-watchful eye of her father, his family, and the other adults in the church. The only ones who knew about their affections for one another were her siblings. As a fourteen-year-old girl Elise could not help but share her excitement with her sister, two years her junior, and spend many evenings recounting every conversation and parsing every word spoken by Richard.

One day shortly after Elise turned fifteen, she came home from school and, from outside the house, could hear the raised voice of her father and the pleas of her younger sister. She walked inside and discovered her younger sister cowering before her father, whose hand was raised to strike her, apparently not for the first time. Through the shouts of her father, Elise surmised that he had caught her younger sister holding hands with a boy from her school. He accused her of disobeying his authority and of being a thirteen-year-old tramp. As his hand rose in the air to strike her again, Elise's younger sister shouted, out of self-preservation, "But Elise has been going with Richard for a year!" Her father froze, turned his eyes toward Elise, and for the following hour she experienced the full measure of his fury, both for lying to him and for being such a shameless, promiscuous juvenile.

That night, after the monster went to bed, she packed her few belongings and walked the three miles of dirt and gravel roads to Richard's house. She knocked on his window and managed to wake him without disturbing the rest of the family. Through her tears she shared the story of what had transpired just a few hours earlier. She was never going back, she insisted, and while she did not have a plan beyond that, she was resolute in her desire to run away. Richard sat against the side of his house, thought for a while, and finally made the decision for the two of them to elope.

His father had been on a two-week drinking binge and was lying in the den, completely comatose. He managed to get Elise into the house without waking his mother or siblings. They slept for just a few hours and rose well before dawn. He packed his only other pair of pants, two other shirts, his knife, and a picture of his mother, stuffing his belonging into a small shoulder bag. He crept into the den and found his father's money purse lying beside his coat. He quietly opened the purse and found a five dollar bill, two ones, and thirty cents in change. Richard took it all, believing he was more than justified in doing so.

As the sun began to make its way above the horizon of Van Hill, Tennessee, Richard and Elise were hitchhiking their way to Knoxville. There they would find a justice of the peace and get married, both find jobs, and eventually see Richard get accepted to the University of Tennessee. Elise continued to work and pay the bills as Richard graduated from the university and was accepted to the University of Tennessee law school. After graduation, through the connection of a classmate, he and Elise moved to Mapleton, Georgia, where they lived for the next twenty-five years. They had a son and a daughter, both enrolled at the University of Tennessee. Neither child had ever met their grandparents. Richard and Elise never returned to Van Hill and had no idea about the whereabouts of their family members.

"Henry," Richard said, after they had spent thirty minutes or so sharing their story with me, "you did just fine today. I know you feel badly that in your nervousness you forgot parts of your sermon, but you did just fine. Mr. Tillery thinks you are the best thing in the world for preaching only five minutes. I heard him telling someone in the parking lot that he will be able to come to church, eat lunch, and still tee off before noon if you keep this same schedule for Sunday mornings."

"But Henry," he continued, "I know that you are not going to keep this same schedule. As you become more comfortable in your public speaking and in your ministry here, you won't have Sundays like this anymore. Plus, Henry–and I really want you to hear this–God is up to something in all this. I wish I could understand it more so that I could explain it better, but I know deep down that God is going to use you to change our church. I'm so tired of seeing a congregation just go through the motions. I'm tired of hearing people like Mr. Tillery celebrate the fact that he only had to listen to preaching for five minutes. I so badly want to see our lives center around God. Henry, I had almost given up hope that it would ever happen. But in the pastor search experience, God spoke so clearly to me, and I want you to know that. I want you to know that I'm praying for you every day. Keep listening to His voice and following His lead, and no matter what else happens, stay centered on Him."

I left Richard and Elise's house that day more encouraged than I'd been in weeks. I felt I could rush the gates of Hell armed only with a water pistol. I had no idea just how much I would need that sense of determination over the coming months. There were many times I wanted to just run away. There were other times I could clearly see God working. Through it all, I just tried to hang on and pray I survived.

For the time will come when people will not put up with sound doctrine. Instead, to suit their own desires, they will gather around them a great number of teachers to say what their itching ears want to hear.

2 Timothy 4:3

Chapter 16

Sunday, July 13, 1997

I adjusted my position in the mauve-and-blue-colored wingback chair. It revealed in both its style and tattered material the number of years it had been since it was manufactured. The flowered pattern and faded colors matched well the other furnishings and decorations in what was commonly called the "church parlor." It had once been a large classroom dedicated to the religious education of junior high school students. When the population of teenagers diminished to the point that it was no longer feasible to separate the junior and senior high teenagers, the two groups were combined into one space. For a short period of time the room became a storage area for anything not quite ready to be discarded–signs for a men's dinner, a youth group backdrop for a dinner theater fundraiser, and decorations for a ladies' game night were all haphazardly thrown into the room.

The room was eventually transformed in 1987 after a particularly exciting meeting of the Women's Missionary Union. Commonly called the WMU, this auxiliary group was formed in the late 1800's as a way for women to be involved in praying for and assisting Baptist missionaries throughout the world. Their quarterly publication listed the names of missionaries, their country of service, and their birthdays. Women would commonly gather together to discuss these mission efforts and to pray for these families serving in foreign countries.

By the early 1980's, the WMU group at First Baptist Mapleton consisted of eight women, all over the age of sixty, and all either widowed, divorced, or very desirous of going to any event that allowed them to be away from their husbands for a few hours. They met every Tuesday evening for a meal and fellowship. For several years, the meetings would often continue late into the evenings, but in 1986 the group determined, by unanimous vote, to end all meetings by seven-thirty. There had been a lengthy and rousing discussion concerning a new television program, Matlock. The show aired every Tuesday at eight o'clock. Ending by seven-thirty would ensure sufficient time to rush home, remove makeup and wigs, and settle into a comfortable chair before being wowed by the classically handsome and incredibly clever Andy Griffith.

In the fall of 1987, the group held its usual meeting, beginning precisely at five o'clock. The meal each week was "potluck," and normally consisted of leftovers from the Monday night dinners prepared by the members of the group. Each had become accustomed to preparing more food than necessary for the Monday evening meal, then placing the remaining portion securely in a Tupperware container to be used the following day. The women met in a Sunday School classroom containing a table and folding chairs with cushions. Most of the members met in this same classroom on Sunday mornings and had either purchased or crafted a seat cushion, making the hard, wooden chairs at least a little more bearable.

Mrs. Ethel Jones was a sixty-five year old widow who served as the president of the group. Her husband, Luther, had died quite unexpectedly at fifty years of age from what was later determined to be a congenital heart condition. Mrs. Jones had lived the last twenty years of her life as a widow woman who was very quick to describe in great detail the incredible misfortune she'd suffered in life. She had a proclivity for quoting and misquoting Bible passages related to suffering, and would connect them to her own life story in such a way that one thought she'd penned the words herself.

"We lost so much after the death of Luther. It was so hard, but I reminded myself that the Lord giveth and the Lord taketh away. Blessed be the name of the Lord."

Mrs. Jones had recently acquired, as a gift from her daughter, a microwave oven. While initially very suspicious of this new technology, Mrs. Jones had come to appreciate the efficient and comparatively instantaneous manner in which meals were able to be prepared. Her daughter had paired this gift with a book, *Microwave For One*, which contained a full array of recipes for the unfortunate soul dining alone each evening. Mrs. Jones, though, did not see the title of the book as being rife with a tragic sadness. Instead, she thumbed through the pages every morning, struggling over the decision of which delectably instant delight she would prepare for her evening meal.

She became particularly infatuated with a recipe for Chicken Parmesan and had found the microwave instructions perfect for preparing a single serving. Armed with a pocket calculator and her own ingenuity, she had attempted to triple and quadruple the required ingredients in order to have the necessary leftovers for the potluck WMU meetings. While presentable and even edible, the chicken was particularly chewy. This presented quite a problem for those members of the group who had traded their God-given teeth for a set of dentures.

The members of the group attempted to avoid the dish prepared by Mrs. Jones, but her insistence that all members at least just try a portion of her entrée meant that each week others were forced to choke down a portion of the rubbery poultry. After a few months of struggling through the gastronomical ordeal, Mrs. Betsy Chapman decided a change was needed. Upon the completion of the meal, she asked the group if she could share a personal concern. They all quickly agreed, hoping to hear a bit of gossip to fuel their private conversations for the next few days.

"As most of you know," Mrs. Chapman began, "I am

having to spend more and more time dealing with Johnny." Johnny was her adult son who had never managed to keep a job for more than two weeks. When a paycheck or unemployment benefits would expire, he would show up at his mother's house looking for food, money, lodging, or a combination of all three. "Therefore, I would like to make a suggestion that we change our meeting procedure on Tuesdays. My friend, Janice Burgess, has a lady who cooks for her twice a week. She is an excellent cook and her prices are reasonable. I say we ask this lady to cook the meal for our meeting. Then we will not have to prepare these items to bring each week." Three other ladies quickly voiced their support for this change.

Mrs. Jones, surprised by this suggestion and the apparent willingness of the other members to so frivolously spend their limited income on this luxury, asked, "Where would she prepare the meal? The only kitchen we have is in the Family Life Center. Surely you do not expect us to meet there, do you? Now, Betsy, I can certainly sympathize with your situation. Lord knows I'm no stranger to suffering and many times I have had to find my strength in the cleft of the rock. After the death of my dear Luther, there were many days I would just pray that the Lord would make me lie down in green pastures and anoint my head with oil. Some days I would just pray, 'Lord, into thy hands I commit my spirit.' But the Lord saw my suffering and heard my prayers and always gave me just enough wisdom to know how to accept the things I cannot change and the courage to change the things I cannot accept."

"I do understand the suffering you have been through with little Johnny. As I always say, 'The Lord helps those who help themselves' and you have certainly tried to get that young 'un to do some helping of himself. I know it has taken a toll on you and I pray that the Lord has plans to prosper you and give you hope in this situation. But as much as my heart feels for you, I do not see how this proposal will work with our group. I just cannot see how we could have our meetings in that big, unsightly gymnasium."

At eighty-one years of age, Mrs. Catherine Steeleman was the senior member of the gathering. Her husband had served as the president of Mapleton National Bank for several decades before his death in 1983. He was a prominent leader at First Baptist and, before his passing, had served in the role of church treasurer for as long as anyone could remember. Mrs. Steeleman had grown especially weary of Mrs. Jones's microwave delicacies and had spoken with Betsy Chapman prior to this meeting. Anticipating the objection of meeting in the Family Life Center, Mrs. Steeleman offered a bold solution to their dilemma.

"As most of you are aware, First Baptist was dear to the heart of my late husband. He supported the church in so many ways, but the way he knew best to support the church was through his financial giving." Mrs. Steeleman had a way of reminding the group quite often of her and her deceased husband's financial gifts to the church. "Upon his death, he left a sum of money to be used specifically for facility upkeep. I know that the pastor and deacons have set aside this money to be used when that old boiler goes out, but I believe that I could request the money be used for a different purpose. They are aware that I, just like my husband, still want to financially support this church I love, and they would not want to disappoint me."

"My suggestion to them will be to take those funds and use them to renovate that old Junior High classroom that has become nothing but a junk room. I say we turn it into a nice parlor for the church. There is another classroom next door that could be converted into a small kitchen. That way, those having dinner meetings in the parlor would have a place to prepare food. Of course, we will need to carefully monitor the use this room, but I think it would be perfect for our meetings."

"Now, if it pleases this body, I would like to make a motion that all future meetings take place in our Family Life Center, with a catered meal, until the church is able to complete this parlor project. All in favor?"

The motion passed. Only Ethel Jones objected over the frivolous spending on a caterer when the pot-luck format was sufficient. The pastor and deacons unanimously supported a motion to use the money given by the late Mr. Steeleman for the remodeling of the former Junior High and adjacent classroom. The parlor and adjoining kitchen were completed in six months.

Until she died in 1991, Mrs. Catherine Steeleman never again ate chewy Chicken Parmesan.

This was my first church council meeting since

becoming the pastor of First Baptist a month earlier. The chairman of the board of deacons sat immediately to my right. According to the church constitution and by-laws, which had last been updated in 1922, the deacon chairman was responsible for moderating all church council meetings. The current chairman and moderator of this meeting was Mr. Dwight Norman, a gentleman who was a retired foreman from the Duncan Company Plant. Duncan Company opened its doors in 1949 as a producer of spun yarn to be used in the manufacturing of carpet. With the population growth and demand for housing which occurred after the second World War, and with the move away from hardwood flooring to carpeted floors, the carpet industry became extremely profitable. The plant typically employed between three hundred fifty and four hundred employees and became the lifeblood of Mapleton. Many residents of the town graduated from high school, began the next week working at the plant, and remained there until retirement. The other businesses in town–clothing stores, grocers, the hardware store, attorneys–they all owed their survival to the paychecks being given to the several hundred workers at Duncan.

In 1980, the Duncan brothers, whose father opened the plant, began to quietly search out an interested buyer for their business. The high interest rates charged for borrowing money made it economically impossible for them to continue acquiring the capital needed for updating machinery and purchasing materials. After several months of searching, they found a buyer from Atlanta. Exactly two years after the new owner took possession of Duncan Brothers, he closed the plant and moved all the machinery to another yarn factory he owned in Dahlonega, Georgia. It was a good financial move for him to consolidate the two plants and to have the business in closer proximity to the carpet manufacturers. For the town of Mapleton, though, it was a financial disaster. In one day, three hundred sixty-eight people lost their jobs and their paychecks. Some people moved to the new factory in north Georgia and a few found jobs in other places. Most stayed in Mapleton and tried to find employment at the few businesses who seemed to be hiring. As people moved, housing prices dropped, the local tax revenue dropped, and offerings in churches dropped. It was not until 1988, when a chicken processing plant was constructed just outside the city limits that the local economy and city coffers began to stabilize.

Mr. Dwight Norman had been employed at Duncan Brothers since his graduation from high school in 1951. He had eventually become a foreman, overseeing a shift of nearly one hundred employees. He was a tough supervisor who ran the business as if it were his own. Yarn manufacturing was all he had ever known, and when the plant closed its doors in 1983, Dwight Norman found himself to be a fifty-one year old unemployed former manager with few skills transferable to another profession. He received an offer to move to the new plant in Dahlonega, in a downgraded position at a lower salary, but his wife refused to leave the place she'd lived her entire life. Plus, she had a good job as a teacher at the middle school, and with the money they'd managed to save, the two could survive on her salary. Dwight had few hobbies, detested golf, and did not much enjoy staying at home and piddling in a garden. So, he poured himself into the life of the church. He was quickly nominated to be on the board of deacons and eventually became the chairman. By the time I arrived in Mapleton, he was serving as chairman for the third time in ten years. Dwight Norman was the de facto CEO of the church, and as I later learned, ran the church in much the same manner as he ran his shift of employees at Duncan Brothers.

To his right sat Mrs. Ethel Jones, now seventy-five years old and still the president of the Woman's Missionary Union. The meeting of the WMU by this point normally consisted of Ethel and five other women. Other than the move from the Family Life Center to the Church Parlor for the Tuesday evening meal, there had only been one change to the WMU meetings. After Matlock went off the air in 1995, the ladies occasionally continued their discussions beyond the previous seven-thirty deadline.

To the right of Mrs. Jones sat Mr. George Jenkins, the chairman of the finance committee. Mr. Jenkins was a Certified Public Account and perhaps the most introverted, reticent individual I had ever met. He possessed such a dull, insipid, uninteresting personality that when he entered a room, it felt like someone left. I had met with him on two occasions prior to the church council meeting and had quickly ascertained that a discussion of any topic other than financial matters was a one-sided conversation. His countenance was like that of a mortician, and he almost seemed to derive pleasure from dispensing information on the financial maladies of the church.

To his right sat Mrs. Marlene Smith, the chairperson of the personnel committee. Mrs. Smith was a short, round, vivacious individual who possessed the exact opposite personality of Mr. Jenkins. She had never met a stranger and bubbled with excitement over the slightest bit of good news or new piece of information. "Oooh," she exclaimed walking into the church council meeting, "someone bought new flowers for the parlor. They are soooo lovely. I just love them and they brighten the room soooo much. Aren't they lovely y'all? Why, just lovely!" Unfortunately, Marlene was endowed with two major character flaws. The first was that once she began to talk, which was the moment her eyes opened in the morning, she would not stop. It was difficult to ever speak in the presence of Marlene. Secondly, due to her love of hearing her own voice, she had an overwhelming obsession with any form of gossip. These two character flaws combined to make a third flaw: she would often listen to part of the gossip, fill in the rest of the details with her incessant chatter, and then repeat stories that were half-truths or virtual lies. Everyone understood that a story told by Marlene Smith was either partially or completely inaccurate.

To her right sat Miss Mary Westwood, the part-time music director. Miss Westwood was the music teacher and choral director at Mapleton High School, where she'd been for nearly twenty years. She was fifty years old and had never been married. For years, various individuals in the church had attempted to get her married off, but Miss Westwood just could never seem to find the right individual. Her father had completely adored her, doted on her constantly, and praised her profusely. No man, in her mind, had lived up to the standard of her father, and so she continued to wait for the right man to come along.

These individuals–Mr. Norman, chairman of the deacons; Mrs. Jones, chairperson of the WMU; Mr. Jenkins, chairman of the finance committee; Mrs. Smith, chairperson of the personnel committee; Miss Westwood, the part-time music director; and me, the newly installed pastor–comprised the church council of First Baptist Church. Our task was to meet quarterly and to determine the activities for the coming months in the life of the church.

Mr. Jenkins, as chairman of the deacons, moderated the meeting. After leading the group through a discussion of the normal agenda, he addressed the only new item of business.

"As most of you are aware, the Maple Festival is coming up very soon. I think we need to discuss our plans for Maple Sunday. We normally designate the first Sunday of the Festival to be Maple Sunday. Let's see, according to my calendar, that should be Sunday, October 19. Any objections to putting that on our calendars?"

"Oooooh, I'm so excited," Mrs. Smith jumped in. "I just love Maple Sunday! Do you know last year that Jimmy and Juanita Drummond both came to our church on that Sunday. They normally go to the Methodist church, but they both quit going after Jimmy had his affair and they almost split up. I'm so happy they stayed together even if it was just for the children, but still, at least they are together. And to see the two of them sitting in church together was such a wonderful surprise. Do you think maybe they will come again this year? Should I invite them? Maybe I'll give her a call later this week and tell her. So what was that date again?"

"Excuse me." I jumped in when it seemed that Marlene was finally taking a breath. "What in the world is Maple Sunday?"

"Oh, Pastor," Mrs. Ethel Jones said, much to the chagrin of Mrs. Smith, who I could see was busting to be the one to tell me all about Maple Sunday. In deference to her senior, she sat back in her chair and allowed Mrs. Jones to continue.

"Maple Sunday is when we have an entire service centered around the Maple Festival. You do know about the Maple Festival, don't you? Oh, no? Well, Mapleton was named after the Japanese Maple Tree, which is much different than your run-of-the-mill Maple tree. You have undoubtedly seen these trees lining the streets of our town, although you may have not been able to identify the significance of their presence quite yet. Every fall, the leaves of these trees will turn a bright red. Not a Christmas red, but a deep vermilion. The streets are lined with these beautiful red brackets on either side, and they are absolutely stunning. Every year we have a Maple Festival for a week to celebrate the changing of the leaves. My husband Luther just loved the Maple Festival. They've not been as pretty to me since he passed away, but

I guess there is a season for everything under the sun, and a time for rejoicing and a time for suffering. My years of suffering sure have been for a long season now."

Everyone just sat still, not sure exactly how to respond to Mrs. Jones.

"As most of you know," she began again, this time with a tightness in her throat and dabbing a tissue to her eyes, "this year's festival is especially important to our family. Tragedy has struck our family again, and my daughter is working hard to make sure this is the best festival yet. I've told her that her work will not be in vain and that the Lord is watching her and saying 'well done, my good and faithful servant' as she toils away. I promise all of you in here that this year's festival will be a wonderful time for our community to come together."

An uncomfortable silence fell over the room as Mrs. Jones' voice trailed off. Everyone else seemed to understand her reference to the tragedy in her family and gave a collective sympathetic nod as she spoke.

I looked around, seeing if anyone was willing to enlighten me further as to the exact nature of Maple Sunday. They all seemed to be very interested in whatever they held in their laps. I finally spoke, breaking the awkward silence. "Pardon my ignorance here, but help me to understand what exactly Maple Sunday is all about?"

It was the open door Mrs. Smith needed. She quickly jumped in before Mrs. Jones could regain her composure and continue enlightening me. "Oooh, Pastor, it is such a wonderful Sunday. Everyone wears their red—not Christmas red, mind you–but Maple leaf red. The mayor comes and speaks and normally our state senator will speak and one year we even had the governor come and speak on that Sunday! The church is full on Maple Sunday. It is so exciting to see all the people here in church and the red colors. Not Christmas red, you understand. But Maple leaf red. All the colors are so beautiful. It is such a wonderful way to begin Maple week, don't y'all think? I'm so glad we have a Maple Sunday every year. Our church really contributes to the community by hosting this."

I was still a somewhat confused as to the nature of the service. "So we do this on Sunday morning instead of having a worship service?"

"No, no, no," Mrs. Smith replied with a chuckle. "This *is* our morning worship service. We have a sermon and sing hymns just like a normal service. It's just that we have the mayor or some other dignitary speak for a few minutes about the Festival and what it means to this community."

"So, the remainder of the service is a normal worship service?"

Mrs. Jones cleared her throat before Mrs. Smith could speak, indicating her desire to enter the conversation but an unwillingness to verbally battle for the right to be heard. Mrs. Smith sat back in her chair, yielding the floor to Mrs. Jones.

"Pastor, I think what we are trying to tell you is that the entire service sort of centers around the Maple Festival. The mayor or some other community leader speaks about it directly, but the remaining elements of the service are indirectly related to the festival. The children's message, for example, may focus on the changing of seasons. The songs are about nature. Your sermon might be focused on the beauty found in God's creation. It's all a way that we can celebrate together this joyous occasion. Lord knows we need to be together as a community and to lean upon our brothers and sisters in our times of suffering. Just like the children of Israel relied upon one another to help them get through those times of suffering under Pharaoh, we need to help one another. Like I always say, two are better than one. If one falls down, it's hard to get up on his own, but if two are there, and they both fall down, it is much better."

Sensing my discomfort with a service focused on the Maple Festival, and in a rare instance of speaking without being asked a direct question, Mr. George Jenkins decided to add his thoughts on the situation. "Pastor, as you are aware, in order to pay our bills and your salary, we need an average offering of just under two thousand dollars each Sunday. We normally take in less than that amount during the summer months and considerably more than that amount in December. But always, and I mean *always*, October is our biggest giving month of the year. And it is all because of Maple Sunday. That Sunday's offering alone is normally over ten thousand dollars. The offering we collect on Maple Sunday makes a substantial impact on being able to fund our operations here."

Mr. Dwight Norman, chairman of the deacons, decided it was his time to speak. "I think what our finance committee chairman is trying to say to you, Pastor, is that it is probably not the wisest idea to try and change Maple Sunday. If it ain't broke..."

Mrs. Jones jumped in to complete his sentence. "Then don't go fixing what has been firmly established. You don't need to put out a fleece and bowl of water on this one, Pastor. If you do not like Maple Sunday, then just understand that this kind of suffering produces faith and that faith will produce a perseverance that will help you get through many more Sundays of suffering. Lord knows I learned after the death of my husband how to suffer in church, and it has helped me persevere through many sermons."

Before I could make another comment, Mr. Dwight Norman decided it was time to conclude the meeting. "Good, then, it's settled. October nineteenth is Maple Sunday. Miss Westwood, would you mind closing us with prayer?"

I heard not a word of what our music director prayed. My mind was consumed with confusion over what in the world I would preach on Maple Sunday.

There is a time for everything...a time to be silent, and a time to speak.

Ecclesiastes 3:1,7

Chapter 17

Monday, August 25, 1997

Mrs. Dale Davidson had served as the president of the Maple Festival Committee for at least three decades. As the wife of Charles Davidson, arguably the most prominent attorney in the town, and as a Mapleton native hailing from an upstanding family, it seemed she was born for this particular position in life. She poured herself into the planning and promotion of the Maple Festival and spent long hours on the phone and meeting with community leaders. She had a congenial manner combined with a forceful undertone in her requests.

"Surely, your business wants to contribute to this important community event, right?" She would ask proprietors each spring, as she began to plan the promotional booklet for that year's coming Festival. She would normally add something like, "I would just hate for people to think that you do not support our community and decide to not patronize your business." Several owners would secretly complain to one another that Dale Davidson should have been born into a Chicago mafia family.

The previous year, just a few months after the Maple Festival, Charles and Dale Davidson's son had been killed in a tragic car accident. Mr. Davidson had coped with his grief through doubling his formerly daily ritual of bourbon and water. For a number of years he would, at exactly four-thirty in the afternoon, fix his first drink, consisting of one part Maker's Mark bourbon and two parts water. He would consume this drink as he finished his work, then fix another for the short drive home. After dinner, he would imbibe a third while watching television. Always under control and never dramatically impaired, Charles Davidson viewed his drinking as a way to relax from the stress of his profession.

After the death of his son, the daily ritual moved to three o'clock, unless he was in court, and the number of drinks doubled. He began to lose the former control he had over his drinking, and there began to be talk around the firm about the need for Mr. Davidson to take an early retirement. When sober, he was an incredibly effective attorney, but the number of those hours seemed to be rapidly decreasing.

Dale Davidson, on the other hand, dealt with her grief by pouring herself into her work. The spring following her son's death, she dedicated herself to making that year's Maple Festival the best the town had ever seen. "In memory of Charlie," she would often say. "Unofficially, we are dedicating this year's Festival to Charlie." While her grief was sincere, she very shrewdly used this tragedy to more than double the normal business and private sponsorship of the Festival.

Charles and Dale Davidson were members of First Baptist Church. Both of them were raised in the church and Dale's mother, the only still living of their parents, remained a faithful member and the president of the Women's Missionary Union. She lived alone but had managed quite nicely, especially since her daughter and son-in-law had recently purchased for her a brand new, modernized microwave. She had become so adept at preparing meals with this microwave technology that she asked her son-in-law if he would check around at his law firm and see if anyone wanted to purchase her twenty-five year old oven. After a fair amount of debate, Charles Davidson was able to convince her that this would not be necessary and there may just come a day that she would need her oven.

Much to the dismay of Mrs. Ethel Jones, it had been years since Charles had been to church on a Sunday morning. The funeral service for Charlie was the first time he had been in the sanctuary for so long that when he commented to his mother-in-law about the "new" carpet, she sarcastically replied, "It was new fifteen years ago when they purchased it, honey." Over the years, she consistently dropped not–so–subtle hints in his presence about attending church, but was never able to guilt him into coming. He worked hard, he said, and Sunday morning was his time to relax, read the Sunday edition of the Atlanta Journal– Constitution, and to have some peace and quiet.

Dale did attend on occasion, but most Sundays stayed home with her husband. The one Sunday she never missed, though, was Maple Sunday. She made it a priority to be at the church early, well before the official beginning of the service, so that she could stand in the foyer and greet everyone as they entered the sanctuary. Every year she had given a brief greeting to the congregation on behalf of the Maple Festival Committee and to "personally invite y'all to participate in this year's festivities." It was her contribution, she said, both to the community and to First Baptist, to ensure that Maple Sunday and the Maple Festival were both done with a high level of excellence.

Although I knew her mother well, I had not met Dale Davidson before she came to my office to discuss the service. "My mother," she said after our initial introductions were made, "just thinks you are the cutest thing in the world. She loves getting to eat with you on Wednesday nights and listening to you pray for her sick friends."

I regularly sat at a table of individuals that included Ethel Jones at our weekly Wednesday evening church fellowship meal and prayer meeting hour. The program consisted of reading through the list of members' and their relatives' latest surgical procedures, medical diagnosis, or hospital stays. At the end of the discussion on the various ailments, the pastor was expected to offer a perfunctory prayer to the Almighty on behalf of all those who were suffering. I had, to that point, performed satisfactorily enough in this area, according to Mrs. Davidson.

"You certainly have won her over," she continued. "By the way, she is very concerned about you finding a wife and is asking all of her friends if they have any granddaughters available. I'm just giving you fair warning on that."

"Thanks for the heads up," I said with a smile. "I certainly need all the help I can get, but I do get nervous about blind dates contrived by grandmothers. I never know what I'm getting myself into."

"Well, don't say I did not warn you. Look, I want to talk to you about Maple Sunday. My mother told me that the church has already designated October nineteenth, which we are promoting in our literature. I expect this year that the attendance that day will be even higher than in previous years. As you've heard already, I'm sure, we are unofficially dedicating this year's festival to the memory of my son, Charlie." She choked back tears, understandably still struggling with the untimely death of her child. "Pastor, I wish you could have met him. You would have loved him so much. So full of life and passion. I'm not sure why the Lord decided to take him from us – it has torn us apart – but we are persevering nonetheless." She paused for a moment to gather her composure and her thoughts.

"Now, we would have made this year's festival officially in memory of Charlie, but I'm aware that if we did that, then every person in Mapleton who loses a relative would ask me to designate future festivals in memory of their loved one, and there is just no way we can do something like that. But, since Charlie meant so much to this community, we feel that it is only fair to recognize the enormity of his loss at this time.

"As you know, normally the mayor speaks on Maple Sunday, but I just spoke with his office and learned that he is having back surgery in a couple of weeks and will not be able to make the service this year. So, what I think would work is for me to give my normal greeting but then to also speak, on behalf of the mayor, about the importance of the community coming together during this time. I plan on using part of that time to talk about Charlie and how he is looking down from Heaven on us and rejoicing in the support this community gives to one another.

Now, I know that time is limited, so I am planning on doing all of this in ten minutes, which still gives you more than enough time to preach. By the way, I do have a list of people who have helped with the Festival this year and all of them are expected to be in the service. I think it would be appropriate for you to recognize them at some point, maybe at the conclusion of the service, just before you voice the closing prayer? What do you think?"

"I'm not sure what I think," I said. "Is this normally the way it's done?"

"Well, Pastor John liked to recognize them at the beginning of the service, but I'll be honest with you: I never liked that. I've noticed over the years that many people seem to have trouble getting here on time. I just cannot understand why people are late to the Maple Sunday service. They miss having the opportunity to see who has put in all these hours to help the Festival become reality. So, if you are comfortable with it, I think we should do the recognition at the end of the service. I will give you the names and their corresponding roles on the committee. Whether you want them to stand or just call out there names, I'll leave that up to you. I mean, you are the pastor of the church, so it's your choice!"

I simply nodded in appreciation of her allowing me this small freedom. We discussed a few other details of the service; she thanked me for my time and left my office. I returned to my desk, leaned back in my chair, and exhaled deeply. For several minutes I simply stared at the wall in front of me. I knew that I needed advice. I picked up the phone and dialed the number for Dr. Smith. Fortunately, he was in his office and answered on the third ring.

"Pastor Miller! Good to hear from you. How is the pastorate today?"

"Lovely. Just lovely. Have you got a few minutes for me to bounce a few things off of you?"

"Fire away, pastor."

Keep your lives free from the love of money and be content
with what you have, because God has said, "Never will I
leave you; never will I forsake you."

Hebrews 13:5

Chapter 18

Tuesday, September 16, 1997

After my first disastrous sermon, I managed somewhat better deliveries in the Sundays that followed. I continued preaching through the book of John, utilizing the hours spent in cram sessions with Dr. Smith. With the length of my homilies extending beyond the five minutes of my first sermon, I did notice the silence of some members who expressed such roaring praise after my initial Sunday. A few others, including my friend Richard Davis, were extremely complimentary. Some of these were intrigued by the messages and asked about further study aids. I began to compose a devotional book to be given out and used by the members through the week as a way to read other Biblical texts related to the topic. I naively had one hundred and fifty printed for the first Sunday. That evening I went back to the church for a meeting, walked into the foyer of the sanctuary, and discovered one hundred and thirty five devotional booklets remaining. Only fifteen individuals had taken advantage of my offer. That same evening, George Jenkins, the chairman of the finance committee, called me at home. "Do you know how much it costs to print these materials?" he asked me. "We do not have money in the budget to print all those booklets every week! How many of them were taken, anyway?"

I was scared to tell him the truth. "I'm not really sure, Mr. Jenkins. How about this: what if I only print twenty-five, and I limit the devotional material to one eight and a half by eleven sheet of paper? Will that be okay?"

He grunted and eventually consented to this proposal.

Over the next several weeks, I came to understand better the dynamics of the congregation. There were a few–a handful, really–who were desirous of hearing Biblical truth and gaining an understanding of God's revelation to the world. The majority, though, simply tolerated my preaching and were thankful when my sermons were shorter in length. There seemed to be an undercurrent of dissatisfaction with my sermons, and I started to notice a slight decrease in the already sparse Sunday morning attendance.

One Tuesday afternoon in September, Mrs. Marlene Smith, chairperson of the personnel committee, called the office and asked if she could stop by and meet with me. Without giving me much of an opportunity to answer, she informed me that she had to stop by the post office and the dry cleaners and she needed to make one phone call before she left the house but would be at my office in less than an hour. Realizing the amount of time I might have to spend on the phone if I asked a follow-up question, I quickly assured her that I would be available.

At four o'clock, I answered the knock at my door and was greeted with a loud and ebullient "Hello, Pastor!" Marlene walked into my office and squeezed into one of the two wing back chairs across from my desk.

"Good to see you, Mrs. Smith," I said.

"Listen, Pastor, as I've told you before, call me Marlene. I know I'm old enough to be your mother. Heck, I've got two boys who are older than you by several years. But you are now my pastor and there is no reason for you to call me Mrs. Smith every time you see me. So, just Marlene from now on. Agreed?"

I smiled and nodded my head as I took a seat behind my desk.

"Now, I know you are wondering why I am here today. First of all, I want you to know that I am very excited that you are our pastor now. I know I've told you that before, but I'm still excited. It is so wonderful to have someone so young preaching every Sunday and representing our church to the community. You have brought a breath of fresh, youthful air to our congregation, and I am so glad that the search committee found you."

"As you know, I am the chairperson of the personnel committee. There are three other church members on the committee, and our job is to meet every quarter and to discuss any issues with the staff members of the church. Of course you know the staff currently consists of you, Doris, Mary, and Sammy."

Doris was the part-time secretary who worked on Mondays, Tuesdays, and Wednesdays. She was a retired school teacher and was paid a paltry salary of one hundred and twenty dollars per week for her services. She and her husband had divorced some thirty years before, and she'd never had any children. Her life revolved around the church. She would have worked for nothing if the church had not been able to pay her, which she knew might very well be a reality one day.

Mary was Miss Mary Westwood, the part-time music director. She was paid seventy-five dollars for the Sundays she led music in the morning worship service, which was virtually every Sunday of the year. On the rare occasion she missed a Sunday, Mr. George Jenkins made sure she did not receive her check that week.

Sammy was the part-time custodian who also worked at the local high school. He cleaned the church two days a week. Unlike the other employees, he was required to clock in and out so that Mr. Jenkins would know exactly how much he was to be paid.

"Now normally," Marlene continued, "there just isn't all that much to talk about. Doris and Mary are paid so little that we could never get anyone to do what they do for what we pay them. Sammy does a good job and Lord knows George doesn't pay him for one minute more than the poor guy works."

"But several people have approached me and they have asked me whether or not the personnel committee is happy with your performance so far. The truth is our committee has not officially met since you came to our church, but we probably should meet soon. And, well, pastor, I am going to have to bring up to the committee this issue since several people have asked me about it."

"What issue is that?" I asked, somewhat more forcefully than I intended.

"Well, your performance as pastor."

"What specifically about my performance?" I managed to keep my voice under control with my second question.

"Well, Pastor, it's a little hard to define."

"Give it a shot." This time I managed a smile as I spoke.

"Well, here is the thing, I guess. You do a good job with your sermon delivery. And your content is really good and interesting. As much as I loved your predecessor, Pastor John, most of the time when he finished preaching I had no idea what he had talked about. That is not true with you. Your sermons are clear and very, well, insightful."

"Thank you, I think. I'm having trouble understanding where the problem is."

"Well, it's like this. You're just a little too serious. I mean, you never tell any jokes in your sermons or stories about people in the congregation. Pastor John was really good at giving us updates on people he'd gone to see and lightening the mood with some funny story about a church member. We just do not ever hear that from you."

"I guess, what I'm trying to say is, even though your sermons are good, I don't ever leave church feeling good. Even though Pastor John's sermons were bad, I always left church feeling good." She paused, sat back in her chair, and gave me a half-hearted smile.

"Pastor, you have all the makings of a great preacher, but you need to have a little more levity in your preaching. You talk about God and sin and the cross a lot in your sermons, which is fine in small doses, but you really seem to spend a lot time on those things. Make us feel good about ourselves. Give us something positive to take away from the services that will help us get through our week. If you do that, I think all this chatter about your performance will go away."

<hr />

That evening I called Dr. Smith and summarized for him my conversation with Marlene. "Doctor Smith, I'm really struggling here. I do not think these people want the kind of pastor I'm turning out to be. I could change, but it's not me. I'm not good at telling jokes and, even if I were, why would I spend valuable time on Sunday morning telling jokes rather than explaining the truths found in God's word? What do you think I should do, Dr. Smith?"

There was silence on the other end of the line. "Hello? Dr. Smith?" I said, wondering if the connection had been lost.

"I'm here, Henry. Listen, sometimes I wonder if I missed the voice of God when I pushed you to accept this position. I know it's hard and, honestly, it may get even harder. And these people may decide they no longer want you to be their pastor and they may fire you. If that is the case, then I'm sure that God had some purpose in it all. But Henry, and please listen carefully, do not give in to the temptation of becoming an entertainer. God has you there not to make the people feel good, but to show them God. You keep doing that. Give them the powerful truths we've studied in Scripture. Henry, keep doing what you have been doing, and you let God handle the rest."

My people come to you, as they usually do, and sit before you to hear your words, but they do not put them into practice. Their mouths speak of love, but their hearts are greedy for unjust gain.

Ezekiel 33:31

Chapter 19

Sunday, October 19, 1997

Mary Westwood chose to open the Maple Sunday service with the singing of the hymn, *For the Beauty of the Earth*. Before instructing the congregation to stand, she proudly informed the nearly five hundred congregants of a slight wording change she'd made in the song. After clearly explaining this creative insertion, she raised her hands into the air, signaling those seated before her to stand and for the pianist to begin playing the introductory melody. At the right moment, the congregation joined with Miss Westwood in singing:

> For the beauty of the earth,
> For the glory of the skies,
> For the love of which from our birth

Over and around us lies;
Lord of all, to Thee we raise
This our hymn of grateful praise.

For the wonder of each hour
Of the day and of the night,
Hill and vale and MAPLE tree and flower,
Sun and moon and stars of light:
Lord of all to Thee we raise
This our hymn of grateful praise.

As the congregation sang the inserted word, "Maple," into the classic hymn, Miss Westwood beamed with pride over her ingenious, creative addition to Maple Sunday. When completed, she instructed the congregants to be seated, and Mrs. Dale Davidson rose from her chair on the platform. With great regality, she took her place behind the pulpit and began her speech to the assembled citizens of Mapleton. As promised, Mrs. Davidson spoke for exactly ten minutes. She thanked those in attendance for participating in this important service and personally invited them to the other Maple Festival events. She implored the congregation to support the local businesses who sponsored the Festival, reminding them that these businesses loved the community and deserved their patronage. She spoke with great eloquence and fervor about her love for Mapleton and the hours she devoted every year to ensure the success of this community celebration. She then paused, allowed her shoulders to almost imperceptibly sag, and in low, soft tone, said, "You all are aware of what my family has been through this past year. The pain has been unbearable at times, and there have been days that Charles and I both have thought we would not make it out of the darkness and despair. But you...our friends...our community...you have been so wonderful to support us. Many people kindly offered to take over the reins of running the Maple Festival this year, sensing that a break from the work might be what I needed most. I appreciate so much their sentiment, but pouring myself into this Festival has been my therapy. I have dedicated myself this year to doing this in memory of Charlie."

She paused, choking back her tears.

"He loved Mapleton and he loved the Maple Festival. Every year he looked forward to the games, the greasy fair food, and the fireworks on the last night. He loved to see the whole community celebrating together and loved getting to speak with so many different people. I feel that this year, as we enjoy this annual celebration, that Charlie will be looking down on us and smiling, wishing us to have the very best Maple Festival yet. Thank you and God bless you all."

As she turned to sit, the congregation rose to their feet in thundering applause.

After another hymn, the offering, and a choir special, it was time for me to take my place behind the pulpit and deliver my first Maple Sunday sermon. I'd struggled for the last several weeks over what I was to say on this day.

Several members of the congregation had informed me that the crowd on Maple Sunday would be more numerous than Easter Sunday, and it was my chance to impress those in the community with my oratorical skills. There had been a lot of pressure to pick just the right text and preach a better-than-average sermon. Some may decide to return, several people felt obliged to inform me, if they like what they hear on Maple Sunday.

"I want to thank all of you for being here today," I began. "If you are visiting with us, I want you to know that we are honored by your presence and hope you will return soon." I looked out over the congregation and realized that the vast majority of faces were unfamiliar to me. Whether they were visitors or habitually absent members, I did not know. It was the largest crowd I'd ever seen in our sanctuary. There were a few remaining seats in the balcony and in the very front pews of the church, but most rows were comfortably full. There was an excitement among the congregation, due in large part to the energy created from a large crowd.

"As you probably know by now, I am the new pastor here. I began my ministry this past summer. This is my first pastorate." I paused in a moment of realization. "In fact, this is my first full time job." A low chuckle rippled through the congregation.

"I understand that in previous years, the pastor has delivered a message on this day about the importance of community, or the beauty of creation, or a message on inclusiveness, and how we really have more in common than differences."

"But I want to speak to you about another topic this morning. In the first chapter of the New Testament book of Colossians, we read these words, penned some two thousand years ago by the Apostle Paul:

"The Son is the image of the invisible God, the firstborn over all creation. For in him all things were created: things in heaven and on earth, visible and invisible, whether thrones or powers or rulers or authorities; all things have been created through him and for him. He is before all things, and in him all things hold together. And he is the head of the body, the church; he is the beginning and the firstborn from among the dead, so that in everything he might have the supremacy. For God was pleased to have all his fullness dwell in him, and through him to reconcile to himself all things, whether things on earth or things in heaven, by making peace through his blood, shed on the cross."

"There are four ideas in this passage that I want to share with you this morning. The first is that all of creation–the flowers, the grass, even the Japanese Maple trees–were created by Jesus Christ. The creation account we find in the book of Genesis is echoed here, but emphasizes the role of Jesus Christ in the creation process."

"The second idea is that he, Jesus, is today the head of all creation, and that through Christ everything is held together. He is the glue of everything we see. If Jesus Christ somehow suddenly ceased to exist, we would all instantly, along with the rest of creation, rupture into a million pieces and our tiny parts would fly into space. We are held together by power of Jesus Christ."

"Thirdly, this Jesus who has supremacy over all he has created came to earth two thousand years ago, took on human flesh, and died a cruel death on a Roman torture and execution device we call a cross. Three days later he rose from the dead, and through that death and resurrection we can be reconciled to God."

"The fourth idea is this, it is *only* through Jesus Christ that we are able to be reconciled to God. Without a relationship with Christ, you are an enemy of God. But through Jesus Christ, you are fully reconciled to God. You are fully accepted by God. No matter what you have done; no matter how far down the path of sin you've trod; no matter how many times you have blown it, when you come into a relationship with Christ, you are fully forgiven and completely accepted in the sight of God."

"I realize that many of you are here today in celebration of the Maple Festival. I've had the opportunity this weekend to see what so many of you have attempted to describe to me: the changing of the leaves and beautiful red canopies lining our streets. As much as we are able to enjoy their beauty, let us never forget that they are but compasses, pointing us toward their Creator. They, like all of creation, are only here because of the creating and sustaining power of Jesus Christ. In that regard, the trees are like us. But, unlike us, the Maple trees are not in need of a savior. I have that need. You have that need. Without Jesus Christ, there is no hope of a relationship with God. Through Jesus Christ, there is complete assurance of an unbreakable relationship with God. My prayer is that all of us in this room, every time we see the beauty of a Maple tree this week, would have our thoughts and affections drawn toward the One who created each and every leaf. Amen."

And so it was with me, brothers and sisters. When I came to you, I did not come with eloquence or human wisdom as I proclaimed to you the testimony about God. For I resolved to know nothing while I was with you except Jesus Christ and him crucified.

I Corinthians 2:1-2

Chapter 20

Tuesday, October 21, 1997

In the days following that sermon, I heard a number of second and third hand comments about the service and my message. A few expressed their appreciation for the sermon. Most were upset that I came across too dogmatic and rigid. Three members–on three separate occasions–felt the need to communicate with me what they heard Dale Davidson tell a group gathered outside the church after the service that day. "That kid knew we had people from lots of different backgrounds in the church that day. Heck, Dr. Weinstein was there because I personally invited him! He was extremely nervous about bringing his Jewish self to a Baptist church, but I assured him that it would be fine. Now, I know he will never come to

Maple Sunday again after hearing that. Didn't anyone at the church tell that preacher boy what to say on Maple Sunday? Who's in charge there now anyway? Furthermore, and I don't mean to sound petty, but he never once mentioned Charlie in his sermon. I met with him weeks ago and told him that this year's Festival was unofficially dedicated to the memory of Charlie. There is no way he can claim ignorance about that! Why in the world wouldn't he at least have said something? Isn't anyone in charge over there at the church now? Who tells that preacher boy what to do, anyway?"

I later learned that even after that Sunday, I still have a few supporters–Richard, Elise, and a handful of other members–most having served on the pastor search team and perhaps felt a sense of personal responsibility for my success. Surprisingly, two of my biggest defenders came from unexpected sources. Mrs. Ethel Jones, mother of Dale Davidson, continued to tell anyone who would listen, that she thought I was doing a fabulous job. She, like her daughter, was slightly annoyed that I had not mentioned her grandson in my Maple Sunday sermon, and she very politely mentioned that to me one evening. But a couple of months before Maple Sunday, she had issued–and I had accepted–an invitation for the two of us single people to dine together on Monday evenings. Every week I had faithfully consumed a chewy microwave meal prepared by Mrs. Jones while we talked about the community, the church, God, or how much she enjoyed reruns of Matlock. She was not about to publicly criticize me and risk losing her Monday night dinner date. To anyone who would listen, she would rattle on about my ministry and the good I had done for the church and the community. When questioned about specifics, she had a difficult time defining her particular views. Anyone who knew Mrs. Jones well understood that her defense of me was almost wholly based upon the enjoyment of her weekly engagement with a younger man.

My second unexpected supporter was Mr. George Jenkins. Truthfully, he did not care what I said or did not say on Sunday mornings. He was really not all that concerned about who I visited or did not visit in the hospital. His chief interest rested in the fact that my salary was forty percent less than what the church had paid to Pastor John. This adjustment enabled the church, for the first time in years, to pay her bills without dipping into the already diminished rainy day fund. He was quick to point out to anyone who would listen that the church would most likely not be able to get the kind of cheap labor they had in me with anyone else. "Better not run him off," Mr. Jenkins would say. "We'll never be able to afford another pastor again."

Those few supporters notwithstanding, my stock value in the church was beginning to plummet. I could sense that quiet conversations were taking place about how to get rid of the preacher-kid. If my sermons did not lighten up soon, they were saying, then I would have to go.

Dwight Norman called me on Monday morning and asked if he and Marlene could meet with me first thing on Tuesday. I knew the meeting would be tense. I spent most of the day Monday fretting over the next day's conversation. I felt strongly that I had spoken the words God wanted me to say, and yet I could not help but be somewhat discouraged by the critical remarks of those in attendance. I slept very little on that Monday evening.

At exactly eight o'clock that Tuesday morning, I heard a knock at my office door. Marlene Smith and Dwight Norman walked in together and sat in the chairs across from my desk. "Now son," the chairman of the deacon board began, "I think you know why we are here. There are a lot of people upset right now. This was Maple Sunday, and you really should have toned down the Jesus stuff. Marlene here tells me she has already had a conversation with you about all of this, and that you seemed to be open to her constructive criticism. So, son, I'm chalking all this up to the fact that you are young and inexperienced, and I'm sure you'll get better at discerning what to say and what not to say in your messages."

Marlene jumped in as soon as Dwight took a breath. "Pastor, I think the whole service was meant to be so uplifting and exciting, and your sermon just put this heavy weight on the celebration. I mean–just think about it–the sanctuary was packed with people, which is so rare these days. And everyone wore red–not Christmas red, remember, but Maple red. The room had a festive atmosphere and everyone wanted to celebrate. Even Dale's comments about her son were uplifting–sweet little Charlie looking down on us as we enjoy the festival this year. The people gathered had an expectation of hearing something positive from you, and then you give this message about us being enemies of God and salvation only through Jesus Christ? We had a lot of community leaders there who are not necessarily church-goers, and you told them that they are enemies of God. I mean, pastor, what in the world were you thinking?"

She shifted in her chair but continued speaking so that neither Dwight nor I could interject a comment. "Now pastor, I think you are losing a lot of support, and you certainly are making it difficult for us to defend your sermons. Don't you think you could tone things down slightly?"

"Marlene," I said, and then looked over at the deacon chairman, "Dwight. Thank you both for coming in today. I have certainly heard your comments and plan to take everything you've said into consideration. If you don't mind, could you give me some time to pray about this, and then we can meet later and continue this discussion?"

Both agreed and, after a few other cursory comments, left my office. I knew there was no reason to argue with either of them. Fifteen minutes later, I had my resignation letter written and stuffed inside an envelope. I placed the letter deep within my desk, confident that I would need to retrieve it soon.

The Lord saw how great the wickedness of the human race had become on the earth, and that every inclination of the thoughts of the human heart was only evil all the time.

Genesis 6:5

Chapter 21

Wednesday, October 22, 1997

I was standing just outside of baggage claim at the McCarran International Airport in Las Vegas when I heard, "How youse doin', Miller!"

I suffered through an awkward and suffocating bear hug from my former roommate, Law. Travelers whisked past us, curiously staring at this large, hairy man with his arms securely wrapped around my body, bouncing me up and down.

"My mudder and fadder told me to be sure and tell you hello. Dey sure did enjoy meetin' ya at de wedding dis past summer," Law continued after finally putting me down, allowing oxygen to once again enter my lungs. "Hey, youse remember Celli, right?"

Law's tiny, timorous bride stood nervously by his side, looking somewhat abashed at her husband's loud, attention drawing antics. "Hi, Henry," she quietly began. "Good to see you again."

I reached out and gave her a friendly, one-arm embrace. "Cecilia, great to see you too," I said. "I can't believe you are still with this Neanderthal. My hat's off to you for surviving the last four months."

I felt the strong force of a fist collide with my left shoulder. "Watchit, Miller. Just cause youse can't find a girl, don't go messin' wit us."

"Henry, just ignore Law. He gets like this when it has been more than an hour since he last ate. He is still grumbling because they only gave him one bag of pretzels on the flight here."

"Seriously, Henry, can youse believe dat junk? One measly bag of pretzels? Good ting Celli don't eat much and gave me half of hers."

At some point in their dating relationship, Law had nicknamed his wife, "Celli," apparently a shortened version of the name her parents bestowed upon her at birth. The way he pronounced this pet name, it sounded like he was saying the word, "silly."

"Celli, which one of dese is your bags gone be on?" Law waved his arm in the direction of several carousels in the baggage claim area. "I wish you could have done jest a carry on. We'se not gonna be here but a few days. Miller, youse got bags to get too?"

I pointed to the small piece of luggage sitting upright

beside me. "No, this is it. Made it easier getting through the Atlanta Airport without having to check a bag."

It had been two weeks before that I'd received a phone call from Law. After his matrimonial weekend and honeymoon at a cabin on Lake Erie, Law had begun a job working in the accounting department of a large steel manufacturer. He had been there only a few weeks when his boss told him that he would be going to Las Vegas for a convention on the latest accounting rules and regulations in the manufacturing industry. His supervisor's wife was pregnant with their first child, he told him, and the due date was the week before the conference. His wife had told him that if he went to this conference and left her with the newborn, she would file for divorce before he placed the first coin into a slot machine. It took him less than two seconds to decide on forgoing this year's accounting convention.

Knowing that Law was recently married and anxious about leaving his bride for a few days, his supervisor informed him that as long as he paid for her flight, she could go along. The room and meals were covered by the company, he said, and the accounting seminars were only for a few hours in the mornings. Plus, there was another supervisor in the company who would be going as well, and his wife would be traveling with him.

Two weeks before the convention, it was discovered that the other supervisor had been embezzling funds from the company. He was immediately fired and charges had been filed. His room, food, and conference fees for the Las Vegas convention had already been paid and were nonrefundable.

Law's supervisor came to him and said, "Look, we do not have anyone else we can send to the conference. All of us are tied up dealing with this embezzlement mess. If you have someone you want to bring along, then go ahead. It's better than the room just sitting empty."

That evening I received a phone call from my former roommate. "Come on, Miller. All youse have to pay for is youse flight. De room and de food is paid already. Youse need to get out of that town for a while anyways. Come on and hang out wit me and Celli for a couple of days. Who knows, Miller? Youse might just meet a girl while we'se out dere."

Law was right; I did need to get out of Mapleton for a few days. Although I was slightly uncomfortable with the thought of being a third wheel to Law and Cecilia, I knew that getting to spend some time away from the church and with an old friend would be great therapy for me. I called Delta and was not only able to find a cheap, round-trip flight, but one that landed in Las Vegas only an hour before Law and Cecilia's flight from Buffalo.

"Youse guys ready to grab a taxi?" Law said after we retrieved Cecilia's bags. Normally I would have objected to such frivolity and insisted upon taking a shuttle, but Law was clear that these kinds of expenses were being covered by his company. We wound our way through the Las Vegas streets and heavy traffic for about twenty minutes before being delivered to the lobby doors of the New York-New York Hotel. "Youse gonna love dis place, Henry. My boss told me dat it's de newest hotel in Vegas and looks like de

236

New Yok skyline. Me and Celli will fit in jest fine at dis place. Youse a souturn boy and might feel outta place, but we will take good care of you."

Law was right about me loving the hotel. It was the most amazing place I had seen in my life. The outside of the hotel was constructed to resemble the New York City skyline. The several towers imitated the Empire State Building, the Chrysler Building, the New York Public Library, and other New York skyscrapers. A one hundred and fifty foot model of the Statue of Liberty stood in front of the hotel, surrounded by a small lake representing the New York Harbor. Anyone entering the hotel from Las Vegas Boulevard did so through an exact replica of the Brooklyn Bridge, constructed at one-fifth the size of the original.

The interior was designed to make patrons feel as if they were walking around the streets of New York City in the 1930's. We entered into an old-style wood paneled lobby and immediately were struck by the wide-open, cavernous space. Interior shops rose three and four stories inside the enormous lobby of the hotel. We looked down and noticed the passageways between restaurants and shops were constructed of cobblestone, and wrought iron streetlights hovered over the large casino, dining, and shopping areas. Every detail gave one the feeling of being transported in time to old New York.

In Law's earlier description of the hotel, he failed to mention what was undoubtedly its most impressive feature: a full-sized roller coaster traveling through the lobby of the hotel. Designed to resemble a New York subway and dubbed

The Manhattan Express, the roller coaster began its ride in the lobby, passed through the casino, exited the hotel, performed a couple of loops, and then ended its journey back in the lobby. I had never imagined such architectural and engineering feats were even possible. As I stood with my mouth agape and my eyes looking around, I am sure I looked the part of a simple, small kid seeing the big city for the first time.

Law went to the lobby desk and checked in. The hotel contained over two thousand rooms, and it took us several minutes to navigate our way to the Century Tower, take the elevator to the thirty-third floor, and locate our accommodations. I opened the door to my room, dropped my bags, and immediately walked over to the windows looking out over the Las Vegas strip. Directly across from New York, New York sat the MGM Grand Hotel and Casino. Its emerald green glass sparkled in the bright Nevada sunshine. An enormous lion, the symbol of the MGM Hollywood film studios, sat proudly at the entrance to the hotel. On the ride from the airport to the strip, our taxi driver urged us to walk across the street and through the MGM hotel. "It opened just a few years ago," he said. "And is the largest hotel in the world-over five thousand rooms. You will get lost in there." As I stood and looked down on this massive edifice, I could not imagine how a hotel could be larger. Even from my elevated view, I was unable to determine its exact beginning and end.

Situated diagonally across from our hotel was the gleaming white Tropicana Hotel. I would later walk through the hotel and learn that it was constructed in the 1950's with a Cuban theme, reminding patrons of a time before the communist revolution in Cuba, when Americans traveled often to this vacation destination.

Across the street from the Tropicana sat the Excalibur Hotel, designed with a medieval ambiance. I was unable to see this hotel from the vantage point of my room, but would later see its castle-like towers rising up into the sky. The four hotels on the corner of this busy intersection were all linked by raised pedestrian walkways, allowing patrons to traverse from one hotel casino to another without having– or being allowed–to cross the street below.

"Pretty dang amazing, ain't it, Miller?" I'd forgotten to close my door, and Law suddenly appeared just behind me. "Been lookin' at de same ting from our window. Can youse believe dat MGM hotel over dere? You know dat's where we'se gonna see de show tonight, don't you?

Law had already secured tickets for us to see the Vegas show, *EFX*, starring David Cassidy. His boss had explained to him, and then Law explained to both Cecilia and me, that David Cassidy was a name that we should have known. Around the time the three of us were still in diapers, he was an actor, musician, and teen idol. He was now the headliner for this show, known to be the most expensive, large-scale production in Vegas. I had asked Law several times what the show was about, only to see him shrug his shoulders and say, "Someting bout a guy going trugh a world of magic. But de effects are s'possed to be incredible."

"Come on, let's go see if Celli is ready yet. I want

to walk around and see de strip before we eat dinner and go to de show tonight." Law's meetings did not begin until the next morning, and so we had a few hours to explore the city that afternoon. We spent the next several hours wandering in and out of the most amazing hotels I had ever seen. We walked several blocks to Caesar's Palace, a hotel designed to invoke thoughts of the Roman Empire. Replicas of ancient Roman sculptures adorned the hotel lobby and outdoor spaces. A model of the Trevi Fountain, the popular sculptured fountain located in Rome, Italy, sat just outside the entrance to the hotel shopping area. These shops were located inside what was labeled, *The Forum Shops*, named after the commerce and governmental section of the ancient city. The facades of the guest room towers were modeled in the form of ancient Roman Architecture, complete with numerous columns, arches, and architraves throughout.

From our vantage point standing on Las Vegas Boulevard, we could see the golden windows of the Mirage Hotel on the right side of Caesar's. To the left was the Bellagio, still in the construction process. As we walked past the site of this new hotel on our way back to New York-New York, we overheard a tourist telling another that the Bellagio would be the most expensive and ornate hotel ever constructed in Las Vegas. "Even Caesar's Palace will look like a Motel 6 compared to what this is going to be," we heard him say as we walked past the two men engrossed in conversation.

After wandering up the strip for a couple of hours, we finally made our way back to our hotel rooms to shower, get dressed, and grab a quick meal before walking over to the MGM theater. I had no idea that within just a few hours, my life would be forever changed.

———————————————

"Man, dat sure was some strange stuff," Law said as we exited the MGM hotel and made our way toward the steps leading to the pedestrian bridge. The sidewalks were streaming with people walking in every direction. Earlier that afternoon we had traversed the sidewalk of Las Vegas Boulevard with ease, but now, after the setting of the sun, we found ourselves navigating through a sea of humanity. It seemed as if the evening streetlights had birthed an entirely new population of people, desperately craving the entertainment afforded by the buffet of activities.

"Yeah, I'm not really sure I understood the whole thing," I replied to Law as we wove our way through the crowd. "So that guy was led on a journey through time, and then he actually became King Arthur, P.T. Barnum, Harry Houdini, and H.G. Wells? And it was so that he could renew his faith in magic and find his true love?"

"I tink de person who wrote dat musical was smokin' some weird stuff," Law said, sort of with a grunt and a huff.

Cecilia managed to break into our conversation as we waited on a group of apparently inebriated, giggling forty-something-year-old women to weave their way past us. "The problem with you boys is that you both do not understand culture and art. The show was designed to take you through these other, imaginary worlds so that you could feel the power of magic...of miracles actually happening."

"Cecilia, tell me again how a beautiful, sophisticated, intelligent girl ended up with a Neanderthal like Law?"

Cecilia laughed and said, "See, Henry, that's why you should have been paying attention to the show tonight. Miracles really do happen."

"I don't know why I brought eider one of youse guys on dis trip. You both tink youse so funny."

"We are just kidding Law," I said as we hit the steps heading to the elevated walkway.

"Yeah, honey, I meant that it was miraculous that I was so fortunate to get you," Cecilia said, with a slight smile and just a hint of sarcasm. Law didn't pick up on the teasing nature of her comment."

"Oh, Cilly, youse de best. Hey, Henry, youse want to head to de casino for a while?"

"You two lovebirds go ahead. I'm probably pushing it to even be in this place. If anyone in my church found out that I came out here, I at least want to be able to honestly say that I did not gamble. Plus, I'm pretty exhausted. I think I'm going to head back to the room and get a good night's sleep. You kids have fun."

We had just crossed the street and stood on the side of the pedestrian bridge closest to our hotel. Cecilia suddenly stopped and pointed at the Excalibur Hotel. "Law, let's go to the casino in that hotel. I just want to see what the hotel looks like. You do not care which casino we go to, do you?"

"No, dat's fine wit me. Henry, we will see youse in de

morning."

Law and Cecilia turned and walked in the direction of the pedestrian bridge between our hotel and the Excalibur. I turned and headed down the steps to street level and the entrance to New York, New York. The crowd on this side of Las Vegas Boulevard was not nearly as dense. It was obvious that the activities and entertainment provided by the MGM Hotel drew a large number of patrons.

I veered from the sidewalk toward the model of the Brooklyn Bridge and from there to the doors heading into the hotel. I was about ten feet from the entrance when I heard a sound, much like the sound of a whimpering puppy, coming from behind me. I turned around, but saw nothing. I started walking back toward the bridge. I took two steps and once again heard the same sound—a whimpering noise—but this time it had more of a human quality. I realized it came from the area to my left. Still, I could not see anything or anyone in that direction. I walked toward the brick pillar on the outside of the bridge. When I got within a few steps of the pillar, I could see a pair of shoes and hands wrapped around legs jutting out from behind the large brick structure. I took another step forward and the picture was complete. A young girl sat on the ground, against the pillar and out of the sight of anyone passing by. Her knees were pulled tightly to her chest and her arms wrapped around her legs. Her head was buried in her knees and I could see her back moving up and down in quick, spasmodic motions. She was completely silent at this point, obviously attempting to remain concealed in her location. With her head down and her dark hair covering her face, she did not notice my approach. I stood in the same place for several moments, wondering whether to address her or to continue my earlier journey into the hotel.

"Hey, are you okay?" I stayed a few feet away but squatted to my knees so that we would be at eye level. Her head jerked up with a snap, obviously surprised that someone had discovered her location. A beam of light cut across her face, and I could see that she was wearing a lot of makeup. Her face was covered with blush, her eyelids had a blue color heavily caked on their surfaces, and eyes were outlined in black. Her tears had apparently run through this liner, causing dark streams to run down her cheeks. Her hair was jet black and straight. It was difficult for me to discern whether it was a wig or just colored, but I knew right away that it was not natural. Even in the darkness, I could see that her eyes were green, and they stared at me with both a shock and scorn.

"I'm fine. Just go away," she replied, once her surprise had subsided.

"Okay," I said, relieved that I would not have to get involved in the situation. I started to rise, but then caught her eyes again. There was something in the way she looked at me that made me stop. There was an anger and hardness in her face, but behind that facade was someone pleading with me for help. "Are you sure?" I said, this time from a standing position but leaning over with my hands on my knees.

"Yes, I told you. I'm fine. You can just go away. Well,

that is, unless you want some company for the night. What do you say? You lookin' for a good time?"

Although it should not have, her statement caught me off guard. I'd heard from plenty of people about Nevada having legalized prostitution. Although technically illegal in the city of Las Vegas, the services were performed under the pretense of offering 'escort services' to patrons. The funds were run through the escort service and gave the appearance of being a legal business. Even in the few hours since we'd arrived, I had seen the sidewalks littered with advertisements for their services. On virtually every corner stood individuals with stacks of leaflets, forcefully offering these to passersby. Most of these advertisements for prostitution services were tossed onto the sidewalks and parking lots.

"Umm...I think I'm good," I somehow managed to stammer. I stood straight up now, ready to make my exit.

"You sure?" she quickly replied, now brimming with a newfound confidence. She saw that the tables were turned and now I was the one who was uncomfortable. "I'll give you a really good deal."

I wanted to tell her that I honestly had no idea what 'a really good deal' was in the world of prostitution. As far as I knew, it could have been fifty dollars or a thousand dollars. And while I had a general concept of what the payment provided, I could not begin to guess whether it meant an entire evening together or just long enough for the services to be rendered.

"Ma'am, I'm not interested. I just wanted to see if

you needed any help."

"You really want to help me? Then take me up on my offer. I need the business." With her last sentence, I noticed her voice cracking somewhat, as if she were fighting back a sob.

"I'm sorry. It's not that you are not attractive. It's just – well, I'm sorry that I cannot help."

"You must be gay."

"Not exactly."

"Married. Which, by the way, she will never find out."

"No, I'm not married."

"You're not gay and you're not married, and I'm telling you that I'll give you a real good deal. Okay, I've got it. You must be broke."

"Well, not exactly broke, but certainly very cheap." A slight, almost imperceptible smile formed on her lips with my last statement.

"Then the best way you could help me out is to move on so I can see if someone else is interested."

"I hate to point out the obvious here, but you are not going to get much business hiding in the dark. I walked right past you and did not see you until I heard you crying. "

"Then shut up, go away, and let me get out of this place and go somewhere else."

"Fine. Have a nice life." I turned and walked back toward the entrance to the hotel. I had walked only four or five steps when I thought I heard someone whispering in my ear. I quickly turned my head to the side, looking around to see who had silently moved beside me. I looked both left and right and saw no one. I shook my head, starting walking, and again heard a distinct whisper. This time the voice was clear, and I quickly realized that the whisper was less audible and more internal. "Go back," it said. I paused, wondering if this was a simply me imagining something. Again, the phrase reverberated deep within my spirit. "Go back." Somehow, instantly, I understood the whisper being the voice of God and the instruction to once again offer assistance to this girl. As much as I tried to dismiss it, this impression upon my soul would not let go. I felt deep within me that if I ignored this urging, it would suffocate my spirit. For some indefinable reason, this calling was irresistible.

I turned around and looked back toward the bridge. The girl had returned to her balled up position and her head was again buried in her knees. I did not hear her crying or notice her body shaking, but it was obvious she was not in a hurry to find a willing client. I walked back in her direction.

"Tell me what exactly a 'good deal' really is," I said. She looked up at me with a surprised expression. I could see that she was attempting to determine the reason behind my question. Was I asking simply for academic purposes, or was I actually interested in her services? After a five or six second pause she said, "Three hundred dollars for an hour. I normally charge four, so you're getting deal."

"How about this? I'll give you a hundred dollars to sit with me for thirty minutes and eat dinner. I'll even buy the food. There is a great pizza place just inside the hotel. You can eat and be back looking for business in thirty minutes."

She gave me a suspicious stare, unsure of how to

respond to this strange offer. "Show me the money first," she finally said. I pulled out my wallet and grabbed five twenty dollar bills. I only had sixty dollars in cash remaining. "Here it is," I said. "I'll give you one of these twenties now and the other four after the meal."

She sat there for a few more pensive seconds, then shrugged her shoulders and said, "Why not?" She rose to her feet, grabbing her small handbag in the process. As she stood, I was able to see that she was wearing a black leather miniskirt and a dark, button up blouse, both very tight against her skin. She was perhaps five feet, four inches tall with a small-framed body. She was thin, but not abnormally so. Her hair fell around her shoulders, and I could see that it was most definitely a wig. It was coarse and jet black. Her fair skin tone revealed that she must have possessed a naturally lighter colored hair. She had a hard edge in her appearance, but there seemed to be a softness lying just below the surface. With her heavy makeup it was virtually impossible for me to guess her age, but I estimated she was somewhere close to my own.

She strode over to me, snatched a twenty-dollar bill out of my hand, and inserted it underneath her bra. "After you, big spender" she said with a sly smile and a hand extended toward the entrance to the hotel. I turned, opened the door for her, and followed her into the lobby. As I walked behind her, I silently prayed, *God, I sure hope you know what you are doing.*

We sat on opposite sides of the high top table with a large pepperoni pizza between us. The pizzeria was one of the more reasonably priced restaurants in the hotel, and I was thankful my new friend was willing to split a pizza.

"So, what is your name?" I asked, once we had gone through the process of ordering our food and finding a table.

"You're paying for this time, so my name can be whatever you want it to be" she replied with a seductive, throaty whisper.

I sat there with my lips pressed together and a slight smirk forming across my face. In the interlude, I was able to get a better look at this girl sitting across from me. In the dim lighting of the restaurant, I noticed that her skin revealed a youthfulness lying underneath the heavy makeup and promiscuous clothing. The green in her eyes was a bright, almost chartreuse color, as if the sun was behind an emerald and the green glowed with a yellow tint. Her skin was pale and smooth, reminding me of the porcelain doll my sister kept on her shelf in her room. Although completely hidden by the wig, I could tell from her eyes and skin that her hair was probably a blondish brown color. I imagined that she possessed a natural look that was quite attractive, like the kind of girl who could wake up in the morning and walk out the door without having to spend a lot of time in front of the mirror.

"Look," I said after letting her last statement hang in the air for a few moments. "I'll give you the five minute rundown of who I am and why I'm sitting across from you, and I'll be totally honest. Then, if you feel like I have been less than truthful with you, you can grab a couple pieces of pizza, I'll give you the eighty dollars, and you can walk away and forget this whole deal. If you believe I've been truthful, then you return the favor with a five-minute, honest version of your story. Deal?"

She inserted the front end of a piece of the pizza into her mouth, then very casually nodded her head and shrugged her shoulders, as if saying, "Alright, why not?"

"My name is Henry Miller and I'm from Charlotte, North Carolina," I began. "I'm twenty-two years old and I'm the pastor of a church in a small town in Georgia. I became a Christian after my first year in college and through a weird series of events I'm now a very young, very inexperienced pastor of a church consisting mainly of senior adults, most of whom would have heart attacks if they knew their pastor was sitting in Las Vegas talking to a girl he'd just promised to pay a hundred dollars. I've been the pastor there for only four months and I'm pretty sure that they are going to fire me soon, which is good because I've already been accepted to law school at the University of North Carolina and would like to start there next fall."

"I came here with my college roommate and his wife. We went to a show earlier at the MGM, then they headed over to the Excalibur to gamble and I decided to go to bed. That is when I heard the sound of you crying and found you curled up in that dark corner. When you told me to leave you alone, I was relieved and headed toward my room. Then, a very strong feeling within me told me to go back to you. I cannot adequately describe to you how strong the feeling was, but I will tell you that parting with a hundred dollars is not easy for me."

"I have no idea why I felt that strong urge or why exactly I'm sitting across from you right now, but that is the honest truth of who I am and why you are eating pizza this evening with a pastor."

She had only eaten a couple of bites before putting down her pizza and listening intently to my story. When I told her I was a pastor, her mouth fell slightly agape, obviously bewildered at why someone in my profession chose to dine with someone in her profession. As I finished, she took a sip of her drink, swallowed, and then placed her drink back onto the table.

"Wow. Well, if you were not honest, I do not know why you would make up anything like that. I mean, if you had told me you were a war hero in Desert Storm or the son of a big time multimillionaire, I would have been tempted to call you a liar. But who in the world would make up stuff like that?"

She paused just long enough for me to worry that she was going to ask for the eighty bucks and take off.

"Your turn," I said, hoping her defenses had dropped just enough for me to coax her ahead in telling her story.

She paused and glared at me with those clear, bright green eyes. After a few seconds she looked down at her plate, pushed her pizza around, and took another sip of her drink.

"I grew up in Manitou Springs, Colorado, a small town just on the outskirts of Colorado Springs. My mom grew up in that area, graduated from high school and began attending The University of Colorado at Colorado Springs, or what everyone there just calls UCCS. Her family was not very well off, and so she worked as a waitress almost every evening in order to pay the bills. She met a guy one night at the restaurant, they had a few drinks after work, and the next thing you know she was pregnant with me and the guy was gone. She dropped out of college and raised me as a single mom. She never dated and, honestly, I never remember her even having one date. She was not going to allow any man to hurt her or me, and so she became both mom and dad to me. She worked hard and managed to pay the bills and keep food on our table."

"When I was in the eleventh grade, my mom was diagnosed with breast cancer. Her doctors said that they had caught it early and with aggressive treatments, she would have a high chance of beating it. They gave her a lot of chemo. I hated seeing her so sick from it. After the treatments, she went into remission, and so I thought everything was going to be okay."

"I graduated and went to school at UCCS. I met a guy my freshman year and he seemed to be the perfect guy. We started dating, and after a while I started spending a lot of nights at his apartment. He asked me about moving in with him, but I wanted to stay living at home with my mother. It had just been the two of us for so long that I hated to leave her. He could not understand my decision and began to treat my mother very badly anytime he was at our house. I told him to stop, and he would for a while, but then his anger turned toward me. I thought I loved him and, honestly, had become so emotionally dependent upon him that no matter how mean and violent he was, I just could not break it off."

"Toward the end of my freshman year, my mom started feeling sick. She returned to the doctor and got the news that her cancer had spread to her liver. The outlook was not good, he told her, but it again was in the early stages and aggressive treatment would give her a fighting chance. The only problem was that mom had quit paying her insurance premiums so that she could help with my tuition. I did not know that she had quit making those payments–I would have dropped out of school if I'd known–but she did and so then we were faced with the fact that the only way she could get treatment was through Medicaid. She would be forced to go to another hospital and deal with a brand new doctor and would probably not get the absolute best care."

"I spoke with my mom's doctor and asked him what he and the hospital would take if we paid cash. I worked out a plan with the hospital so that for roughly two thousand dollars a month, she could get the treatments she needed. I knew there was no way that my mom could come up with that kind of money and pay the bills too. So, I went to my boyfriend. His parents had both passed away when he was young and his inheritance had been placed into a trust account. He was not extremely wealthy, but very comfortable and seemed to always have enough money to buy whatever he desired. I asked him for a loan; just enough money to help us get through the first round of treatments until I could come up with a plan. He told me that it would be a waste of money and that my mom should just use Medicaid. I begged and pleaded and he finally told me to get out of his apartment and his life. We'd been together for a year and had practically lived together at times, and suddenly it was all over. Within the span of a few days I'd not only been given this devastating news about my mom, but had lost my boyfriend as well."

"I dropped out of school and immediately began applying for jobs. One door after another was shut in my face. At some point in my search process I began to realize that even if I got a good job, there was no way I was going to be able to cover the bills that were piling up while my mom was unable to work. Life seemed to be spinning out of control and there was nothing I could do to help my mother."

"A friend of mine from high school told me about her cousin who worked in Nevada as a prostitute. Said her cousin made a six-figure salary working only nine months of the year. This friend gave me her cousin's number. I threw it into my pocketbook and originally intended to just throw it away. For several more days I watched my mom struggle with trying to get an appointment with Medicaid and worrying about her future. The pain of seeing her suffer became unbearable. I made the decision to call my friend's cousin. I figured I could work for four months and make more than enough to see my mom get treatment for the first year."

She paused and looked away from me, into the lobby area. Her head turned back and her eyes stared at the table between us. "That was nearly two years ago that I made that decision, and obviously I'm still living and working in Nevada."

With her head still down, staring at her uneaten pizza, I asked a question to fill the silence. "So what about your mom?"

Another long pause, and this time I saw a tear fall from her face onto the table below. She breathed in slowly and deeply, exhaled, and then replied, "She died a year ago. She did all the treatments exactly as the doctor told her, but when the cancer spread to her liver, it started raging out of control." She looked over toward that lobby area again, her focus and her thoughts apparently in another world.

"The irony of the whole thing is that I came here, started working, and so I was able to pay for her to have the treatments. But then because I was working here, I missed spending a lot of time with my mother. I flew home at least every other week to see her, normally staying Monday through Thursday and then getting back here by Thursday afternoon to start working the weekend crowd. But still, I missed so many days with her. And then after doing this to get her the treatments she needed, she goes and dies anyway."

There were several seconds of silence between us. She never looked up from her plate. Finally I said, "I'm so sorry," unsure what else to say in that moment.

She looked up at me and a smiled formed on her lips. She had allowed herself to feel the emotions of that past pain, and now decided to suppress those feelings. She shrugged her shoulders, put her hands up in the air, and said, "So, since I had nothing else to do in Colorado and nothing really keeping me there, I came back here and continued working. So that's basically it, preacher boy. What do you think?"

I sat back in my chair, looked over at my dinner companion, and with a smile said, "If you would indulge me, I have three follow-up questions." She raised her arm and looked at her watch. "You've got five minutes according to our deal. Better ask them fast."

"Okay. The first question is this: what is your name?"

She chuckled, realizing that nowhere in the conversation had she actually revealed her name to me. "My professional name is Trixie. The name my mother gave me is Grace."

"Grace. I like that name. Is it a family name?"

"Is that your second question?" She asked with a broad grin across her face. "Never mind. I'll give you a pass on that one. She gave me the name because she said that in her life she needed a lot of grace, and she hoped I would be the kind of person who would show grace toward others and have grace shown toward me. I'm not sure if either one of those has been true in my life, but that is how I got my name."

"Question number two," I said. "Why were you crying earlier?"

"Hmph. I'd almost forgotten about that. Yeah, that is why I'm leaving you in about three more minutes. See, I work for an escort service. People call the company and my boss arranges the meetings. Earlier this evening I met a customer here in this hotel. After our, uhem, session together, he refused to pay. Kicked me out of his room. I called my boss who called the hotel room but discovered that the guy had already checked out and was gone. Unfortunately, whenever that kind of thing happens, I'm still responsible for the payment. When I walked out of the hotel earlier, the fact that I'd just been stiffed combined with this weekend being the anniversary of my mom's death...well, all the emotion came rising to the surface and I just needed a moment to cry. That's when you saw me. And, since that dude cheaped out on me, I've got to go earn some money tonight so that I don't have to dip into my savings to pay my boss."

She took a sip from her drink, grabbed her purse, and stood from her chair. "Henry, your thirty minutes is up. It was nice to meet you and I hope you have a great life. Now, I need my eighty bucks." She held out her hand in front of me, waiting for her promised payment. I reached into my wallet and pulled out the eighty dollars plus an additional twenty.

"Grace," I said, "here is twenty more dollars if you will allow me to ask my final question." I became painfully aware of the fact that I now had only forty dollars in cash.

"Alright, preacher boy, but make it quick. I need to go and find some big money customers before all the high rollers find someone else for the evening." She slid back into her chair but kept her purse in her hand, indicating her desire to quickly answer the question and leave.

"Grace." I paused and reached my hand across the table, placing it very gently against her arm. She did not pull away as I expected, and her facial expression changed. Her former "let's get this over with" demeanor softened as I spoke. "Is there any chance you would want to give all this up and start over somewhere else?"

She snickered, pulled her arm away, and wrapped both around her body in defensive posture. "And do what exactly?"

"Anything. You said you went to college for a year already. Have you thought about finishing?"

"Henry, what I did not tell you earlier was that my mom's treatments ended up costing a lot more money than what the doctors originally told us. I started working here, but even as good as the money was, it was not enough. In desperation, I borrowed money from my boss. A pretty good bit of money. I've been working this past year to pay off that debt. Then jokers like tonight come along and they don't help things at all. Henry, I'm trapped here. I cannot leave. There is no way I can pay it back unless I keep doing what I'm doing."

"Grace, there is always another way," I said, almost in a whisper. I looked intently into her eyes, trying to discover the real girl behind the hard veneer she exhibited.

She quickly turned away, looking toward the lobby, again looking at nothing in particular. I was sure that she was searching for potential customers and was just a few seconds away from leaving the table. Part of me desperately hoped she would do exactly that and I could get out of this terribly uncomfortable ordeal. Another part of me knew that I would be incredibly disappointed if she did.

After several long seconds, she turned her face back to me. "Okay, Henry, you just earned another fifteen minutes, free of charge. Let's talk."

We sat at the table for another two hours.

Many waters cannot quench love; rivers cannot sweep it away. If one were to give all the wealth of one's house for love, it would be utterly scorned.

Songs of Songs 8:7

Chapter 22

Tuesday, November 4, 1997

R ichard called me at my office and asked me to come to their house for dinner that night. "We've got some great news for you," he said. "I'm going to let Elise and Grace tell you about it, so do not ask me any questions. I'll see you tonight."

Just a few weeks earlier, Grace's life had completely changed. We sat at the high top table in the pizzeria for nearly three hours before she finally made the decision to leave Las Vegas and, with it, her nearly two-year career in prostitution. Law exploded with indignation when I explained the situation to him. "Miller, youse done lost youse freakin' mind!" He exclaimed, trying to talk me out of helping Grace. "Look, man, youse don't really know whats youse getting youself into here." After some begging, pleading, and promising on my part, he finally acquiesced and agreed to help me carry her luggage to the airport.

We landed in Atlanta and drove straight to Richard and Elise's house. Fortunately, both were home. I spent the first thirty minutes introducing Grace, and then asked if she could go into another room while I spoke with the two of them privately. I then fully explained the situation; how we'd met in Las Vegas and how I had felt, more than ever before, God's leading for me to help her. I then asked them to consider, very quickly, if they would be willing to house Grace for the next few weeks until she could get a job and a place of her own. I was asking a lot, and I told them as much. I knew the whole thing sounded absurd, and I would completely understand them refusing to help, but I sure hoped they wouldn't refuse. They both sat quietly for a while, then Elise turned to Richard and said, "I think I'll go show Grace her room." After Elise exited, Richard turned to me and said, "Henry, we are more than willing to help you out here. I just really hope you know what you are doing."

The next week, Richard hired Grace to file papers and answer the phones at his law firm. Being a small town, people began to ask a lot of questions. Richard was incredibly inept at lying, and so the best he could do was to simply say, "She is a friend of our pastor, and we are helping her out for a while." I saw Grace nearly every day, and rumors began to fly around town. Most people said she must be an old girlfriend from college who had gotten into some kind of trouble and called on me for help. Whenever church members or people from the community would ask us questions, we remained sufficiently vague in our answers.

Grace began to attend a women's Bible study with Elise on Monday nights. I was excited for her to become friends with Elise and to be a part of this Bible study. Additionally, I had my regular date with Mrs. Johnson on Monday evenings, and so it worked out well for Grace to have another activity to occupy her time. The group consisted of eight to ten women from a variety of churches. The group rotated homes to meet in, but Elise always led the study.

The first night Grace attended this study, Elise was in the middle of a series on the New Testament book of Ephesians. Elise introduced Grace to the group, and then opened her Bible and began reading from the second chapter:

For we are God's handiwork, created in Christ
Jesus to do good works, which God prepared in advance
for us to do.

Grace sat quietly as Elise explained the depths of mercy God has bestowed upon us. Elise expounded upon the word, 'handiwork,' telling the group that the word also meant, 'masterpiece'. Grace sat forward in her chair and listened intently. "Through His grace, God not only sees you as forgiven, but as His masterpiece, created by Him for His great purposes," Elise said to the group. As the other women discussed this concept, Grace sat and contemplated this truth.

Later that evening, as I was enjoying one of Mrs. Jones' microwave desserts, Grace quizzed Elise while they drove back to Elise's house. "Is all that stuff you were saying tonight really true? I mean, God sees us as His masterpiece and all that you said about Him viewing us as His treasure? How can that really be true? Or, let me phrase it another way: with all the stuff I've done in my life, how could God ever view me that way?"

Elise pulled her car into the driveway of her house. She shut off the engine, and for the next several minutes spoke with Grace about God's mercy, and how everyone, no matter how good or bad they are in the eyes of the world, is in desperate need of God's forgiveness. She told Grace that no matter what she'd done in her past, when she became a follower of Christ, God saw her as completely pure. Every moral failure was wiped clean and she was forgiven. Through Christ, she could become His masterpiece."

"But you have no idea what all I've done," Grace retorted. "In the last two years, I have given myself to innumerable men; basically anyone who was willing to pay the going rate. How could God forgive all that I've done?"

"Because, what Jesus Christ did on the cross was that powerful. Powerful enough to wipe away all your sin. Powerful enough to make you adored in the eyes of God. When you release control of your life over to Christ, you gain that incredible status before God."

Elise told me later how Grace sat there for the longest time without saying a word, simply staring at the glove compartment in front of her. Finally, Elise noticed tears streaming down her face and falling into her lap. When Elise reached over and grabbed her hand, the waterworks burst forth. Grace turned and buried her head into Elise's chest and spent the next fifteen minutes sobbing. Finally, she pulled back from Elise but did not let go of her arms. Like a desperate child before her parent, Grace simply said, "Help me, Elise. Help me to do this."

That night Grace experienced the most powerful grace in the world.

⸻

I showed up to dinner, nearly busting to hear the news after Richard's teaser earlier in the day. While we were eating dessert, Elise coaxed Grace into telling me what happened the previous evening. With some degree of reluctance, and without the use of any church-verbiage, Grace described the transformation that had taken place in her heart. "Elise explained it to me in a way that just made sense," she said with a shy, almost embarrassed expression on her face. "A major piece of something was missing from my life, and last night I found it."

For the next several minutes, Elise and Grace talked about their conversation the previous evening. As they each took turns filling in the details of the event, I found myself unable to take my focus away from Grace. I knew that something had drawn me to her that first night we met in Las Vegas, but I assumed that it was all for the purpose of God using me to help this girl leave a destructive lifestyle. Since she arrived in Mapleton, I found myself thinking about her often and looking forward to times that we could be together. I chalked it up to my connection with her through a dramatic event and quickly dismissed any of my perceived romantic feelings. She was, after all, a former prostitute, and I was a Baptist pastor who had never even really kissed a girl. In my mind, anything beyond a friendship between the two of us had been out of the bounds of reality.

But as I sat there and listened to her talk about the Bible study, I felt myself unable to suppress the feelings rising within me. Although a romantic relationship between the two of us seemed far-fetched, I found myself suddenly dreaming about our life together. For several years I had assumed that my life would be lived as a bachelor. It was not that I did not desire female companionship; rather, even at my young age, I found myself believing that perhaps it was just not in the cards for my future. I had taken a job in nowhere, Georgia, where my dating opportunities at this point had consisted of a weekly meal with a female septuagenarian. I had become extremely pessimistic concerning my chances for marriage. At twenty-two years old, I had considered myself to be a confirmed bachelor.

But as I sat at the table, something that had been dormant was suddenly awakened. The longer Grace talked, the more those previously untapped feelings began to swell within me. Her natural beauty, heavily masked the first time we met, was unmistakable. Her hair, skin, and eyes combined with a radiant smile to give her a wholesome appearance. If I had not been privy to the knowledge of her recent past, I would have assumed her to be the typical girl next door. I found myself gazing at her cheekbones and her smooth, ivory skin. Her bright green eyes had such a brilliance, like emeralds set in an alabaster frame. Her silky hair looked so delicate as it brushed against the side of her face. As she and Elise talked, I found myself studying every one of her features.

"Henry? Henry?" My mind finally came back into the present. "Henry," Elise continued. "So, are you worried at all about that?"

Completely clueless as to what should or should have not worried me, I stammered momentarily, searching for an adequate answer. Finally, worried that I may embarrass myself further with a terribly wrong reply, I decided to confess. "I'm so sorry. I had a counseling session today with a person facing a particularly difficult issue, and my mind wandered briefly back to that meeting." I lied, but it was better than saying, "I've been ogling Grace for the last few minutes, and that is why I did not hear anything you guys just said."

"Grace was talking about what happened at the office this morning. She was working at the receptionist's desk when a girl came in who wanted to meet with an attorney. The girl said she needed someone to help her get child support out of her son's father. The girl was young, perhaps nineteen or so, and obviously distraught. All the attorneys in the office were busy with other clients, so Grace asked the girl to wait in the lobby. After a couple of minutes, Grace looked into the lobby area and noticed the girl had her head in her hands and was obviously crying. Grace went in the lobby area, sat beside her, and started a conversation with her. Long story short, Grace was able to share with this girl about God's forgiveness through Christ. The girl seemed to be very open and wants to meet with Grace to talk further."

"That's great!" I said. "Wow, Grace, I'm really impressed. What a great story."

"You obviously missed the second part of her story," Elise continued. "In the process of sharing the truth about God's love with this girl, Grace told her own story. Her *complete story*."

"You mean the whole deal? The prostitution and everything?"

"I just felt like this girl needed to hear that God could forgive her," Grace chimed in. "She was having the hardest time accepting the fact that God could forgive her sin. When she heard my story, her entire countenance changed. At that point, she actually believed that God's grace could cover her sin."

Richard spoke up for the first time in several minutes. "Grace, I think you did exactly what you were supposed to do. Your honesty about your past may be exactly what God uses to completely change this girl's future. You do not need to question, in any way, what you said to her this morning."

"But," Richard continued, "if this girl tells anyone else..." Richard's words hung in the air for a moment, "well, this is a small town, and people talk. We just need to be prepared for a lot of questions."

"I'm so sorry," Grace said. "I just was not thinking clearly, I guess."

Richard leaned over the table, put his hand on top of Grace's, and quickly said, "Grace, you have no reason whatsoever to apologize. What you said to this girl was exactly what God wanted you to say. Your past is your past. God has forgiven you and others should as well. You do not have to answer to anyone. I only say this because I know that all of us, but Henry especially, will be hit with questions if this gets out."

"You're right, Richard," I said. "And you know, it is what it is. We will answer truthfully, and if there are people who object to Grace being a part of our church because of the choices she made in her past, then we

will have a little stoning party. Richard, you can play the part of Jesus, and ask all those who are without sin to cast the first stone. We'll see that place clear out fast."
Richard and Elise chuckled, but Grace simply cocked her head, obviously unaware of the Biblical reference and unappreciative of my poor attempt at humor.

"And I'll deal with whatever happens at my firm," Richard said.

"Grace," I said with a big smile on my face, "I'm happy for you." She smiled back and gave a sheepish, "thanks" in reply. When her gaze at me lingered for a second longer than normal, I felt my heart skip a beat. *If we are worried about the gossip now*, I thought, *what in the world will it be like if I fall in love with this girl?*

The words of a gossip are like choice morsels; they go down to the inmost parts.

Proverbs 18:8

Chapter 23

Thursday, November 20, 1997

Small towns are notorious for thriving on gossip. I discovered very early after moving to Mapleton that the rumor mill operates virtually 24/7. Even my most mundane daily tasks would often be a topic of conversation between two residents. As I strenuously chewed on microwave pot-roast one Monday evening, Mrs. Ethel Jones very casually said, "So, Pastor, I heard you went to the Piggly Wiggly yesterday afternoon."

Surprised that someone thought my shopping was newsworthy enough to pass along to Mrs. Jones, and even more surprised that she thought it interesting enough for our dinner conversation, I simply replied, "Well, I needed groceries."

"Uh huh...see, I was just wondering if you thought

it was acceptable for a pastor to shop on the Sabbath? Lord knows I'm no stranger to suffering and there are certainly times that an ox is in a ditch and the only resolution is to work out your salvation with fear and trembling, but have you thought about people seeing you at the store on a Sunday?"

I had never once considered the patronizing of Piggly Wiggly as a violation of the Sabbath. Obviously, it was of some concern to my dinner hostess, so I simply replied, "I've never thought of it in that light before, but maybe it is a violation. I guess I could wait until Monday nights to go to the grocery store, but that would cut into our time together."

I could see Mrs. Jones making the mental calculation that the chastisement of my Sunday shopping could possibly cut into her Monday evening companionship. She quickly responded, "Oh, no, I don't think it's wrong at all. Mrs. Causey called me last night and asked me what I thought about it. She was the one who saw you at the grocery store."

"Is Mrs. Causey a Christian woman?"

"Oh, yes. She is a fine, upstanding member of First Methodist."

"Well then, what was she doing at the grocery store on the Sabbath?"

Mrs. Jones had to think about this one for a moment. She finally shrugged her shoulders and said, "Like I said, she's Methodist. Who knows what weird things they believe?"

———————————

While even the most uninteresting, routine events in the lives of local citizens were often discussed as if they were deserving of coverage on the evening news, when a major occurrence or scandal happened, it would become the foremost topic of conversation throughout the city. Such was the case when the truth of Grace's past became exposed. Richard was the first to be confronted with a phone call from a church member. It was the Thursday morning after Grace's Tuesday conversation with the girl in Richard's office. The caller feigned concern for Richard's reputation and the potential loss of clients as the truth about his house guest became more public. Truthfully, Richard said, she was prying for as many details as she could possibly obtain, presumably with the hope of being replete with information as she relayed the latest Mapleton scandal. He did not confirm nor deny anything, deciding that his best answer was to direct others to have a conversation *about* Grace *with* Grace. Naturally, no one agreed to that course of action, arguing that it was really none of their business, and they would not feel right speaking with a person they did not know about this personal matter.

Shortly after the phone interrogation of Richard, Mrs. Marlene Smith made a surprise visit to my office. As the chairperson of the personnel committee, Marlene felt it her obligation to keep me up-to-date on the feelings of the congregation concerning my pastorate. Almost like receiving weekly tracking polls of my popularity rating, Marlene would call or stop by my office to inform me of what she had heard in the hallways, or at a restaurant, or in a phone conversation with a church member. The previous week she had informed me that, according to her estimates, roughly one third of the active members were pleased with my ministry, one third were dissatisfied, and the other third really did not care. "I think that if you will just please try to preach some sermons that make people feel good," she said as she rubbed her pudgy hands together, "then you will be able to win over some of these people who are not your fans right now." I'd simply smiled and thanked her for the suggestion.

On this Thursday morning Doris, the part-time secretary, was not in the office. I was attempting to finish my sermon when I heard a quick knock followed by the opening of the door and the head of Marlene Smith sticking through the opening. "Pastor, are you here? Oh, good, there you are. Do you have just a minute?"

I let out an imperceptible groan, knowing that a meeting with Marlene was never just a minute. I turned from my desk and greeted her with a smile. "Sure, Marlene, come on in."

She entered my office and squeezed into one of the chairs opposite my desk. "Pastor, I will cut right to the chase here. There is a girl living with Richard and Elise

Davis. Now, I have seen her at church a few times and I thought I heard that she was Richard's niece and in need of some help right now. I have seen you talking to her sometimes and, like many others in our congregation, hoped that maybe she was a potential pastor's wife for you. Honestly, Pastor, there really aren't that many young single girls here in Mapleton, so I was hoping that perhaps Richard and Elise were trying to set you up with his niece. Anyway, just yesterday I heard some news that was awfully disturbing. I heard that she was in fact a . . . well . . . Pastor, I'm not exactly sure how to say this, but a girl of ill repute. Pastor, do you know what I mean when I use that term?"

Marlene paused only momentarily enough for me to nod "yes" to her question.

"Now Pastor, I'm not really sure exactly how this girl has arrived in Mapleton, and I plan on talking to Richard and finding out why she is living in his house, but my main concern in speaking to you this morning is that you would be careful about being seen with this girl. I would hate for people in our congregation to get the impression that you are socializing with a girl of this reputation. I realize you are good friends with Richard and Elise, and certainly you need to continue to minister to them as members of this congregation, but I would keep my distance if I were you. Your approval rating among the congregation would plummet if members discover you are socializing with this young lady. I'm just trying to look out for you, Pastor."

She finally took a breath, pausing long enough for me to jump into the conversation. "Marlene, her name is Grace, and she is staying with Richard and Elise as a favor to me. I'm the one who met her first."

A look of shock and dismay became immediately visible on her face. "What? Pastor, please tell me you did not, ahem, how do I say this, engage the services of this girl? I mean, Pastor, I know you are a young, single man and that certainly you have temptations, but that would be an act so horrible that you could not stay on here as the pastor of this church!"

"Marlene, take a deep breath. You know me better than that. Of course I did not engage her services. I met her, she needed help, and so I offered some. And, just in case you are interested, she actually became a follower of Christ a few nights ago. Elise had the chance to talk to her about forgiveness and salvation offered through trusting in the work of Christ. Isn't that awesome?"

"Of course, Pastor, we are certainly glad for that. But are we sure we want her coming to this church? I mean, today we have a former prostitute coming here, what will it be tomorrow? Former drug dealers? Former prisoners? Just think about it, Pastor. Are we opening a door here for bad people to come to our church?"

"I hope so."

She cocked her head and just stared at me with an incredulous expression. I had never seen Marlene quite this speechless. Her mouth hung open, obviously desiring to speak but unsure of what to say in response to my last statement. Finally, she let out a huff of exasperation. "Pastor, I just do not get you. I try and try to help you to improve your standing among this congregation, but you just refuse to take my advice. Now, I'm not exactly sure what you are up to in this whole thing, but I'm telling you that I cannot defend you when people call me and complain about this girl being in our church. You still have my support, but you sure are making it hard for me when people come and complain. I sure hope you know what you are doing."

"Marlene, I treasure your support and your friendship," I said with a smile and a relaxed tone in my voice. "I cannot think of anyone in the church who would make a better personnel chairperson than you. Thank you for your concern."

As Marlene walked out of my office, I had one overwhelming thought: *Lord, if only she knew what was about to happen.*

There are three things that are too amazing for me, four that I do not understand: the way of an eagle in the sky, the way of a snake on a rock, the way of a ship on the high seas, and the way of a man with a young woman.

Proverbs 30:18-19

Chapter 24

Saturday, December 6, 1997

Richard asked me, "Henry, are you sure about this?"   "Richard, as sure as I have ever been about anything in my life."

We sat in the den of Richard and Elise Davis' home. This couple, easily old enough to be my parents, had become my closest friends in Mapleton since my arrival six months before. I ate dinner in their home two or three times a week and Richard regularly ate breakfast with me on Monday mornings at a café located in the downtown section of Mapleton. He usually spent that time encouraging me after the previous Sunday's profusion of criticisms related to my sermons or my ministry in general. He would disabuse me of my desires to resign by reminding me of how clearly God had orchestrated the necessary events for me to come to the church. After our Monday morning breakfasts, I would have the fortitude necessary to face another week of ministry at First Baptist.

"Well, Henry, no matter what happens, you know that I will support you one hundred percent."

"Thanks, Richard. I appreciate it. There is no doubt I will need it in the coming weeks."

At that moment, Elise and Grace walked into the den. This Grace looked nothing like the one I'd met two months earlier outside of my hotel in Las Vegas. The black wig was removed, revealing her naturally light brown, cream-colored hair. Gone was the caked-on make-up and dark eyeliner. Instead, the girl before me had little, if anything, painted onto her face. She wore a white, long-sleeved T-shirt over faded blue jeans and a pair of Asics running shoes. She looked much more like a college coed than a Las Vegas prostitute.

"So where are you two headed?" Elise said, with a knowing grin spreading across her face.

"It's a surprise for Grace," I quickly replied. "All I've told her is to dress casual and to wear comfortable shoes. Grace, looks like you follow instructions well."

"Thanks," she replied with sarcasm. "Since you won't tell me what we are doing, then I have no choice but to follow your fashion advice. From the way I've seen you dress, I would assume that most people would caution against that, so I'm really taking a chance here."

"Alright, enough with the criticisms of my very trendy but under-appreciated style. We need to go if we are going to avoid traffic later."

"Traffic? Please tell me where you are taking me, Henry!"

"Come on, let's go."

———————

Without having to fight typical weekday traffic congestion, we were able to make the drive from Mapleton to Stone Mountain in just over an hour. The sky was a brilliant blue on this cloudless Saturday morning. We exited I–285 onto Highway 78 and drove the few remaining miles to the park. The park was developed in the 1950s around a granite dome rising nearly seventeen hundred feet above the earth. On one side of the mountain, one can see the largest relief sculpture in the world containing the images of three leaders of the Confederacy in the American Civil War: Jefferson Davis, Robert E. Lee, and Thomas "Stonewall" Jackson. The park contains shopping, a Civil War museum, antebellum homes, and a number of hiking trails and water activities.

We entered the park and drove immediately to the parking lot closest to the base of the mountain and the beginning of a hiking trail leading to the summit. This was the first trip for either of us to Stone Mountain, but I had managed to glean some ideas and details from Richard on how to best structure this day. The park seemed to fit perfectly into my plans.

We parked the car and I led her toward the place where the trail started up the mountainside. Richard informed me that he and Elise had walked the trail a number of times and, except for a few steep sections, was not particularly challenging. "At your ages," he said, "it will be a breeze."

The walk took us approximately twenty minutes and, just as Richard had described for me, only the last hundred yards or so proved to be of any difficulty. We finally reached the summit and made our way around the fence line guarding the steep cliffs on the edges of the mountaintop. From our vantage point, we could see for miles. The skyscrapers of downtown Atlanta were easily visible, as well as the silhouettes of several distant mountains. We found a large rock on the portion of the summit farthest from the trail and from the couple dozen people gathered on top of the mountain. We both found places to sit on top of the rock. For a few moments we allowed the cool breeze to flow over us as we looked out over the vast horizon.

It was a peaceful scene and normally I would have felt quite copasetic in such a moment. My thoughts, though, were focused not on the amazing beauty around us, but on the words I needed to say. I could feel my heart beating wildly in my chest and my pulse pounding throughout my body. Even though it was a brisk, early winter day, an almost scorching heat seemed to cover my arms, my legs, and my scalp. My hands felt clammy, as if I were holding onto a warm, wet dishrag. I knew I needed to speak, and yet in every attempt the words would catch in my throat and refuse to form on my tongue. Finally, after several deep breaths and a quick prayer to the Almighty, I decided it was time to jump into the deep end of the pool.

"Grace," I began, hearing a nervous quiver in my voice as I spoke that first word. "Grace," I repeated, "thanks for coming with me today. I've wanted to come here for a while. I really appreciate the company."

"Of course. I mean, thanks for bringing me. This is great."

"Grace, I have something to ask you, but I need you to just listen to me without interrupting before you answer my question. I have been in Mapleton since June, and since then I've continued to ask God, 'Why in the world do you have me here?' I mean, virtually every week I think they are going to fire me, and to be honest, I just cannot believe they have not already done so. During that time I kept asking God to show me His purpose in all of this, but I never received an answer. That is, until recently. See, when I met you, it was the second time I heard the voice of God. Very clearly there was this urgent feeling within me that I needed to offer you some sort of help that first night we met. As far as I knew at the time, that is all it was–just offering someone help. But over the last couple of weeks, and especially this week, I have heard the voice of God with an incredible amount of clarity."

I stopped and looked out over the horizon. The wind blew hard against my face, causing my eyes to water. A strong emotion began to swell within me, and I suddenly felt myself fighting tears produced by more than the breeze. I looked back at Grace, then reached out and took her hand in mine. Although we had been in each other's company on numerous occasions, this was the first time we had ever physically touched. A look of surprise suddenly appeared on her face, but she made no effort to pull back her hand. I adjusted my hold and allowed our fingers to intertwine. I then placed my other hand on top of her free hand while turning my body to face her directly.

"Grace," I continued. "I have very quickly fallen madly in love with you." I noticed her eyes grew wider as I nervously spoke those words. "For the longest time I believed I would never fall in love with anyone, but now I realize that I was just waiting for the right person. You are that person, and there is no way I can express to you how much I have been captured by you."

Her mouth opened to say something when I quickly said, "Hold on, I told you that I needed you to hear me out for a just a moment." She closed her mouth and gave me a flirty little pout, as if she were hurt but willing to consent to my request.

"Not only have I fallen in love with you, but in the past few days, I have had yet another moment of clarity from God. Even more than the calling to come to First Baptist, and even more than that urging to help you when we met in Vegas, God has shown me His will and made it so crystal clear, there is no way I can deny it."

I released her left hand and reached into the pocket of my jacket. At virtually the same moment, without letting go of her right hand, I allowed my body to slide down the rock and placed a knee on the ground. I then held up a ring, and the single, solitaire diamond sparkled in the bright sun. Her mouthed dropped open as I said, "Grace, will you marry me?"

As we drove into Mapleton, I glanced in Grace's direction and noticed her eyes fixed on the engagement ring. During the ride home she asked me question after question about the ring–where I purchased it (at the only jewelry store in Mapleton); how long I'd had it (about two days); what was the size of the ring (half a carat); how did I know her ring size (lucky guess)–and about a dozen other questions. Her immediate *yes* answer on top of Stone Mountain had brought me both a sense of joy and trepidation. I felt confident it was what I was supposed to do. I also had a strong sense of the ensuing storm coming as this news became public information.

To some who were confident of their own righteousness
and looked down on everyone else, Jesus told this parable.

Luke 18:9

Chapter 25

Monday, December 8, 1997

G race arrived at the law firm office just before eight o'clock on the Monday morning after our Saturday visit to Stone Mountain. After a lengthy discussion on Sunday, we had both determined that it was best for her to wear the engagement ring in public and for both of us to be brief but forthright in our answers to the expected questions. She worked at the reception desk without interruption until just before lunchtime, when the Mapleton rumor mill would get just the primer it needed to run full speed.

Juliet Sanders was the wife of Robert Sanders, one of the two founding partners of the firm. While Juliet did not officially work outside her home, she did spend a considerable amount of time in the spring and summer months as a wedding coordinator. The job served both her need for activity and to constantly engage in the latest gossip swirling around Mapleton.

Every Monday she met her husband at his office at eleven forty-five before going to the Mapleton Country Club for lunch. It was a tradition they began when their children were younger so that they could have some time for adult conversation in the midst of a busy week. Over the years, Robert had discovered that Juliet's insistence on lunch had very little to do with her desire to converse with him. What she really enjoyed was going to "the club" on Mondays and gathering information on the events of the previous weekend.

She walked in on this Monday, as was her custom, and was told that her husband had a client in his office and would be with her shortly. Disturbed by having to wait, and certainly not lowering herself to waiting in the lobby, she let out a huff and found an empty chair behind the reception desk. Just a few feet away, Grace knelt on the floor with a mound of manila folders stacked beside her. She was in the process of organizing the muddled folders that had been haphazardly thrown into piles the previous week. Juliet furtively studied Grace for a few moments. She'd recently learned, along with the rest of Mapleton, the truth about Grace's past. She was slightly uncomfortable with Grace working in the firm, and had told her husband that she'd better not catch him flirting with his new secretary. She reminded him of her exceptional ability to know everyone's business, and if she ever discovered that his relationship with "that girl" was anything but professional, she would leave him and take every penny he had.

After a minute or two of indiscriminately glancing in Grace's direction, she suddenly noticed a slight glimmer coming from her left hand. She carefully studied Grace a few more seconds, and when Grace lifted a folder from the floor to place inside the filing cabinet, she again saw the bright shimmer reflecting from her hand. Unable to contain her curiosity, Juliet stood from her chair and walked over to where Grace leaned over the bottom filing cabinet. Juliet stood there momentarily, hovering over Grace, who was completely unaware of her presence. Finally, Juliet cleared her throat and said, "What is that on your finger?"

Startled by this sudden voice, Grace nearly fell over onto the floor. When she regained her composure, she realized that Juliet was looking directly at her engagement ring. "Umm...yeah, I got engaged this weekend. Do you like the ring?"

"Who exactly are you engaged to?" Juliet asked tersely, ignoring Grace's last question.

"Uh, Henry. Henry Miller. He is the pastor at First Baptist Church."

Juliet huffed and with a tone of exasperation said, "I *know* who Henry Miller is. He is the pastor of my church." She paused for a moment, carefully studying Grace. "So you are telling me that you are marrying Henry Miller?"

Grace was unsure what to say. She realized that this person standing before her was not simply asking a question; rather, she was clearly making a statement that Grace did not deserve to marry me. Juliet's tone implied that someone with her history was not good enough to be my bride. It was the same struggle that Grace had in accepting my proposal. Dozens of times she had asked me if I were serious, or if I knew what I was asking, or if I really wanted to be with a girl like her. After hours of conversation and my dogged determination, she finally accepted the fact that I really did want her to be my wife.

But as Juliet incredulously fired her questions, all of Grace's insecurities came rushing to the surface of her mind. Unable to control this sudden onslaught of emotions, tears suddenly began to stream down her face. She looked at the carpet below her, attempting to hide the obvious emotional pain. Juliet noticed the tears and suddenly realized her words had stung Grace deeply.

Juliet was certainly no saint, but neither was she a malicious person. Her heart became overcome with conviction at the pain that she had caused. Based on the information Juliet had gathered from others, she had crafted in her mind an image of Grace as being a cold, calculating whore. Suddenly, on the floor below her, sat a young girl absolutely crushed by her foolish words. As much as she disapproved of her past, Juliet felt a rush of sympathy for Grace. Juliet knelt down beside Grace, put her arm around her, and said, "I'm so sorry. That came out completely wrong. I guess I'm just really surprised that Henry is getting married. Is this a secret?"

"No," Grace sobbed. "I don't guess so. I mean, we are planning on getting married next month, so people will know soon enough I'm sure."

"Do you have a wedding coordinator yet?" Juliet asked.

"Uh, no, I don't think so," Grace replied through her sniffles. "Are we supposed to?"

"Oh, yeees, honey. And I know just the person," Juliet said with a broad grin.

That week, the Mapleton rumor mill was in full operation. By Wednesday, there was not a person in town who did not know that the pastor of First Baptist Church was getting married to a former prostitute.

For I too was a son to my father, still tender, and
cherished by my mother.

Proverbs 4:3

Chapter 26
Saturday, December 13, 1997

It was a full week after I proposed that I finally worked up the nerve to call my father and tell him that I had become engaged. He was understandably shocked, his initial response being, "Son, I wasn't even sure you liked girls. So, I'm thrilled to know that you are attracted to the fairer sex." He then quickly followed with, "Son, here's the deal–we did not even know you had a girlfriend. Don't you think you could have at least told us you were dating someone before deciding to get married? Who is this girl? How did you meet? When did you propose?"

"Dad, everything has just kind of happened really fast. By that, please do not assume she is pregnant. It's not one of those kinds of quickie weddings. But we have only known each other for a short while and are getting married in just over a month."

"Son, I really do not know much about these things, but here's the deal–I think that is pretty quick to plan a wedding. Where are you getting married? Where is this girl from? Have you reserved a church?"

"Uh, Dad, she is from Colorado, but we are not planning on going there to get married."

"Son, you want me to call the office at Eastover Methodist and see when our church is available? Do you have a set date already?"

"No, I appreciate it, but I do not need you to call the church. We are getting married here. At First Baptist in Mapleton, and, yeah, Dad, we have a date set. We are getting married on January twenty-forth. Six weeks from today."

There was several seconds of silence before my father finally said, "Son, be honest with me now. Are you sure she's not pregnant? I mean, here's the deal–I'd rather you just go ahead and tell me now rather than me finding out later."

"I promise you she's not pregnant. Dad, I know this will sound really weird, but we are getting married quickly because God wants us to. This whole thing is something He has orchestrated." As soon as I said the words, I knew how far-fetched they sounded to my father.

"Son," my dad said after a heavy pause, "your mother and I have tolerated this whole religious path you've been on. Honestly, we've both assumed you would grow out of it after a little while and head on to law school like you'd originally planned. But now...well...son, has this girl gotten you into a cult? Do they have red Kool-Aide at their meetings?"

"Dad, it's nothing like that. I'm Baptist now, which isn't all that different from Methodist. And the girl isn't in a cult. She really didn't go to any church until she met me. Dad, I know it is hard to get your brain around all of this."

There was dead silence on the other end of the phone line. I imagined my father looking up at the ceiling in the house, wondering what in the world his son was doing with his life. Finally, after several seconds of neither one of us speaking, my father finally said, "So, what is her name?"

"Grace."

"When do we get to meet Grace?"

"I want us to come to Charlotte next week, if that's okay."

"Yeah, of course it is. Son, are you sure about this?"

"Dad, do you remember telling me the story of how you and Mom met? Do you remember how crazy you were in your pursuit of her? Taking that chance in chapel that day and giving that fake accent on the phone just so you could find out her name? Remember telling me how insanely jealous you would become when another guy on campus even spoke to her? And how you guys didn't have jobs or any solid plans when you proposed to her? And how all you knew was that you loved her and that was enough? Well, Dad, I feel the same way about Grace that you felt about Mom. I'm that crazy in love with her, and that is why we are getting married."

Again, there was silence on the other end of the line. I could sense my father thinking about his rebuttal to my argument. *Yeah, but that was a different time or we were young and foolish and were lucky we survived.*

After several seconds of silence, he simply said, "Do you want me to tell your mother, or do you want to tell her yourself when you get here?"

"Umm, Dad, if you don't mind, go ahead and tell her, and tell her to start gathering addresses as well. We'll bring the wedding invitations with us. You guys can get to know Grace while we address envelopes."

Arrogant foes are attacking me...

Psalm 54:3

Chapter 27

Sunday, December 14, 1997

As my usual Sunday custom, I arrived at the church several hours before the beginning of the morning worship service. The sun had yet to make its introduction to the day. I was accustomed to arriving at the church very early on Sundays to complete my preparations for the message. In the fall, when the days grew shorter and the nights longer, the early hour of my arrival felt even earlier. I held tightly to my cup of coffee, hoping it would soon accomplish its purpose and aid me in brushing away the mental cobwebs.

As I exited my car and walked toward the entrance to the church office, I noticed a shadowy figure standing beside the doors. I stopped, my senses suddenly heightened as I quickly assessed the situation and determined my next course of action. I stood approximately fifteen feet from the entrance, and started to call out to the person, knowing that I still had a chance to run if I did not receive an answer that alleviated my fears. Just as I opened my mouth to speak, the figure stepped out of the darkness and into the light of the distant street lamp. I immediately recognized the voice calling out to me.

"Pastor. We need to talk."

Mr. Dwight Norman, the chairman of the board of deacons, stood before me. He had a wearisome, solemn expression on his face. "Dwight," I said. "Any chance it could wait until after the worship service?"

"No chance at all. We need to talk now."

I reached into my pocket and extracted my keys. I opened the door to the office, waved my arm, bowed low, and said, "After you, Mr. Chairman." I expected at least a faint smile at my over-exaggerated display of respect. With nothing but a blank stare, Dwight led the way into my office.

After settling into our chairs, Dwight said, "Pastor, I need you to be very honest with me."

"Of course Dwight. I've never been anything but."

He just stared at me with an expression displaying both doubt and intrigue. "There are wild rumors flying around that you are about to marry a prostitute. Is that true?"

"No, Dwight. That is a lie."

A look of both surprise and relief immediately emerged on his face. "Uh, well, Pastor, all I can tell you is that there are lots of people, including most of the deacons, who are convinced you are getting married. I'm glad to know that the whole thing is just a nasty rumor."

"Now Dwight, I did not say that I was not getting married. I am getting married. Your question was whether or not I'm marrying a prostitute. I am not marrying a prostitute. Now, you asked me to be completely honest, and I told you I would be. So, in the spirit of full disclosure, you do need to know that she *was* a prostitute. But she no longer is. She is now a fully forgiven follower of Christ. And yes, we are getting married next month, right here at First Baptist."

Dwight sat back in his chair, breathed in deeply, and with his arms fully extended rubbed his hands forcefully against his knees. I could tell see his mental wheels turning, searching for a response. He seemed to be measuring his words very carefully before he spoke. Finally, after a long silence, Dwight said, "The technicality of this issue aside, you are telling me that you are marrying this girl who, as you say, was a prostitute, right?"

I simply nodded my head in assent.

"Pastor, I'm sorry to tell you this, but I've spoken with a number of the deacons about this issue. This is just unacceptable. Think about how embarrassing this is for our church. First Baptist will become the joke of Mapleton. Our pastor...our leader... married to a whore?"

I quickly rose from my seat, leaned over my desk, and stared directly into the eyes of Dwight Norman. In a low, deliberate voice I growled, "Dwight, I'm going to give you two seconds to apologize for that last statement before I come over this desk and rightly defend the girl I'm going to marry."

Dwight quickly raised his hands in a defensive posture. "I'm sorry, I'm sorry," he said. "I should not have said it that way. But don't you see, Pastor, what a problem this is going to be? Are you going to fight every person in town who makes a snide remark about your wife? We cannot have our pastor constantly being arrested for battery. Lord knows that cheap old George Jenkins would not write a check to bail you out of jail."

I slowly eased back into my chair. I realized what Dwight was saying was right. I could not become so aggressive every time someone said something about Grace, no matter how unjustified. I had not thought about this side effect of marrying her. There would be talk, and lots of it. I needed to prepare myself for the moments when some sanctimonious soul would make a disparaging remark about my wife.

"You're right, George," I said. "I've not thought about that."

"Look, Pastor, I want you to know that I have been your supporter in so many ways. I think you are a good preacher and you've made me consider things I've never thought about before. But this thing has gotten out of hand." He paused, took a deep breath, and continued. "The deacon board is planning to meet this Wednesday, and there will be a motion to ask for your dismissal as pastor."

My expression did not change as I locked eyes with Dwight. While the comment about Grace caught me off guard, I knew this motion was coming. From the moment I recognized his voice outside the church, I knew exactly what he would say to me. I had prepared myself for this conversation. Observing my steadfast demeanor and hearing no response from me, Dwight continued speaking. "Now, Pastor, there are a couple of ways out of this. The first is for you to call off this marriage. Just tell the deacons you made a mistake and you were blinded by love or something like that, and I'm sure that they will understand."

"Not happening, Dwight." He could see the determination on my face and hear the resolve in my voice.

"Okay, fine. Then here is the other way to avoid this motion being presented on Wednesday. You stand up in the worship service this morning and resign as pastor. Tell the church you've decided to go to law school after all, and that you are going to go home to Charlotte and spend some time there before beginning school this fall. Heck, tell them you've decided to spend the winter in Colorado skiing, I don't care. But make your resignation effective today."

Again, he could see no reaction on my face, so Dwight continued. "If you will do that and simply leave quietly, then we will offer to give you three month's salary. That will at least put a little money in your pocket for a while until you can find something else. I've already spoken with George Jenkins and, as much as he hated the idea of paying someone who was not working, he said that he could agree to those terms. By the way, he is one of the few deacons who does not want us to ask for your resignation. He said that he did not think we'd be able to get another pastor for what we are paying you, and he really did not care who you married as long as you did not ask for a raise."

I could not stop the slight smirk forming on my face at the thought of the miserly George Jenkins defending me simply for economic reasons. "Look Dwight," I responded, "I know you guys feel like you have to do what you have to do. And honestly, I do not blame you. If I were in your shoes, I may do exactly the same thing. But Dwight, this whole thing is not my idea. It has been God leading me every step of the way. Now, I know that is not easy to believe, and I may not believe it myself except for the fact that I've experienced it so powerfully."

"Pastor," Dwight quickly responded, "I just don't think that is going to fly with the deacon board. Many people throughout history have done crazy things and attempted to place the blame on God. I'm not sure that pinning this on Him is going to get the deacons to suddenly support you in this decision."

"I know, Dwight. I've already thought about that. Look, Grace and I are leaving this afternoon to go to Charlotte. We are going to spend several days there and celebrate Christmas with my family. So I will not be here on Wednesday night. So here is what you can tell the deacons: I am still marrying Grace, and I will not resign. If you pass this motion, then we will take it to the church. If the church votes to fire me, then so be it. I'll step down and I will leave Mapleton. If the church votes to keep me on as pastor, then maybe God really does want me to stay here."

"Pastor, I'm sorry to hear this. I'd hoped this could be handled much more discreetly."

"I understand, Dwight. Thank you for being so forthright with me."

The chairman of the deacons rose from his chair and, without speaking, left my office. I did not see him in the worship service that morning.

*Do not be afraid. Stand firm and you will see the
deliverance the Lord will bring you today.*

Exodus 14:13

Chapter 28

Wednesday, December 31, 1997

It later became known as the infamous *New
Year's Eve Showdown* at First Baptist. According
to the by-laws, any called church-wide business meeting
required two weeks notice to the congregation. Exactly
two weeks prior, postcards had been mailed to every
member of First Baptist announcing the business
meeting to be held at six o'clock in the church sanctuary.
The call for the meeting had originated within the
board of deacons, and there had been an abundance of
conversation concerning the unusual timing of such an
event. There was concern, naturally, of many being either
unable or not desirous of attending a church meeting on
New Year's Eve. After an hour of discussion solely devoted
to the timing of the meeting, the chairman finally decided

to move forward with a vote. Although the motion to hold a church business meeting on New Year's Eve passed by only two votes, a dissenting deacon did concede that the holiday would probably not diminish attendance much at all. "I mean," someone heard him mumble, "there will be more fireworks here than anywhere else in town that night."

For as long as anyone could remember, First Baptist Church hosted what was known simply as "prayer meeting" every Wednesday night. In the 1960's and 70's, according to some of the older church members, prayer meeting began with a meal prepared by the church dietitian. Tables were placed in the gymnasium of the Family Life Center, and members of the church would pour into the building after their work or school day and dine together. Once the crowd was satisfactorily stuffed, the few adults who were not part of a class, a committee, the choir, or teaching children were expected to remain in the gym for the prayer meeting. The pastor was normally the one to lead this time, which consisted of going through a printed and distributed list of prayer requests submitted to the church office. The majority of the requests related to physical maladies of members or their families. The pastor would stop occasionally as he read through the list to allow those present to share the latest news on an illness or surgical procedure. The pastor would close the time praying for God to watch and care for all of those who were suffering. After he voiced the concluding "Amen," he would teach a brief Bible study, normally sharing a thought or two on some current event of the day as well.

In the 1980's, as younger families began to migrate away from First Baptist, and as the schools and recreation leagues began to become less faithful about dismissing practice early on Wednesday afternoons, the attendance at the weekly prayer meeting began to plummet. What had been a gathering of two to three hundred members at its height dropped to just a few dozen. Classes were canceled, committee meetings became rare, and any children or youth who happened to attend simply remained in the gym with the few adults gathered.

By the time I became pastor of the church in 1997, the prayer meeting had moved from the gym into a large classroom adjacent to the parlor kitchen. The normal crowd of somewhere between one and two dozen faithfully gathered every Wednesday evening to dine together and, in keeping with tradition, to read through the prayer list and keep one another abreast on the latest happenings in the church and community.

On New Year's Eve, despite the holiday, the church had the largest gathering on a Wednesday night in anyone's memory. Nearly four hundred people assembled in the sanctuary. As had been my custom every Wednesday night, I began the meeting by reading through the prayer list, stopping occasionally to ask the large crowd gathered before me if there were any updates to the printed material. Each time, my question was met with complete silence. Every person in the room wanted me to get through the list with as much haste as possible. I knew this crowd was not present on a holiday evening to pray for their friends and relatives. I understood well why the sanctuary was full on a night normally reserved for gathering in homes or in city venues to celebrate the conclusion of a calendar year. I finished reading through the list, offered a brief prayer, adding a silent petition for my own situation. When I raised my head and looked out over the faces staring back at me, I could see both anxiety and anticipation in their eyes. They were ready to begin the discussion that would ultimately culminate with a church-wide vote.

After voicing a concluding "Amen," I thanked everyone in attendance for coming to the church on New Year's Eve and their desire to take part in the church business meeting. I then informed the church that I would call on Mr. Dwight Norman, the chairman of the deacons, to serve as the moderator for the church business meeting. I turned from the pulpit, walked off the platform, and found a seat on the front pew.

Dwight walked up the two steps to the platform and took his place behind the pulpit. He opened a manila folder containing one sheet of paper and said, "The First Baptist Church of Mapleton will now enter into a specially called business meeting. You have all received the required two-week notice for this meeting and the written motion being presented. I will read the motion for the purpose of the minutes, then we will enter into a discussion concerning the motion. The motion has already been approved by the board of deacons and is being recommended for adoption by the church. The motion reads as follows: *We move that First Baptist Church no longer employ the services of the senior pastor, Henry Miller, effective December 31, 1997."*

"Now, since this motion comes from the Deacons, there is no need for a second. We will now enter into a time of discussion, followed by a vote. According to the constitution and by-laws of First Baptist Church, a congregational vote to dismiss the Senior Pastor must have seventy percent approval of the membership in attendance. After our discussion, we will take the vote by secret ballot, but we do need everyone to place your name on the ballot so that we may confirm that you are indeed a member. The ballots will be destroyed after the count is complete."

"Before we open the floor for discussion, we will have two individuals speak. I will be the first. The deacons have asked me to explain why we passed this motion and believe this to be the best course of action for our church. After I speak on their behalf, Pastor Henry Miller will come to the pulpit and give explanation for his actions. Afterwards, we will allow there to be a full discussion of the matter."

Dwight then gave a very clear and honest

presentation to the congregation of my intentions to marry a girl who had previously been employed as a prostitute. He was careful to only speak to the facts and avoid any volatile language. He explained with complete accuracy our Sunday morning meeting, thankfully omitting any reference to my outburst of anger. He spoke of the offer by the deacons to give me a generous severance package if I agreed to resign, although he did not share the specifics of that package. He then expressed what he said was the sentiment of the majority of deacons: this marriage would be a scandal at First Baptist Church and throughout the community of Mapleton. It was best, in their estimation, if I were released from my duties, given two week's severance, and sent on my way. "We tried to bring this matter to a resolution without having this called meeting, but Pastor Henry refused to accept our offer. Although it was not our desire to end up here tonight, this is where we find ourselves. I will now call on Pastor Henry Miller to speak."

Dwight sat down in one of the chairs as I made my way back to the platform and stood behind the pulpit. "I'll be brief in my remarks because I know many of you have questions and comments you'd like to share. First of all, it was never my desire to bring anything but good to this church. If my actions and my expressed intention to marry Grace have caused you embarrassment, then I'm sorry I've made you feel that way. In everything I've done, I've always acted in a way that was above reproach, and I believe am doing so in this present case as well."

"Secondly, I want to confirm the accuracy of what Dwight just shared with you. He is correct that Grace was a prostitute. But I believe that the operable word here is *was*. She is no longer a prostitute and, in fact, recently became a Christian. Sure, her past is awful, but isn't there complete forgiveness in Christ? If God has forgiven her, does anyone else have the right to condemn her?"

"Thirdly–and this is the most important part–I want you to understand that I am madly in love with Grace." I paused momentarily, overcome with the emotions I felt toward the girl who would soon become my wife. "The second and third hand comments I hear about her tear me to pieces. No matter what you think about Grace, I see a girl who is beautiful, loves God, and has made me a better man. No matter what happens, my love for her will not change. Even if you vote for this motion, I will have no regrets. Marrying Grace is more important to me than a job."

I returned to my seat on the front pew and watched as Dwight once again stepped behind the pulpit and said, "We will now open the floor for discussion. Anyone wishing to speak, please go to one of the microphones set up in the aisles."

Over the course of the next two hours, a vigorous and heated discussion took place inside the sanctuary of First Baptist Church. I heard almost nothing spoken that evening. As I sat in my pew, my thoughts and heart were directed toward Grace. She was at Richard and Elise's house, away from the drama and fireworks. I desperately wanted the meeting to end so I could go and spend New Year's Eve with my fiancé.

After the discussion, a vote of the congregation was taken. Five men were charged with counting the ballots. After twenty minutes of waiting in the sanctuary, the congregation was relieved to see Dwight walk in with the official results. He walked to the platform, opened a sheet of paper, and slowly read the handwritten script before him:

"On the motion that First Baptist Church no longer employ the services of the senior pastor, Henry Miller, there are 249 votes in favor of the motion, and 156 votes against the motion. The total is 61% of the votes. The constitution requires 70%, so the motion fails. Henry Miller remains as pastor of First Baptist."

How handsome you are, my darling! Oh, how charming!
And our bed is verdant.

Song of Songs 1:16

Chapter 29

Saturday, January 24, 1998

After we exchanged vows and rings, Dr. Smith declared to the congregation, "I now present to you, for the first time ever, Mr. and Mrs. Henry Miller!" There was only a spattering of applause from those gathered. Breaking with the traditional form of clapping for the newlywed couple, most people gathered that day simply sat in silence. As the organ played Mendelssohn's *Wedding March*, Grace and I walked arm in arm from the platform, up the center aisle of the church, and into the foyer. We turned and walked through a side door leading into the parking lot, then walked through another door and into my office. There we met Dr. Smith and thanked him for taking the time to perform our ceremony. He congratulated and hugged both of us. "I know you guys want to get on the road, and I need to head back to Macon. Henry, call me next week. You two drive carefully."

Grace and I changed out of our formal clothes and into more casual attire. We exited the side door to the parking lot and my waiting car. Less than fifteen minutes after the end of the ceremony, we were heading east, away from the contentious atmosphere of First Baptist Church and toward the historic city of Savannah, Georgia.

While neither of us had ever been to Savannah, the movie *Midnight in the Garden of Good and Evil*, had premiered in theaters the previous year. Both of us, on separate occasions, had seen the movie and become intrigued with the old southern town. When making plans for our honeymoon, we quickly agreed on this location. I made reservations at The Mulberry Inn, a historic hotel located just a short walk from Savannah's famous River Street, with plenty of shopping, restaurants, and locally owned taverns. According to the receptionist, we would be able to travel from there to several of the historic sites. She even arranged for us to take a *Midnight in the Garden* tour, compliments of the hotel as their honeymoon gift to us.

We arrived at the Mulberry just before six o'clock. We left my car waiting under the porte cochere while we checked in at the reception desk. The hotel employee informed us that our car would be valeted and our bags would soon be placed in our room. Neither one of us had eaten in several hours and decided to visit the hotel restaurant while we waited for our luggage to be taken to our room.

Although I should have been famished, I found myself unable to do more than push the delicious looking food around on my plate. I confessed to Grace that of all my trepidations about our marriage and life together, her sexual experience and my lack thereof sat at the top of the list. I feared that our time together would be disappointing to her. She patiently listened to me as I opened my heart and nervously shared my thoughts about our first night together as husband and wife.

She calmly waited for me to finish my rambling, then reached over and placed her hand on top of mine. She started to speak, but caught herself choking back tears. After a few seconds, she looked into my eyes and said, "Henry, of all my fears about marrying you, this part of our relationship has been at the top of my list as well. There are several reasons. First of all, I have spent the last two years of my life completely divorcing physical intimacy from emotional love. I worry that bringing those two back together will not be so easy, although with the way you have melted my heart emotionally, I am less concerned than I was at first. Secondly, so many times I still feel guilty over my past. I wish so badly that you could be my first. I wish that I could give you that gift tonight. But I've thought about it so much, and there is no way I can change the past. And in a way, you will be my first. Ever since that night that Elise told me what it means to be forgiven by God, my life has been completely different. I have been a different person. And so, in a way, tonight will be the first time the new me has experienced what we will experience together." She then took her fingers and intertwined them into mine. "And I'm so thankful it is you I get to be with tonight. I love you, Henry Miller."

That week in Savannah, was without question the most wonderful week of my life.

I will say of the Lord, "He is my refuge and my fortress, my God, in whom I trust."

Psalm 91:2

Chapter 30
Monday, February 15, 1998

After returning to Mapleton from our honeymoon in Savannah, we both continued to endure the seemingly unrestrained gossip and the judgmental stares of church members and residents. There were no more direct confrontations toward either one of us. The now famous business meeting had settled the issue of whether or not I would be allowed to remain as pastor of the church, but the underlying current of disapproving chatter remained. We fortunately found great refuge in the home of Richard and Elise. They continually reminded us to trust in the Lord and to ignore the jabs and sneers of those who thought they could sit in pious judgment.

Since our wedding, the atmosphere of the Sunday

morning services at First Baptist had changed, although at first it was very slight and almost imperceptible. Several of the members who had been so faithful in my first few months had ceased attending on Sundays. Other members and residents, some who I did not know, started to attend. The overall effect on the attendance was negligible, but there was a noticeable shift in the response of the congregants to my sermons. I noticed those attending with Bibles in their hands as they entered the sanctuary. When I would read from the Bible, I could see several individuals looking not at me, but down at their own copy of the Bible, reading along with me. I even saw some individuals with small journals, apparently taking notes as I expounded upon the morning's text. I began to notice a real shift in the desires of those attending on Sunday. More than just going through the motions of a religious ritual, there was an attitude of expectation. Many seemed to want to meet with God, hear from God, and learn more about His character and His ways. Something was happening at First Baptist, and I wondered if perhaps God Himself was finally starting to show up on Sundays.

Two weeks after returning from our honeymoon, I met Richard for our weekly Monday morning breakfast meeting. After taking my first sip of coffee, I asked Richard for his thoughts on the previous Sunday morning service.

"I tell you, Henry, it seems that a fresh wind is just starting to blow through our church. Now don't get me wrong. It's not windy in there yet, but it's like there is finally some air movement after years of sitting through a stale, stagnant environment. God is up to something, and there are a number of people who are starting to search for Him beyond the traditions and religious customs we've become accustomed to for so long now. I'm praying Henry, and I know you are as well, that *whatever* is happening will keep happening and will grow stronger."

"I've sensed the same thing, Richard. Just like you said, it's not a complete change from where we were, but it's like the dead corpse just moved a finger, ever so slightly. I'm praying that God will keep breathing life into our church body."

Richard nodded his head, took a long drink of his coffee, and then set his cup on the table in front of him. "Henry, there is something I want to tell you," he said with a somber tone in his voice. The way he said the words, I immediately began to worry that he or Elise had just been diagnosed with a terminal illness.

"Henry," he continued, "I had a long conversation with Mabel Johnson the other day. She called me and asked if she could come by the office and speak with me for a few minutes. Well, a few minutes turned into an hour, but it was worth the time spent. You remember, I'm sure, me telling you the story of Mrs. Johnson serving on the Pastor Search Team. She was so quiet in so many of our meetings, barely speaking at all as we would discuss candidate after candidate. But she was listening, and she would take every single resume home and pray over it. She spent hours and hours praying about the process and the man who would ultimately come to be our pastor. You know, Henry, she is the reason that you are sitting here with me today. I still remember the day she said God had revealed it to her that you were to become our pastor."

"She sat in my office and told me about how God had been speaking to her lately about our church and what He was doing. She said, by the way, that her first reaction to your marriage was not positive. She is old fashioned, she told me, and the thought of her pastor getting married to a girl who had worked as a prostitute was a hard pill to swallow. But, she said, God began to reveal to her that your marriage to Grace was what He wanted, and even as strange as it was to her, she began to sense that God was *doing something* through your marriage."

Richard paused. I was just about to put a bite of scrambled eggs into my mouth when he continued, "But Henry, she said that something... well... something bad has to happen first."

I sat there, waiting for Richard to continue, but several seconds passed by and he said nothing further. Finally, I let out a brief, nervous laugh and said, "Richard, what did she mean by *bad*?"

"She didn't know. Well, she did not know anything specific. All she knew was that it was something that would affect you personally, Henry. She wished she knew more so she could tell me more, she said, but that was all she sensed the Lord telling her."

"The reason she came to see me was that she was really not sure whether she should tell you this or not. She did not know whether God had revealed it to her in order that she should simply pray for you more, or if this was a message He wanted passed along to you. She came to me to ask for my advice on the matter. I told her I was unsure, and in a way that only Mrs. Johnson could, she said, 'Well, you pray about it, and whatever God leads you to do, you do.' So, after really thinking this thing over for a while, I decided if it were me, I would want someone to tell me. So, with no more specifics than that, I'm passing along this information to you."

I sat there, too stunned to respond. I shifted in my chair and finally managed to say, "Richard, what in the world do you think I should do with this information?"

Richard sighed deeply then said, "This is one of those times I wish I had the Wisdom of Solomon. Lacking such, all I can advise you to do is to make sure you are trusting in God at all times. No matter what happens, keep trusting."

Oh, my anguish, my anguish! I writhe in pain. Oh, the agony of my heart!

Jeremiah 4:19

Chapter 31

Friday, April 3, 1998

Grace and I held hands and watched the streams of water shoot from one point to another in perfect, choreographed synchronization with Vangelis' *Chariots of Fire*. Surrounded by the lights of downtown Atlanta and standing in the middle of Centennial Olympic Park, built for the 1996 Olympic Games, the moment to me seemed almost surreal. Flags, representing the nations who had competed less than two years prior, were gently waving back and forth in the cool, evening breeze. Fortunately, the weather had been unseasonably warm, the thermometer reaching nearly seventy degrees earlier in the day. Even so, with the setting of the sun and the wind cutting through the skyscrapers of downtown, I felt a strong chill running through me. I released Grace's hand and wrapped my left arm around her shoulders, my right across her body, and pulled her in close to me. The extra protection from the breeze combined with the increase in my pulse rate immediately abated the chill, replacing it with a warm sensation traveling throughout my body.

As the music ended and the final spurts of water receded into the ground, Grace whispered into my ear, "Henry, would it be okay if we went home? I'm getting a little cold."

"Sure," I responded. I took her by the hand and led her to the parking deck and our waiting car. I hoped she would have wanted to spend more time walking through downtown Atlanta, but the evening air was turning cooler than I had expected. We found my car, exited the garage, and started the journey back to Mapleton.

Just as we merged onto the interstate, the car engine warmed enough for the heater to blow warm air through the vents. With one hand on the steering wheel, I managed to maneuver my way out of my jacket and toss it into the back seat. I thought Grace might do the same, but instead she continued to sit with her arms wrapped around her body.

"Are you still cold?" I asked. "I can turn up the heat."

"No, I'm fine," she said, somewhat curtly. All evening she had been less than talkative. Before walking to Centennial Olympic Park, we had dined at the

Hard Rock Café in downtown Atlanta. It was our first opportunity to get out of Mapleton since returning from our honeymoon, and I assumed she would have been extremely excited about spending some time away from the fishbowl of our small town. Throughout dinner, she answered my questions and made perfunctory small talk, but was never fully engaged in the conversation. It had been a long week for the both of us, and so I assumed the distance I felt from her was due to her physical fatigue. Not wanting to have our first fight as a married couple in the dining room of the Hard Rock Café, I chose to ignore her reticent manner and simply hope the remainder of the evening would cheer her spirits.

As we drove out of downtown Atlanta, and Grace's emotional detachment continued, I decided it was time to address the issue.

"Grace, what in the world is wrong with you? You have barely spoken to me tonight. I thought this would be a great night out for us. Have I done something to make you mad?"

I could hear her exhaling deeply. I knew she tended to avoid conflict. In our few months together, I had discerned that when angry or upset, her method of dealing with her hurt was to withdraw, isolate herself, and work though her emotions internally. I had seen this play out a couple of times when we would overhear a snide comment about our relationship. Grace would immediately ask me to drive us to our apartment, where she would invariably go into the bedroom and make it clear that I was not to join her. After some time alone, she would emerge from her isolation and seem to be completely recovered. I would ask her if she wanted to talk about what had been said, but she would simply respond with, "Oh, I'm fine. I just needed to spend some time processing." The first time this happened, I tried to push her further, but she kindly insisted that we find another subject to discuss. "Henry, I promise you," she said, "I am fine now. It just takes me a little time to work through things like this."

I feared that she would respond similarly in this situation, and I would have to spend the evening wondering what was upsetting Grace. If we were in our apartment, I knew that she would escape to the bedroom to avoid this discussion, but she was trapped in a moving vehicle and her only choice was to either sit in complete silence or actually discuss the issue. I could tell that she was weighing these options and wavering between the two.

Finally, after nearly a minute of silence, she spoke. There was a noticeable tightness in her throat. She was nervous, or upset, or both. "Henry," she said, looking straight ahead, through the windshield. She did not turn her body or her head toward me. "I'm bored. The thing that is wrong with me is that I'm bored."

I felt an immediate wave of relief rush over me. I was so worried that I had said or done something to seriously upset her. In my mind, I ran through the previous week's conversations and interactions between the two of us. I desperately tried to recall anything I had said or had done that may have been hurtful or misinterpreted in some way. Unable to pinpoint any potential relationship faux pas on my part, I was thankful to hear her response. It was not that I was completely clueless on how to be a good husband. It was simply that she was bored with my choice of activities for the evening.

I laughed, a natural reaction to my feeling of relief, and said, "Grace, I'm so sorry. I wish you had simply told me what you wanted to do tonight. I just picked something that I thought you might enjoy. It is only nine-thirty. Tell me what you think would be fun. I'm sure there is a movie theater close by. We could go and see a late movie. Or," an idea suddenly hit me. A smile emerged on my face and I reached over and grabbed her arm, "we could find a hotel, spend the night here in Atlanta, and do something fun tomorrow. Anything you want to do. I promise you I'm game."

Grace never moved her arms. They remained tightly wrapped around her body. While she did not recoil at my touch, neither did she respond. She remained still, her gaze forward, refusing to look in my direction. "Henry," she responded, "I don't mean tonight. It's not that I'm bored with going to dinner and walking around Atlanta. I mean I'm bored with my life. I'm bored with the tiny little town of Mapleton. I'm bored with our little apartment. I'm bored with my job at Richard's office." She paused long enough for me to speak.

"Grace, honey, why didn't you tell me this? We can talk about how to fix these things. If you are not happy with your job, we can find you another job. We can move into a bigger place; maybe try and rent a house somewhere for a while. Heck, Grace, I will even start praying about getting another job and moving to another town if you think you are that miserable in Mapleton. You are my first priority. Not my job. Don't worry honey. We can figure all this out."

I looked over and I could see tears falling from her face and onto her coat. She tried to speak, but was physically unable to do so. We drove in silence for a couple of minutes. I normally would have been so uncomfortable with the void in conversation that I would fill it with some random babbling. But I was determined to get inside Grace's mind and hear her thoughts. I drove and waited for her to speak. Finally, she regained her composure and continued. "Henry, you are without a doubt the only man in my life who has really loved me. Even with all that I have done, you have loved me so unselfishly. I am so thankful that I met you outside that hotel in Vegas." She paused, seemingly weighing her words very carefully. "But Henry," she said, with the tears flowing down once again, "it's not just that I'm bored with my job and Mapleton. Henry, I'm bored with *you*."

She began to cry hard, then leaned over in the car

seat and buried her head into her hands. I was so stunned I could not respond. My breathing became labored and I could feel my heart rate increasing. I needed to find an exit off of the interstate and pull the car into a parking lot somewhere, but I could not locate anything immediately ahead of me. I continued to drive, trying to process the words Grace had spoken to me. *It had been less than ten weeks ago that we were married, and my wife was telling me that she was bored with me? What in the world did this mean?*

"Grace," I said after regaining control of my breathing, "I have no idea how to respond to this. What are you saying? What can I do to change?"

"That's just it," she said through sniffles, "I don't know that *you* can change anything."

"Then what are you saying?"

There was a long pause. Finally, for the first time since we pulled out of the parking deck in Atlanta, she turned her body and looked in my direction. "I don't know, Henry. I don't know."

The little sleep I managed to get that night happened on our living room couch.

My soul is overwhelmed with sorrow...

Mark 14:34

Chapter 32

Saturday, April 4, 1998

I awoke on the couch in the living room of our apartment. I had spent the entire night oscillating between wake and sleep; between the agony of my reality and the nightmares that came when I would actually manage to doze off. When the morning sun began to spill through the blinds and into our apartment, I decided to forgo my quest for sleep. I walked into our kitchen and searched though the cabinets for some instant coffee. Neither Grace nor I drank coffee, but I remembered purchasing a jar of Sanka several months earlier for those times when Richard and Elise came to visit.

I finally found the coffee, heated a cup of water in my microwave, and sat at our small, two-person kitchen table sipping on the strongest, foulest tasting beverage I had ever put in my mouth. I could not understand why people willingly chose to drink coffee on a regular basis, but in that moment I was thankful to have the jolt of caffeine traveling through my bloodstream. I determined that as soon as I could clear the heavy fog from my brain, I would make my way into our bedroom and get this issue with Grace resolved. I did not want this matter to linger between us any longer. Somewhere in the middle of my restless night, I made the decision to confront her and keep her in the bedroom until we had worked out an action plan for making our marriage a great one. I was willing to do whatever it took, and I was cautiously optimistic she would feel the same way.

I finished drinking my coffee, put the empty cup in the sink, and walked to the closed bedroom door. I knocked gently at first, hating to wake her if she were actually getting rest, but hoping she would already be up and we could begin the inevitable long discussion. Hearing no answer, I tapped on the door again, this time hard enough to wake her. Again, there was no response. I reached down and turned the knob, thankful to discover the door was unlocked. I slowly opened the door, hearing the hinges creak as I pushed it open enough to peer my head through the opening. The blinds were completely closed, and it took my eyes a moment to adjust to the darkness. I pushed the door, opening it wider and allowing the light from the living room to fill the bedroom. As my eyes focused and I saw our bed, I immediately noticed something was wrong. My hand reached for the light switch as I stepped through the doorway and into room.

The bed was completely made. I did not see Grace. I called out to her, hoping she was in the bathroom. There was no response. I quickly turned the corner, walked into the bathroom, but Grace was not there. I turned back toward the bed, and this time I noticed a sheet of paper lying against the pillow. It was one sheet, folded over, with my name written on the outside. I opened it, and my heart sank as I read the words written in Grace's handwriting:

> *Dear Henry,*
> *There has never been another man who has loved me like you have loved me. That is why I'm sorry that I cannot stay with you. I hope you will find it in your heart to forgive me, and that you will someday find a girl who will love you like you deserve.*
> *Grace*

I read the short paragraph and then quickly reread every word. It was so straightforward and clear, and yet my mind could not seem to process the words. Everything about our relationship had seemed just fine until the last week. The sudden revelation of her discontentment took me by surprise, but the note and her apparent exit from my life was beyond comprehension. I looked around the room and noticed that her things were gone. The closet doors were open and only my shirts and pants were hanging from the metal rods. Her jewelry box was gone. I turned and looked toward the bathroom, and I could see that her make-up bag was missing. She had obviously packed her things in the middle of the night and snuck out of our apartment during one of the few times I actually slept.

I walked over to our dresser and noticed three pictures remained perched on top. One was of the two of us standing on top of Stone Mountain, just a few minutes after I had proposed to her. We had asked someone who walked by to take our picture. We were seated on a large boulder with the Atlanta skyline in the background. Grace held up her left hand for the camera, proudly displaying the ring I had just presented to her.

The second picture was of the two of us on our wedding day, I in my black tuxedo and her in a white wedding dress. Richard and Elise had waited for us in the foyer of the church and took a picture of us embracing, the first photo taken of us as husband and wife. She had her arms wrapped around me tightly and her head buried in my shoulder. Just before Richard snapped the picture, Grace whispered, "I love you, Henry Miller." The photo captured my reaction as I looked down at her with a broad grin across my face.

The third was of us on our honeymoon, in Savannah, seated at a table in a restaurant on River Street. We both looked so happy and relaxed in that picture. It was my favorite picture of Grace; the light seemed to capture her natural beauty and the joy in her smile. We spent nearly three hours in the restaurant discussing our future hopes and dreams. We had even briefly discussed having children and the names we would give to them. Our dinner that evening had been one of my favorite times spent with her.

As I held the picture in my hand, the gravity of my circumstances seemed to overwhelm me. Grace was gone. My wife had left me.

I sat down on the edge of the bed and wept bitterly.

After pulling myself together, I managed to call Richard and Elise. They both came immediately to the apartment after I gave them the summary version of the previous evening and what I had discovered that morning. For a couple of hours they sat and listened as my emotions ran from one direction to another. At one moment I would describe, through nearly uncontrollable sobs, just how much I missed her. Five minutes later a wave of indignation would swell from within me, and I would nearly scream condemnations against her character and what she had done to me. Later, I would declare my resignation over the whole thing and that

I was ready to move on to the next chapter in my life. Through my wild range of emotions, Richard and Elise provided a needed presence and listening ears.

When I completed my tirade, Richard asked if he could pray for me, for Grace, and for the situation. I gladly accepted, although I was not all that sure I wanted him to pray for Grace unless it was a prayer of rebuke. I thought about asking Richard to pray for fireballs from Heaven to reign down on Grace's head, but instead simply leaned forward from my seat on the couch and bowed my head. I was physically, spiritually, and emotionally drained, and Richard could sense that. He reached over, placed his hand on my shoulder, and spent the next several minutes praying for God to give me comfort, understanding, and clear direction for my life. When he finished, Elise offered her own prayer, this time focusing more on Grace and pleading with God to work in her life as well. When they finished praying, I sensed the door of my soul cracking ever so slightly, allowing the first rays of God's peace to come through.

I confessed to Richard that there was no way I would be able to preach the next morning, but I did not want the congregation or anyone else in Mapleton to know why. He told me not to worry at all about preaching, and that he would contact the right people and they would make arrangements for the next morning. I asked both of them what they thought my next move should be. Richard and Elise looked at one another, then Richard looked back at me and said, "Henry, this has been a God thing from the beginning. Remember how you told me that your meeting Grace was *His* plan, and bringing Grace to Mapleton was *His* plan, and how your marriage to her was *His* plan?"

I nodded my head in assent. I could not deny that I had indeed felt that way and had expressed those feelings to Richard.

"Then here is what you need to do. You need to spend the afternoon talking to God and asking Him what you are supposed to do next. He wanted you to marry her, and He needs to be the One to show you what to do now."

I knew Richard was right, but I also knew that I would have a difficult time talking to God at that point. I was hurt, angry, and spiritually depressed. It was going to be extremely difficult to read my Bible or pray in that state of mind.

"Richard, it may take me a while to even feel like talking to God," I said.

"That's okay. God certainly understands. But I would not waste any time trying. The sooner you can talk to God, the sooner you will know what you should do next."

He was right. I thanked both Richard and Elise profusely for coming over, for crying with me, for praying for me, and for being such good friends. They both hugged me for a long time before leaving.

I will get up now and go about the city, through its streets and squares; I will search for the one my heart loves.

Song of Songs 3:2

Chapter 33

Thursday, April 9, 1998

I heard Jimmy saying, "Man, you either have to slide over or you are going to have to sleep in that other bed with Law."

The morning cobwebs were still densely covering my mind. I heard and recognized the voice, but the instructions were not exactly clear. In the haze of the morning, I thought I heard my childhood friend, Jimmy, telling me to do something. Was I dreaming that we were back in high school, and I was spending the night at his house? As the fog began to lift, I heard his familiar voice speaking again. "Seriously, Henry, I am not all that comfortable sleeping in the bed with another guy, and especially one that is married and may forget that he is not in the bed with his wife."

My eyes were still closed, but I suddenly realized that it really was Jimmy speaking to me. We were in a hotel room, sleeping in a queen bed while my former roommate Law slept in the other. The previous evening, we had drawn straws to see who got to sleep solo. I had hoped for the long straw, but I had really hoped Jimmy did not get it. I would have chosen to sleep on the hard floor over sharing a bed with Law. I remember from our days in college that sometimes he would sleep *au naturel*. The last thing I wanted was that hairy beast, without clothes, sleeping next to me. Fortunately, Law drew the long straw, and I got my second choice. Jimmy and I were forced to bunk together.

"Henry, wake up and move over," I heard Jimmy say again. Without opening my eyes, I decided to have a little fun with Jimmy. I reach over and started rubbing my hand against his shoulder. "Honey," I said, "please don't be angry with me. Let's make up right now."

With the speed of a cheetah, Jimmy hopped out of the bed and shouted, "Henry, you've got to wake up, man! You're dreaming, you crazy fool!"

I sat up in the bed and began laughing. "Jimmy, I'm just messing with you man. You don't have to be so dramatic."

"I'm serious. You are going to have to sleep with Law tonight. I just cannot get comfortable sleeping in the same bed with a married man. In the middle of the night, you may forget where you are and the next thing I know you're all cuddling up next to me thinking I'm somebody else."

About that time Law groaned and rolled over from his side to his back. As he turned his body, the sheet lowered, exposing his massive, hairy torso. "Jees, whatchu guys makin' so much noise about, huh? What time is it, anyways?"

"Time for Henry to sleep in the bed with you, Law."

"Come on, Jimmy. You think I can sleep in the bed with that Grizzly Bear? Just look at how much hair that joker has on his body! One look at him proves the theory of evolution. If a scientist ever got a hold of Law, he would think he'd found the missing link!"

"Youse two sissy boys are jest jealous. Both of youse got bodies of twelve-year-old boys. I'm de only real man in the room."

"More like beast," I mumbled.

"I don't care if he is half ape, Henry, you kept touching me all night long. You are sleeping with Law tonight."

"Awe, Jimmy, youse don't need to give him no grief about dat. He's just missing Grace."

Law realized what he said just as the words were coming out of his mouth. "I'm sorry, Henry," he said. "Youse know I didn't mean anyt'ing by dat."

I knew that Law was not intentionally trying to hurt my feelings. We were joking around, and Law, just wanting to cut up, reminded me of a painful truth. I did miss Grace. I missed her badly. And it was my missing her so badly that had the three of us sleeping together in a hotel room.

In Las Vegas, Nevada.

———————————

"Youse fellas ready to hit de streets?" Law had just placed his fork and knife on top of his plate. Jimmy and I had suggested just grabbing something to go, but Law insisted we hit the breakfast buffet before starting our day. At $12.95 per person, I thought the price was a little steep for breakfast, but after seeing the amount of food consumed by Law, I was certain the restaurant did not charge him nearly enough. After consuming three plates, each one piled high with eggs, sausage, bacon, and hash brown potatoes, Law finally waved the white flag of surrender. "Dis ought to hold me over for a couple of hours," he proudly announced to no one in particular.

We had spent the previous night at the New York, New York Hotel in Las Vegas, the same hotel where Grace and I first met. I was fortunate to have two friends who did not hesitate in coming to my side in the middle of my crisis. I had contacted both by phone on the Sunday after Grace's departure. I explained the events of the previous two days, listening to the initial shock of both as they tried to process how something like this could have happened so early in our marriage. Jimmy's response was more thoughtful and reserved while Law spewed forth a barrage of obscenities in his description of the situation. He was careful not to say anything derogatory about Grace, wisely realizing she was still my wife and my feelings toward her were strong. After sharing their sympathetic concerns for me, both Jimmy and Law asked the same question: "What are you going to do now?"

I explained to both about my conversation with Richard and the Saturday afternoon I had spent in my apartment, attempting to pray to and hear from God. I was very honest and told them my initial reaction to the situation was one of resignation. I had done everything God wanted, I believed, and she had left me. I certainly could not be held accountable for her actions, I had reasoned, and so this was my opportunity to move on with my life. I would resign from my position as the pastor of First Baptist, move in with my parents for a few months, and then begin law school in the fall. I had virtually settled on that decision by the middle of Saturday afternoon when suddenly an overwhelming uneasiness came over me. For the first time that day, I started really praying to God. I prayed for some sort of direction in the matter. For over an hour, I prayed, read my Bible, and prayed some more. "Finally," I said to both Jimmy and Law, "God began to speak to me. It was not audible, but it was this very clear, unmistakable voice of God. I knew in that moment what I had to do."

"What in de world does He want youse to do?" Law had nearly shouted into the phone.

"Go and get my wife back."

———————————

Without my knowledge, Jimmy contacted Law on Sunday evening and suggested the two of them join me in my quest to find Grace. I told both of them that I had called a travel agent the day before and booked a flight out of Atlanta early on Thursday morning. Law found a flight out of Buffalo that arrived in Las Vegas shortly after mine. Jimmy found a flight that left out of Charlotte late on Wednesday night. They both called me on Monday and told me that we would meet in the lobby of New York, New York at noon on Thursday. I told both, emphatically, that I had not called in order to coax them into helping me. "Henry, its jest like we'se in college again. I'm gonna take care of youse, no matters what youse say," Law had informed me. Jimmy had shrugged off my refusal for his help as well. I was thankful to have two friends who were so willing to drop everything and assist me in my mission to find Grace.

When we met in the hotel lobby, I embraced both friends and thanked them profusely for their help. We found a table at the same pizzeria where Grace and I had shared our first meal together. Jimmy had arrived the previous night and had already secured a map of the city. There, we formulated a plan to scour the Las Vegas strip and find Grace. We assigned each other hotels spread out over the city: I took the MGM, Law took Caesar's

Palace, and Jimmy took the Aladdin Hotel. Our tactic was to simply walk around these hotels and their casinos, hoping we might find Grace. We knew the plan was the equivalent of finding the proverbial needle in a haystack, but none of us had any better ideas at the time. We agreed to meet back at the hotel for dinner later that day.

I spent the first couple of hours walking through every corridor and around the sidewalks of the MGM Hotel. I used the overpass leading to the Tropicana Hotel and spent the next hour quickly searching through the casino and restaurants. I then crossed the street again and repeated the process at the Excalibur. I then made my way to the fourth hotel perched on that busy intersection, the New York, New York, and desperately searched through every part, hoping I would find Grace. On a couple of occasions, I saw girls whose height and frame were similar to Grace's. In my desperation I would quickly walk toward the girl, only to be disappointed as their faces came into view.

We met for dinner that evening and shared the same stories of our futile quests for Grace. As Law devoured a rib-eye steak and baked potato, he offered an idea that had, for some reason, previously escaped our planning process. "I gots this little flyer ting today from some person on de street. It looks like it is advertising for an escort service. Youse tink dat maybe Grace is working again for one of dese people?"

"Yeah, unfortunately, that is exactly what I think,"

I replied. "It breaks my heart to admit it, but the way she talked to me last Friday night, it was the excitement of the night life she was missing. I cannot imagine she would have left Mapleton and moved to Colorado to take some boring desk job. She was after the thrill of the nightlife. That is why I decided to come to Vegas. Something inside me tells me that she is here."

"Well, here's my idea," Law continued. "I'se tink we needs to go out and finds dese people advertising dese escort services. Den we'se come back here to de hotel room and start calling dem and asking for Grace. Jest tell dem dat you met her one night here and youse want de same girl to be your escort again. What do you tink?"

"Dang, Law, that is a brilliant idea," Jimmy said. "That may actually work. What do you think, Henry?"

I sat there, pensively looking off into the distance. I was desperately trying to remember something Grace had told me the first night we had met. "It may just work, but you cannot ask for Grace," I said. "That is not the name she went by when she was working here. I think she may have told me the name she used, but I cannot seem to recall it."

"So if we jest ask for Grace, dey won't know who we'se talkin' bout?"

"Either that, or they would know that we were lying about being a customer," Jimmy said. "Henry is right. The only way this plan will have a chance is if he can remember her working name."

Suddenly it came to me. "Trixie," I said. "I think she told me she went by the name Trixie."

"Are you sure?" Jimmy asked.

"I'm sure. I think. Yeah, I'm sure."

We spent the next couple of hours gathering as many flyers as we could possibly find. The escort services advertised both males and females and catered to a variety of desires. While my mission helped to distract me from the nefarious nature of what we were seeing, I still found myself sickened at times by the depth of depravity that existed all around us. Most of the advertisements were geared toward men searching for young girls. Some of the advertisements were aimed at men who desired young males. The pictures and the wording of the pamphlets were designed to elicit the most base desires of the human flesh. As I thumbed through the materials and walked through the city streets, I felt as if I had stepped into the ancient city of Sodom and that at any moment fireballs would reign down from the heavens.

We made our way back to the hotel and began sorting the brochures, creating a list of businesses and phone numbers. Once we had discarded the duplicate advertisements, we had the names and numbers for eleven different escort services. Law volunteered to make the phone calls and seemed somewhat excited over the prospect of being involved in an undercover operation. He dialed the first number for *Ecstasy Escort Services*.

After a few seconds, a voice on the other end answered with a greeting and the name of the business.

"Yeah, uh, my name is Bill, and I was here a year ago and met an escort named Trixie," Law said in a disguised voice with nearly perfect diction. "I am back here on business again, and I'm trying to track her down." Law paused as the person on the other end of the phone spoke. "Yeah, she is Caucasian, about five feet four inches tall with green eyes. Last time we were together, she had long, black hair. I think she told me at one point she was from Colorado."

Again, there was a pause on the other end. Law listened for several seconds and did not speak. Finally, he said, "Thank you, anyway," and hung up the phone.

"What did the person say?" I immediately asked.

"Dat he's gots several girls better dan any Trixie girl would be who would gladly serve as my escort tonight," Law said.

"Did he say if Grace, uh, I mean, *Trixie* had ever worked there?" I asked, hopeful that something... anything the guy said might help us in our search.

"He said dey had a Trixie who is six foot one and used to be called 'Trey.' I don't tink dat is Grace."

"You ready to dial again?" Jimmy asked Law. "Your accent was great, by the way. How come you don't speak like that all the time?"

"'Cause I don't likes to sounds like a stuck-up old codger, dat's why."

348

"Just dial the phone, Law. Here is the second one: Playtime Escorts. See what you can find out."

Law repeated his earlier performance and once again was given nothing to help us in our search. He immediately hung up the phone, shrugged his shoulders, and dialed the next number. Again, the person on the other end of the line was not interested in providing any information. Law dialed three more services and received the same results.

On his seventh attempt, Law called Vegas VIP Escorts. He repeated the same spiel he'd given six times earlier. He paused, expecting the same unhelpful response. Suddenly his eyes opened wide and we heard him say, "You mean Trixie works for your company?" We saw him listening intently and jabbing his pen at the brochure, signing to Jimmy and me that this was the one. "Yeah, sure," Law said. "Tomorrow night at 9:00. Uh, you need a credit card number to hold the reservation?" Law looked at me with a confounded expression on his face. His eyes were begging for me to give him instructions on what to do. If I gave my card, then Grace might see my name and know I was searching for her. If Law gave his own card, then Grace would surely become suspicious. How many other Stanislaw Szukalski's could there be in the world? Our only choice was to use Jimmy's card, and hope she did not become suspicious of the name. "Uh, yeah, let me get my card," Law said into the receiver as he reached his hand out to Jimmy and snapped his fingers, signaling for him to hurry and hand over his card. Jimmy slowly and begrudgingly reached into his pocket, pulled out his wallet, and handed his card to Law.

"Yeah, its a Visa, and the name on the card is James S. Rawlins. Yeah, I know I said my name was Bill, but that is just what I go by while I'm in Vegas, if you know what I mean." Law looked at me and shrugged his shoulders. I nodded my head, indicating he was doing just fine and to keep up the act. He then gave the card number to the person on the other end of the phone. "Yes, New York, New York. Room 3208." Law then hung up the phone.

"You think it's really her?" I excitedly asked.

"Yeah, Miller, I tinks so. He said I was in luck. She had been on a leave of absence, but had jest returned. He said de way I described her, it had to be de same girl. She is supposed to meet me here tomorrow night at nine o'clock."

"How come you didn't try and get her over here right now?"

"'Cause he told me right away dat she was not working tonight and was booked tomorrow until nine. I did de best I could do, Miller."

"I know, Law. Thanks man. I don't know if I can just sit around and wait until tomorrow night at nine o'clock. I mean, if she is 'working,' you guys know what that means. I've got to find her before she..." my voice trailed off and I was unable to complete the sentence.

"Henry," Jimmy said, "let's just get a good night's

sleep, and we'll start the search tomorrow just like we did today. I know this is easy for me to say, but worrying about it isn't going to do you any good."

"I know. You're right, Jimmy. It's just driving me insane. I wish we had found her today. But we'll get it figured out tomorrow."

"Hey, since dere are jest two beds and tree of us, how's we'se gonna sleep tonight?"

Jimmy and Law both looked at me. "I guess we'll need to draw straws," I said.

Saul replied, "You are not able to go out against this Philistine and fight him; you are only a young man, and he has been a warrior from his youth."

I Samuel 17:33

Chapter 34

Friday, April 10, 1998

After watching Law unhinge his jaws and inhale three plates of food at the breakfast buffet, we left the lobby of New York, New York and once again went to our assigned hotels. Armed with the knowledge that Grace was most likely working in Vegas, I spent the morning hopefully searching the MGM Grand with a renewed vigor. I quickly walked through the aisles of the casino, between the rows and rows of slot and video poker machines. I went into every restaurant and gift shop. I walked the complete circumference of the massive hotel, hoping to catch a glimpse of the girl who was still legally my wife. After nearly three hours of intensely combing through every corner of the vast complex, I repeated my previous day's journey and took the overpass to the Tropicana Hotel. There, I spent another hour walking through the corridors, the restaurants, the casino, and around the grounds on the outside of the hotel. When I completed my search, it was nearly one o'clock. Law and Jimmy were supposed to meet me for lunch at the hotel. I knew they would be waiting, and Law was generally not very happy when he had to wait for his food. I decided to end my search at the Tropicana and head back toward our hotel to meet my friends.

As I exited the Tropicana, I looked up and saw, across Las Vegas Boulevard, the towers of the Excalibur hotel reaching up toward the sky. I made a quick decision to take the overpass from the Tropicana to the Excalibur, walk quickly through the casino, and then make my way back to our hotel. I crossed Las Vegas Boulevard and entered the elevated passageway leading to the upper floor of the Excalibur. The hotel's medieval castle facade was built with four high turrets and several red and blue pointed towers of various sizes. The raised walkway was built to resemble an ancient curtain wall, connecting an outer defensive tower with the main portion of the castle. The passageway led underneath an iron gate and into the heart of the castle. Just beyond this entrance was the main casino area of the hotel. My plan was to make a quick pass through the gaming area before heading to our hotel for lunch.

I entered the hotel and slowly walked through the

casino. There were plenty of men and women all trying to win big, but no sign of Grace. As I got to the end of the casino, I decided to walk out the back exit and take the side street around the hotel and back toward the intersection of Las Vegas Boulevard and Tropicana Avenue. I turned and began to walk toward the sidewalk when I heard a raised voice coming from somewhere to my right. I looked up and could see the silhouettes of a man and a woman standing in a corner outside of a side entrance to the hotel. They were behind a wall, in a hidden corner probably reserved for storing carts used by bellhops. The angle of the sunshine overhead and the shadow over the secluded area kept me from being able to see more than just two dark figures, but their shouts and body language clearly indicated a heated quarrel was taking place. As I continued to walk, the wall eventually blocked my view of the couple. As I got closer to where they stood, the voice of the man became quite clear. He was upset, evidently, over something this woman had done, or perhaps had not done. I was roughly twenty feet away when I heard him say, "A deal is a deal, and I do not care what you *feel* or do not *feel* like." He dramatically emphasized the word 'feel' each time he said it. "So, whether you *feel* like it or not, we are going back inside." He growled as he spoke each word through clinched teeth.

I stopped and retraced my steps backward, toward the main entrance of the hotel. I veered my path so that I was able to see around the wall and into the alcove where the couple stood. I could see that the man was an extremely large, well-built individual. For a brief moment I considered walking toward the couple and offering my assistance in resolving their dispute. From the look of his body language and the defensive, fearful posture of the female, I sensed that he was not a person with whom it would be easy to reason. I turned around and noticed a car pulling into the hotel driveway, probably only forty feet or so from where I stood. I waved in their direction, hoping they would perhaps alert a hotel porter or security guard that someone needed assistance. The car did not slow down, either not seeing or deciding to simply not acknowledge my signal. I made the decision to walk back to the hotel entrance and inform an employee of the situation. I had only walked a few steps when I heard the female speak. Her voice stopped me in my tracks.

"Please. I'm sorry sir. That is all I can say," I heard the familiar voice timidly say. It was unmistakably the voice of Grace. I immediately turned around again and walked quickly toward the wall, this time around the wall and straight toward the opening into the alcove. As I turned the corner, I realized I could only see a sliver of Grace's right side as she stood against the wall with the large, loudmouth gentleman standing between us. His massive frame blocked most of my view as he stood, with his arms akimbo, hovering over Grace. His head was looking down, and from where I stood it seemed that he was virtually on top of her. I could hear the snarl in his voice as he repeated, "*Sorry* isn't good enough." I saw his hands move from his hips to her shoulders. Although I was unable to see Grace, I could tell that he was firmly gripping her body as he repeated, "Sorry. Just. Ain't. Good. Enough. I'm the customer, and I expect good service!"

Instinctively, I called out, "Grace!" The man turned his head in my direction. He then released his left-hand grip from Grace and turned his body toward me. Now, he was no longer blocking my view of Grace. I could see that she had once again colored her hair a jet black, almost identical to the first night we met. She wore heavy makeup and a tight, black dress. Her face displayed an obvious shock as she suddenly realized the voice she had heard was in fact mine. "Henry?" she shouted with a tone of disbelief.

I stood about ten feet away from Grace and the man who held her tightly with his right hand. "Sir," I said, "I think there has been some kind of misunderstanding."

"You are right about that, kid," he said with a gruff laugh. "This girl here has misunderstood what she was supposed to be doing."

"Sir, I'm not really sure what has happened here, but if you will just release your grip on her, I think we can figure this out."

"Son, I don't know why in the world you think this is any of your business. Won't you just keep on moving, go find your college friends or whoever came out here with you, and leave the two of us alone."

"I would," I replied, "except for the fact," I hesitated before speaking the words sitting on my tongue. I could not believe that I was in this position, having to confront this brute of a man outside of a hotel in Las Vegas. For a brief moment, I started to wonder if it was worth it. Grace had left me, returned to her old lifestyle and apparently found herself in a less than ideal situation. Maybe this was exactly what she deserved. If she had not left me, she would not be in this situation. Had she stayed in Mapleton, even if she were unhappy, we could have worked on our marriage and tried to fix whatever was bothering her. She knew that I was madly in love with her, and yet she made the decision to leave me for . . . *this* . . . trapped by some burly man outside a hotel with his gigantic hand firmly planted on her shoulder, ready to curl his fingers around her throat if she tried to escape. I thought that perhaps I should simply hold up my hand, apologize for interfering, then turn and walk away. Certainly, no one would have blamed me for leaving Grace after she had already left me. I could walk back to the hotel and tell Law and Jimmy that I found her and had satisfied my curiosity. It was time to leave Las Vegas and get on with my life. In that split second, all of those thoughts went through my mind.

"I would just move on," I repeated, quickly realizing another emotion rising to the surface within me, "except for the fact that *she* is my wife."

An expression of both shock and disbelief showed on his face, then slowly faded to a knowing smirk. "You must be drunk, kid. This girl ain't nobody's wife. She works for an escort service, and today she is *supposed* to be working for *me.*"

"I understand what you are saying, but if you will just let go of the girl and listen to me for one second, I think this whole thing could be resolved."

I noticed his hand slide up her shoulder and his fingers wrap around the back of her neck. His thumb pressed against her throat, and Grace's eyes suddenly widened. This man was obviously not thinking rationally. Grace had disappointed him in some way, and his animalistic urges were now taking on the form of physical aggression. "Son," he said, with his empty eyes glaring at me, "you have about three seconds to turn around and leave before I press my thumb so hard that her esophagus caves in."

I found myself completely frozen. I thought about taking a flying leap at the man, hoping he would reflexively let go of Grace and direct his ire toward me. But the chance was risky. He was large and obviously had some form of military training. He would most likely be able to easily handle me while simultaneously squeezing the life out of Grace. "Sir," I said. "If you will just calm down, we can..."

"One," I heard him say. *Dang*, I could not think fast enough. What in the world was I supposed to do? I could not leave Grace with this brute, but this guy was insane. His face was red and his eyes were fierce. I could tell that he was either high or was coming off of a high. I decided one more attempt at reason. "Please!" I shouted, hoping the elevated volume of my voice would get his attention. "Just be reasonable for one second!"

"Two," he said, without raising his voice at all. I knew that I had to make a decision quickly. Perhaps if I turned and walked away, went inside hotel and shouted for help, a security guard or policeman would be close by. We could possibly make it back outside in time to help Grace. Or... the man could grab her and run, escaping into the maze of streets and hotels. I had only a split second to decide.

Here goes nothing, I thought as I threw all of my one hundred and fifty pounds at the man before me. Fortunately, he instinctively let go of Grace in order to defend himself from my attack. Unfortunately, his massive right hand released from her neck and connected with my cheekbone. At the last minute, seeing his fist coming around at my face, I managed to halt my forward motion just enough that his punch did not land squarely on my cheek. His hand grazed my face and continued moving, slamming against the brick wall of the alcove. The man shouted and cursed, shaking his hand in pain. Almost immediately he seemed to recover and refocused his attention on me. This time he threw a punch with his left hand, landing it solidly into my ribcage. The force of his punch threw me against the opposite wall, but somehow I managed to brace myself and keep from falling. I desperately wanted to get this man away from Grace, who was trapped in the corner behind him. I attempted to back up and draw the man out of the corner, but he saw my movement and grabbed me by the back of my head with his left hand. He drew back his right arm to deliver another punch, this time aiming squarely for my nose. He hesitated momentarily, smiling and savoring the experience. I noticed the split second delay and decided to act, throwing a punch, with all the force I could manage, right at his adam's apple. The move worked, and he released his grip on my head and clutched his throat. I immediately backed up, still trying to draw the man away from Grace. He quickly caught his breath and lunged at me, the both of us falling to the ground and sliding toward the open area just outside the alcove. The back of my head hit the concrete, and for a moment everything went black. I blinked a couple of times, and through my blurred vision was able to see that my attacker was now on top of me. One hand was on my throat and the other was raised above his head, ready to smash my skull. Although the fall left me dazed, I understood enough to know that this punch would either put me in the hospital or the morgue. As I saw his fist begin its quick descent, my only thought was, "I hope Grace got away." I closed my eyes and braced for the powerful, imminent impact.

Instead of the expected crushing blow against my head, I felt the slight rush of a breeze and the release of the man's hand from my throat. I opened my eyes just in time to see a set of legs flying across my chest, almost perfectly parallel with the ground below me. I turned my head to the right and saw Law slammed into the side of my attacker, who had been thrust into the wall from the force of Law's headfirst dive into his ribcage. The two fell into a heap onto the ground against the wall. The man who had so viciously assaulted me was momentarily stunned by this surprise attack, seemingly unable to fully comprehend why this unseen force had so suddenly and violently knocked him into the adjacent wall. At the same moment he regained an awareness of his surroundings, Law's right elbow connected with the man's temple, thrusting his head backwards and into the brick wall only a few inches behind him. I saw his eyes roll upwards as he slowly collapsed to his side.

"Lord, Law, you may have just killed the man," I heard the familiar voice of Jimmy say. As I looked up and saw Jimmy with his arm around Grace and his body shielding her from our direction. I turned and saw Law leaning over the brute, checking his neck for a pulse. "Aw, he's fine, but he will have one screamin' headache later." Law turned his head toward me. "Miller, youse okay?"

I slowly tried rising to my feet, still shaken from the full frontal attack I'd suffered. "Yeah, I'm okay, I think. How did you guys know we were here?"

"We'll tell you later. Let's get out of here before this guy wakes up."

"Grace, what in the world happened with that guy?" I asked. We were in our hotel room inside New York, New York. Grace had willingly walked with the three of us from the Excalibur back to our hotel, but had remained silent the entire time we walked. Except for subdued sniveling, she had not made a single sound. I was worried something horrific had happened to her, but I was also struggling with raging feelings of anger toward her. As we approached the doors to the elevator leading up to our room, Law said, "Jimmy and me are goings to get someting to eat. Youse two need to work some stuff out."

As soon as we arrived at our hotel room, she walked immediately into the restroom and closed the door. Still feeling groggy from my brawl with her attacker, I collapsed onto the bed and tried to collect my thoughts. Eventually, Grace would come out of that bathroom. I had so many questions, yet no idea where to begin.

After several minutes, the door to the bathroom opened. Grace emerged, her makeup smeared from her attempt to wipe away the tears on her face. She walked over to the other bed and sat down on the edge. Unable to look at me, she kept her eyes focused on the stretch of carpet between the two beds. "What are you doing here, Henry?" she said.

"I came here to get you back."

"Why in the world would you want me back after everything I've done to you?" Her voice cracked and tears began to again stream down her face.

I stared at Grace for several moments. Her eyes quickly averted my gaze, looking down at her feet. Her teardrops rolled off her cheeks and fell onto the floor below. I reached out and took both of her hands in mine. "Grace. I came here to get you back because," my voice trembled as I struggled with the emotions welling up from within me. "Because I am still madly in love with you," I finally managed to say. She looked up into my eyes. Even through her tears I could see the shock on her face. She didn't have to voice her question. I could see it in her expression. *Why? Why would you still love me after what I've done to you?*

She pulled me toward her and wrapped her arms tightly around me. With her head buried in my chest, I could feel her whole body shaking as she sobbed uncontrollably. For a full minute or so, I just held her in my arms as tears ran down my face and into her hair. I finally managed to gain control of my emotions enough to speak again. "Grace," I said, "when I woke Saturday morning and found your note, it was the most painful experience of my life. I do not care what you've done. I just want you back."

She continued to hold her arms tightly around my torso. Without moving her head, she spoke through her sobs and said, "No one has ever loved me like that."

I turned my head so that my mouth was close to her ear. In a whisper I said, "But I do. I love you *that* much."

We held each other for several more moments. Finally, she released her grip somewhat but kept her body close to mine. Through a sniffle she said, "Henry Miller, you are crazy. I knew it from the first time we met. You are absolutely crazy."

"You're not the first person to tell me that."

"And you know what else? You are the most wonderful man I've ever met. I love you so much, Henry Miller. But . . ," She took a deep breath before continuing. "But, Henry," her voice cracked and the tears began to flow again. "Henry, I desperately want to go back with you, but I just can't."

I leaned back so that I could see her face. "Why Grace? I mean, if you want to come, why wouldn't you?"

She released her arms from around my body and reached into her purse for a tissue. After wiping her nose and regaining her composure, she said, "Henry, the Friday night I told you that I was bored with you – that was only partly true, and it certainly was not the whole story. Yeah, I was feeling a sense of restlessness, but that was just a small part of the bigger picture."

"What do you mean? What exactly is the bigger picture?"

"Do you remember the first night we met and I told you why I came to Las Vegas and began working in this job?"

"Yeah, so you could help pay your mom's medical

bills, right?"

"Right. But what I did not tell you is that the bills were tremendous. I knew I could eventually earn enough money, but the doctor and the hospital were both telling me that if we did not pay, they were going to send my mom to the county hospital where they specialized in indigent care. I was not going to allow that to happen."

She paused and dabbed the tissue around her eyes. "So I took a loan from my boss. An eighty thousand dollar loan with a twenty percent interest rate. I was able to pay the bill and keep my mom at her hospital and with her doctor, but I found myself in major debt. I continued to work, but just could not seem to ever significantly pay down the balance."

"When I left with you several months ago, I still owed seventy thousand. I thought that maybe by going with you to a small town, I could simply vanish. I hoped that my boss would assume I'd died or left the country, and that perhaps he would just forget about the debt."

"Not long after we returned from our honeymoon, I started to notice a guy in town I'd never seen before. He was sitting in his car one day, parked across the street from the law office. Then later I noticed him parked in the church parking lot. I became suspicious that he was a private investigator, hired by my boss, and had somehow tracked me down. I started to live in fear that one day a couple of thugs were going to show up in Mapleton and drag me back to Vegas. I knew that if you were around, you would try to defend me, and I did not want anything like that to happen. I lived in a state of constant fear. It was not fair to you to have to deal with the junk I brought with me into our marriage."

"So I ran from you to keep from having to burden you with all of this. I came back last week and offered to start working again for the same escort service. My boss says that with late fees and the accrued interest, my debt is ninety thousand dollars. It seemed so overwhelming at first, but I figure that maybe if I can get a lot of business, I can have this paid off in a couple of years."

"By working as a prostitute," I said.

Her gaze returned to the floor. "Yeah."

"Is this what you want? To stay here in Vegas, working this job?"

Her shoulders began to tremble as she futilely choked back the tears. "No, Henry. It's not what I want. It's just what has to be."

"No, it doesn't."

So I bought her for fifteen shekels of silver and about a homer and a lethek of barley. Then I told her, "You are to live with me many days; you must not be a prostitute or be intimate with any man, and I will behave the same way toward you."

Hosea 3:2-3

Chapter 35
Easter Sunday, April 12, 1998

As I stood from my chair and walked behind the pulpit, I noticed a handful of individuals–all men–standing along the back wall of the sanctuary. That morning, every pew was packed, and these men had graciously relinquished their seats for others who wished to be a part of the morning worship service. While the crowd normally swelled considerably on Easter Sunday, the lack of available seating on this Sunday was not primarily due to the celebration of the resurrection. The individuals who sat before me were not interested in hearing about the empty tomb, the appearance of Jesus to the disciples, or the two men meeting Jesus on their journey to Emmaus. Had I attempted to preach a typical Easter sermon on a typical Easter passage, those gathered would have been incredibly disappointed.

The more than seven hundred individuals who decided to attend First Baptist on this Sunday morning had heard the rumor that spread like wildfire during the previous week. A female resident of Mapleton had seen Grace getting into a waiting taxi outside of our apartment complex. It was the middle of the night, and she was holding a large suitcase. It did not require great intellectual capacity for this woman to come to a correct deduction about the event. She told a neighbor, who told a friend, who told another about the midnight exit of the pastor's wife. By the time I left Mapleton on that Thursday to head to Las Vegas, the rumor had spread throughout the town.

There were both members and visitors crammed into the pews of the sanctuary that morning. They went through the motions of singing the traditional Easter hymns, *Up From the Grave He Arose* and *Christ the Lord Has Risen Today*. They politely listened as the choir performed a choral version of *To God Be The Glory*. They tolerated the responsive reading led by Mary Westwood. For most in the room, they squirmed in their seats, waiting patiently as the first half of the service took its usual course. As I rose from my chair and stood behind the pulpit, I could sense the collective desire of those who sat before me. They were salivating to hear a word from the pastor who had just been abandoned by his wife.

***

I read a passage of Scripture from the Old Testament

book of Hosea. I briefly told the story of this prophet who was called by God to marry a prostitute. I then walked from behind the pulpit and down the steps leading to the space in front of the platform area. I wanted to speak to the congregation in a style that was not formal in nature. I wanted them to hear from me in a more conversational manner of speaking. I was fortunate that the church had invested in a wireless microphone several years before I became pastor, giving me the freedom to walk out from behind the pulpit and move around while still being heard by the congregation.

"This morning," I began, "I want to speak to you not only as your pastor, but as someone who has a message from God for you. In ancient times, these men were known as prophets, and they were sent by God to give a message to the people. This morning I come to you with a prophetic message."

"Many of you are aware that three months ago I married a girl who had formerly worked as a prostitute. I never dreamed I would marry someone who had a past like Grace's, and yet in the process of meeting her and bringing her to Mapleton, two things happened. The first was that I absolutely fell madly in love with Grace. The second was that God very clearly told me that it was His will for me to ask Grace to marry me. With my heart so captured by her, and God's leading me to marry Grace, it became obvious what I was to do. Last fall I asked her to become my wife, and in January we said our vows to one another in this room."

"While I was happy in our marriage, I was still very

unclear as to why God has led me to Grace. While thankful He had done so, I was struggling to see the bigger picture in my marriage to a girl who had formerly worked as a prostitute in Las Vegas."

"As many of you now know, Saturday week ago Grace left me." I paused, making sure I was able to keep my composure as I recalled the personal pain I experienced just a short time earlier. "That afternoon, after I discovered that she had walked out on me, I spent several hours in hard, fervent prayer. I knew God had directed me to marry Grace. I knew beyond any doubt that it had been His will for her to become my wife. And yet . . . she had walked out on me. I cried out to God in anger, I questioned God's goodness, and I honestly began to wonder if I even believed in Him anymore. I experienced a range of emotions as I struggled with the loss of my wife and the looming loss of my faith in God."

"At some point in my struggle with God, I heard Him speak to me. Please do not think that I mean an audible voice–I do not. Even though I did not actually hear God, the message I heard seemed to be more explicit than anything I've ever heard in person. As I lay on the floor of my apartment, weeping, I sensed God asking me about my love for Grace. I was so angry–both at God and at Grace. I found myself absolutely seething with anger as I had imaginary arguments with both. After giving my life to follow God's leading, I was being rewarded with a wife who abandoned me after three months of marriage. What sense was there in that? After giving my heart to Grace, she was willing to leave me with no more than a brief, handwritten note? How could she be so cruel?"

"Somewhere in the midst of my emotional rage, I again heard the voice of God, again asking me how I felt about Grace." One more time, I paused and choked back the tears. "Honestly, I broke down and wept even more bitterly. I finally understood what God was asking me, and it hurt so much. Even after her abandoning me...even after her callous disregard for my feelings and our vows...even after *all* that hurt," I paused, and then in almost a whisper said, "I was still in love with Grace. Madly, head over heels, wanting to rip my heart out in love with her. That is what hurt so badly. If I had felt ambivalent about our relationship, it would have made her leaving much easier. But that was not the case. Even though I was angry with her, I still loved her so incredibly much."

The congregation sat before me with rapt attention. As I took a breath and a long pause, the room was completely silent as everyone eagerly waited for me to finish the story. "In that moment, somehow, God spoke to my spirit. In my quiet, lonely apartment, God said to me, 'Henry, that is how I feel about the people of First Baptist Church.' It took me a minute to process what God was saying. Then suddenly, in a blinding moment, it all became clear. God wanted me to fall in love and marry Grace as an illustration to you, and to me—to all of us in this room—about His love."

"See, Grace did not just leave me. She left me and went back to Las Vegas. She went back to her former profession. She decided to leave my nearly unconditional love for the temporary, cheap love of men who cared nothing for her."

"God showed me in that moment how His relationship with us is the same way. God has loved us unconditionally, and yet we've left God to chase after other lovers. We've abandoned Him for things like self-importance, ambition, and cheap religious rituals that focus more on making us feel good than exalting God. We have committed adultery against God, cheating on Him with disinterested lovers. Our spiritual prostitution has angered Him greatly, and yet, *He is still passionately in love with us.* Through my own pain and heartache, I was able to move beyond just knowing this truth. *I felt it.* In the same way that my stomach turned as I thought about Grace; in the same way that my eyes filled with tears as I imagined her leaving in the middle of the night; in the same way that my heart sank as I wondered if she were in the arms of another man... God is that much in love with you and me. Even in the midst of our sin and rebellion, God's heart is aching for us to come back to Him."

I walked over to the divider between the front pew and the floor area in the front of the pulpit. I leaned on the wooden rail, nearly on top of those seated in the front pew. "I know what some of you are thinking: 'God told you to marry a prostitute so that you could tell us God loves us? Come on, don't you think we know that?' But the story is about more than God loving us even in our spiritual adultery."

"See, as I sat there that Saturday afternoon, heartbroken over Grace, and yet realizing this powerful truth about how often we are unfaithful to a God who loves us unconditionally, something else happened. I heard from

God again. And again, the message was very clear. I was to go and get Grace back. Somehow I knew that she was in Las Vegas, and that she had gone back to her old profession. And deep within my spirit I could sense God telling me to go and rescue Grace."

"I flew to Vegas and after a couple of days, I found Grace." I chose not to share the circumstances of that find, electing to save that story for another sermon. "When I found her, I discovered that she was not able to easily return to Mapleton with me." I gave a brief summary of the cancer situation her mother faced, and how Grace began working in the prostitution business in order to get the funds for her mom's treatments. I shared the details of her financial debt to her employer, and how this employer had discovered her location in Mapleton. I recounted the conversation Grace had with me in the hotel room – how out of fear she ran from me and back to her job."

"She felt as if she were in bondage to her employer, but that with enough work, she could eventually free herself from that situation." I paused, stood up straight, and looked over the crowd before me. "But as her husband, I was not going to sit by and do nothing."

I backed up from the divider and walked toward the left side of the sanctuary. "Most of you are aware that I had intended to go to law school before coming here to be your pastor. When I was born, my grandparents purchased a number of savings bonds for my education. Fortunately, I was able to obtain an academic scholarship to college and did not need to use these funds. However, I did not receive a scholarship to law school, and I knew that I would need virtually all of those funds to pay for my tuition and living expenses."

"Honestly, I have not touched that money because law school has been my backup plan ever since I came to Mapleton. I was sure that either you would fire me, which nearly happened, or that out of extreme frustration I would pack up one day and leave. When that day came, I thought, I would simply go with my original plan."

"Now I know why I have held onto those funds so tightly. On Friday morning, I called my parents in Charlotte and instructed them to cash the bonds and deposit the funds into my checking account. The value of the bonds was exactly ninety thousand dollars."

"Grace and I went to her boss and paid her debt. In full. She was no longer in financial bondage. It took everything I had, but now she is not only free from that obligation, but she is free to be fully committed to me." I walked back toward the center of the church. It was time to deliver the culmination.

"Two thousand years ago, God chased after each of us while we were in bondage. We were trapped, thinking that we had the power to overcome our sin, but God knew better. So he sent His Son, Jesus Christ, to die on a Roman cross. It took everything he had–*his entire life*–but it was the price that had to be paid in order to purchase us from our sin. And it worked. It was exactly what we needed to free us from the chains of sin and spiritual death."

"And now, though we have cheated on God over and over, He has paid the price for us to be free. Free from our sin and free to love Him with everything we've got." I stopped and looked over the crowd gathered before me. Most were staring at me, waiting for my next word. A few ladies were discreetly wiping tears from their eyes. There was a palpable sense of God's presence in the room. I could sense that He was working in some hardened hearts. Eyes were being opened to the reality of God's love. I could feel Him powerfully drawing people to the cross of Jesus Christ. As I walked from the floor and up the platform steps, I prayed that the congregation would be responsive to God's leading.

"Jesus paid the ultimate price for you, and for me. Now, the question is, will you continue to run after other lovers–lovers who really care nothing for you–or will you fall wholeheartedly into the arms of the only one who has ever truly loved you?" I said the next phrase very slowly, almost in a whisper. "What...will...you...do?"

I turned and sat in the wooden chair on the platform. Mary Westwood, the part-time music director, rose from her seat and stood behind the pulpit. I could see that she was having difficulty maintaining her composure. We had discussed the closing hymn, but obviously God had been working on her heart, and she was momentarily at a loss for words. Finally, she motioned her arms for the congregation to stand and said, "We are going to sing the hymn, 'Jesus Paid it All.' If God has spoken to you today, as He has spoken to me, then join me here at the front of the church to pray."

The organist began to play and the congregation sang the first verse of the old hymn:

Jesus paid it all,
all to him I owe;
sin had left a crimson stain,
he washed it white as snow.

As the congregation sang those words, I looked around the room. Not one person made a move. Everyone simply stood, most singing and a few simply standing and staring off into space. I silently wondered if anyone would actually respond, or if those gathered were already thinking about their Easter lunches and afternoon naps. Were they even listening? Do they even care about how much God loves them?

I bowed my head and offered a quick prayer. As the congregation began to sing the second stanza, I looked up and saw Marlene Smith stepping out from her pew and making her way into the aisle. Her husband, who I rarely saw at church, grabbed her hand before she could begin her journey toward the front of the sanctuary. She quickly turned her head toward him in a look of defiance, assuming he was attempting to dissuade her from going down to pray. He continued to hold her hand tightly as he maneuvered his way out of the pew to join her, and together they walked to the front, knelt on the floor, and began to pray.

I then saw Dwight Norman, the chairman of the deacons, walk from the place where he stood against the back wall. Dwight's attendance at church had been sporadic since the New Year's Eve business meeting. When the vote to dismiss me failed, he had taken it as a personal attack on his decision to bring the matter before the congregation. I'd heard rumors that he was considering leaving the church after his term as chairman was completed.

He walked down the center aisle of the church and stopped just a few pews short of reaching the front. He turned and extended his hand to his wife, who was standing beside her children, several spaces to the inside of the pew. She wormed her way around several individuals to get to the aisle. Once she made her way to Dwight, the two walked hand-in-hand to the front of the church, and there they knelt and began to pray.

Juliet Sanders was the next to come. Her husband was playing golf that day and was not interested in coming to hear the scuttlebutt on the pastor, but Juliet would not have missed it for the world. She was visibly weeping as she nearly ran down the aisle and found a place to kneel and pray.

Ethel Jones, my standing Monday night date, began to slowly make her way down. She was unable to kneel, but found an empty space on the front pew, sat down, and began to pray.

More and more people came, completely filling the space in the front of the sanctuary. Mary Westwood had the organist play through "Jesus Paid It All" a second time, although most in the congregation were not singing. Many knelt in their pew and a few even found spaces on the sides of the sanctuary to bow before the Lord. I stood and watched a scene that was nothing like I ever expected to see at First Baptist Mapleton. People were desperate for God.

I had earlier asked Richard Davis to close the service. As the organist continued to softly play the hymn, Richard found his way to the pulpit and said, "Today begins a new day in the life of our church. We are no longer playing around. From now on, we are serious about following God." He then prayed a beautiful prayer of repentance and thanksgiving to the Lord. People stood and began to mingle with one another. I quickly exited the sanctuary and went to my office, where I knew Grace would be waiting for me.

***

"How did it go?" Grace asked when I walked in. During our flight on Saturday from Las Vegas to Atlanta, I had told her what I was planning to share with the congregation the next day in worship. While she was supportive, she insisted that she would not be present in church. It was too early and she did not want to face the judgmental stares of the congregation. She did agree to come and wait in my office until the conclusion of the service.

"It went well. Very well, in fact. I think God really got hold of some people this morning."

"Henry, I've been down here praying the whole time. I've prayed for you and I've prayed for the congregation. I've also been crying out to the Lord for myself and asking for His forgiveness for what I've done to you."

"Grace, it's like I told you yesterday – it was all part of God's plan, and I absolutely forgive you. I've worked through all of that."

"Henry, there is something else I have to tell you." She paused, and I could see a nervous look on her face. "I did not tell you this yesterday because I had no idea how you would react."

I knew that I could not face one more shock in our relationship. If she was leaving me again, I would lose my mind.

"You remember the big guy arguing with me outside of the Excalibur, right?"

"How could I forget?" I touched my ribcage, still sore from his powerful left hook.

"He was my first 'client' since I returned to Vegas. He was upset because I would not sleep with him."

"You mean you guys never...?" I was unable to complete my question.

"No, we never, and I never did with anyone else either. Since I came to Mapleton last fall, you are the only person I've been with."

I was overcome with joy and confusion. Although I forgave her, I was still struggling with the fact that my wife had been unfaithful to me. It was such a relief to know that she had not been with another man while we were apart.

But I was also extremely confused. She had left me to go back to her profession and to earn enough money to pay her debt. "So, if you were being paid, why did you not sleep with that guy?" I asked.

"Because I felt sick," she said.

"Yeah, that makes sense. I would have been sick too, seeing that beast naked."

"No, it was not that. Well, not *just* that anyway. I was physically sick. I kept having to run to the bathroom and throw up. I finally told the guy that I needed to cancel our 'date' and reschedule. I quickly left the hotel room and he followed me outside. He grabbed my arm as I was walking around the corner of the hotel and pulled me into an alcove. That is when you discovered us."

"Wow, you have no idea how thankful I am right now for the flu bug."

She just looked at me and smiled, measuring her words very carefully. "You shouldn't be."

"Why? What do you mean?"

"It was not the flu. Henry, I'm pregnant. You're going to be a father."